At 3:15 P.M. Monday, October 15, 1973, Stephanie Spaulding looked into a small eye of death and didn't know it. The eye was a Lee-Enfield sub-machine gun with a four-power telescopic sight mounted.

The young man aiming the gun from a prone position in the brush, feet outspread combat-style, had watched Stephanie enter her chauffeur-driven Lincoln Continental in front of her red brick mansion near Pound Ridge.

He was thinking he had never killed a woman, outside of Vietnam. He didn't know if he could do it.

Now the limousine glided toward him. His scope moved to the back seat and a face came into view, almost frighteningly large in the finder. At that moment she was saying something to the chauffeur, her green eyes lively, then laughing at whatever he said in return.

She would die, he thought, without knowing why, which was the death she deserved. He squeezed the trigger and imagined her head exploding, the skull fragmenting, the laugh dying with her soul. . . .

LAST MAN AT ARLINGTON

LAST MAN
AT ARLINGTON

Joseph DiMona

A DELL BOOK

Published by
DELL PUBLISHING CO., INC.
1 Dag Hammarskjold Plaza
New York, N.Y. 10017

Dell ® TM 681510, Dell Publishing Co., Inc.

ISBN: 0-440-14652-6

Reprinted by arrangement with
Arthur Fields Books, Inc.
Printed in the United States of America
Previous Dell Edition #4652
New Dell Edition
First printing—November 1978

"There is always an inequity in life. Some men are killed in a war and some are wounded, and some men never leave the country. . . . Life is unfair . . ."

John F. Kennedy
Press Conference, 1962

BOOK I

ALLEN LOWELL

A letter to George Williams:

November 22, 1973, is the tenth anniversary of our late President's death. For reasons which you will fully understand we will observe this anniversary with the death of the following:
George Williams
James Carson
Thomas Medwick
Everett Mellon
Stephanie Spaulding
Robert Warneky

— 1 —

At 3:15 P.M. Monday, October 15, 1973, Stephanie Spaulding looked into a small eye of death and didn't know it. The eye was a Lee-Enfield submachine gun with a four-power telescopic sight mounted.

The young man aiming the gun from a prone position in the brush, feet outspread combat-style, was Allen Lowell. He had watched Stephanie enter her chauffeur-driven Lincoln Continental in front of her red brick mansion near Pound Ridge, had watched the chauffeur slide into his seat, the door clicking shut, and the car suddenly throb to life and move out of the driveway and onto this road beneath him.

Allen was thinking he had never killed a woman, outside of Vietnam. He didn't know if he could do it.

Now the limousine glided toward him. His scope moved to the back seat and a face came into view, almost frighteningly large in the finder. The cross hairs he placed on her forehead by instinct, observing nothing of the fragile beauty, the deep-set eyes, the fine upcurving nose, the luxuriant black hair that tumbled loosely around her shoulders. At that moment she was saying something to the chauffeur, her green eyes lively, then laughing at whatever he said in return.

She would die, Allen thought, without knowing why, which was the death she deserved. He squeezed the trigger and imagined her head exploding, the skull fragmenting, the laugh dying with her soul.

A moment later the Continental was safely past and Allen stood up, unscrewed the stock of the Enfield, buried the two pieces in his knapsack, and stepped out on the road to hitch a ride. A motorcyclist picked him up and he roared into Pound Ridge, hanging on.

He got off at the station and caught the next train to New York.

At Grand Central he went to the information desk and met, on schedule, a young man in a tan sweater and levis. He gave him the knapsack.

— 2 —

Excerpt from a letter to Allen Lowell, postmarked Toronto, October 18, 1973:

> . . . everything set, but unable to get white stuff. Even if we could, it would be difficult to get it across the border. Hope your plan works.
>
> Mike Gorgio

— 3 —

Beyond the little hill on which the camera crew stood, was a desert. But this was not Nevada, it was an iron mine in upstate New York, and the desert was man-made. Thousands of tons of gritty refuse, the finite fragments of pulverized rock after iron ore was removed, were gushing into a wilderness gulch from a spout which could be seen far in the distance.

It was weird, that spout. You had the feeling that eventually it would fill this gulch—as other gulches had been filled—overflow the hill, tumble into other valleys and ravines and fissures until all was finally smothered in the endless desert of refuse.

"See what they did over there," said the man from Reynolds Chemical. "It didn't work."

Allen Lowell, the film editor with the crew, turned. Five hundred feet behind them he saw an enormous mountain of this same sand with a brave sprinkling of shrubbery on top. But the shrubbery was dead.

The Reynolds man told him what had happened. "They got these pollution freaks raising all kinds of hell up here, so they tried to show them that a mountain of sand with green shrubbery fits right into the beautiful scenery."

"But it didn't grow?"

The Reynolds man laughed. "Nothing grows in this stuff. It's cancer."

They waited in the sun for Harry Andrews to arrive with the explosives. Meanwhile, the Reynolds man had clambered down the hill, leading the wire from the blasting machine to a spot in the sand about eighty feet away. "Can you see me?" he shouted to the cameraman.

The cameraman stared through the viewer of the Arriflex motion picture camera and saw a man in a blue helmet, faded jeans, and dusty cowboy boots, holding a wire. He moved his eye from the viewer and yelled, "OK! Watch the shadows."

There was a grinding noise as a Ford pickup truck made its way up the hill behind them. It stopped and Harry Andrews climbed out. He was a big broad-shouldered fellow with a green kerchief around his forehead to soak up the glistening sweat. He went around back and pulled out some foot-long clear plastic cartridges filled with a white explosive called "chemite," the newest explosive in the industrial field. He threw one carelessly toward Allen Lowell who caught it against his chest easily. A cool one, thought Andrews.

Allen looked down into the gulch where the Reynolds man stood waiting in the sand, then threw the cartridge of explosive as high as he could in the air.

"Holy Christ!" said the cameraman.

Underneath, circling warily like Willie Mays with his life at stake, the Reynolds man stared into the sun and saw a slim tube dimly tumbling toward him. It plummeted into his hands and he barely hung on. He breathed heavily a minute, then trudged through the sand to the group on the hill. "That was hilarious," he said to Allen.

"It's safe. That's what the demonstration is all about, isn't it?"

"You still can't afford to screw around." The Reynolds man was getting angrier by the minute. Allen said nothing. The Reynolds man said, "Why don't you go back to town and hop the first plane out of here."

But Harry Andrews was trying to smooth things over. "I started it, Jim. I threw it to him first."

"Idiot!" the Reynolds man said bitterly, then he turned back to the test spot. He had been against this stupid film from the beginning, but the men at his office said an actual test film to show how safe chemite was would sell the product. Maybe so. But who believes film?

And how safe was it? Unlike "water gel" and other standard explosives, it was not too stable, that was certain. At any moment that little stick could turn into an unstable freak ready to go off right in your hands.

Now he was here risking his life in the rear end of an iron mine four hundred miles from home showing some idiot camera crew how to shoot explosives. Lesson one, today: they blow four types of chemite plus one dynamite. Lesson two, tomorrow: they shoot bullets into chemite, set it on fire, hack it with a cleaver, to show it won't go off accidentally. Not on your life!

An hour later Allen Lowell watched closely as the Reynolds man with the chemite cartridge squatted in the sand next to a green flag. Far to their left was a dynamite stick under a red flag. Farther down under other colored flags were three different types of chemite, all designed for different industrial purposes.

Allen Lowell memorized every move. The Reynolds man took a small pocketknife, cut a three-inch slit in the side of the cartridge, and then stabbed a primer deep into the gelatin explosive. The fuse was fast-burning primacord with which he now threw a half-hitch around the cartridge, then led the fuse back about eight inches and threw another half-hitch around it, relieving the pressure on the primer so it wouldn't pull out. He stood up and led the fuse back to the main wire leading from the blasting machine on the hill, and connected it.

A few minutes later he was safely back on the brow of the hill, hovering over the blasting machine, a gray box with two red buttons and a fail-safe switch. The sun beating down on his face, he looked up at Greg Miller, the director, and said, "I buried the stuff deep enough to throw up some sand. But you'll have to keep it in frame. The wind will blow it to the right."

"We got it," said Miller. "Let's go."

The Reynolds man went through the time-honored blasting ritual. Standing up, he cupped his hands beside his mouth and yelled: "FIRE IN THE HOLE!" Then he turned in other directions and shouted the same words. The shouts echoed over the surrounding areas, meant to warn itinerant strangers, workers, and vehicle drivers. But Allen Lowell was thinking, how dangerous can it be? The explosive is way out in the sand in a gulch. He had seen stuff like it a hundred times in combat.

But then the Reynolds man was clicking the switch, and pressing down on both buttons, and the flat sand, serene and glittering quietly in the sun, suddenly rose in a massive upheaval of earth and fire and smoke. A sound like a clap of God's hands reached Allen's ears and momentarily stunned him.

Jesus, that harmless little cartridge packed a wallop! That chemite was something else. The Reynolds man was staring at the cameraman. "You get it?"

"Perfect," said the cameraman.

In the silence, Allen decided it was the right time to apologize to the Reynolds man. He said to him, "I'm sorry. That could have been you out there."

"You're bloody damn right." The Reynolds man got wearily to his feet. "Let me tell you something, fellow," he said softly. "The first thing we learn about one hundred percent guaranteed safe explosives is that they kill. The second thing we learn is they kill *us*."

They blew the other shots at the other flags, then rode back in a company car to a yellow wooden two-story hotel in the center of Largo Falls.

When they came down to dinner in the small dining room with the flowered wall paper, the proprietor told them the young film editor had checked out. Miller was angry. "He can't walk out on a job without permission. We're paying him."

"It's just as well," said the Reynolds man. "We may all live longer. That boy is strange."

The director said, "We've hired Jeff Bolton twice as a free-lance, and both times had trouble. But he has talent. And——" he stopped.

The Reynolds man looked up.

"He's cheap," Miller said with a shrug. "He has trouble getting jobs so he works for next to nothing."

Allen Lowell drove his rented car to Syracuse, the nearest city with an airport, then flew back to New York. He was a man who did not smile often, but he had to smile thinking of the look on that character's face when he had pitched him the explosive. An impromptu idea—but it had worked. Harry Andrews had watched that soaring explosive as if hypnotized.

In New York he checked into the Holiday Inn on Ninth Avenue under the name Bolton and a few minutes later had opened the project kit—drills, bits, picks, more than he would ever need. The boys in Toronto were taking no chances.

Or so they thought. For they could not know, would not want to know, would never know what they were really into.

— 4 —

Excerpt from Allen Lowell's diary . . . entry October 22, 1973:

Tonight the years of study began to pay off. I took two simple picks from the kit and went up to

16

Carson's room in the Waldorf. Nobody around. I placed one pick in the lock and pushed upward and then moved the other pick around below until it clicked. No problem. Door opened and I took care of his passport.

Left a Kennedy half-dollar on his bed, according to plan.

Took a walk on Ninth Avenue around midnight and saw what I fought for. Derelicts, drug addicts, muggers, colored whores, pimps . . . the parade of civilization 1973.

. . . Sometimes when the darkness is in me I want to kill Williams first, to rip and stab him. But that would be too kind to him. I want him to suffer longest, for he deserves it the most.

Two hours later. I am still up. Can't sleep. I'm so excited!

I have just read what I wrote above and realize I sound like a sadist. I am not a sadist. I am a soldier who can think.

— 5 —

The men in black robes sat nine in a row and looked down impassively into the well of the Supreme Court where a red-faced, immaculately dressed Southern attorney pleaded a civil rights case.

Behind them were soaring Ionic columns and red velvet drapes and a simple clock near the ceiling giving justice a time frame. George Williams, Deputy Assistant Attorney General, Justice Department, walked into the back room behind the banks of spectators and took in the panorama before him.

The justices of the Supreme Court sat behind a mahogany bench on a raised dais. Beneath them was a long simple table at which a court stenographer sat,

17

and on either side smaller tables presently occupied by the attorneys for the state of North Carolina and the federal government. Off to one side sat the clerk of the court and one of the marshals.

Tension filled the court as the Southern attorney made his points in an angry style, but then the hands on the clock reached one and the Chief Justice reached for his gavel and struck it sharply. "I'm sorry to interrupt your argument, Counsel, but it is now time for recess. The court will reconvene at two thirty."

Williams hurried down the aisle, flashing his identification to a marshal, and intercepted John Newhouse, one of the government attorneys. John smiled at him. "You just come in?"

Williams nodded.

"You should have heard corn mash and grits giving me hell. He feels we should be out of the civil rights business for good."

Both of them were now making their way to the cafeteria. Newhouse asked Williams what brought him there.

"I want you to come to dinner tonight. You and Susan."

"Why?"

"I'm going to quit my job."

Newhouse said nothing until they had bought sandwiches and sat down at a table. Then he said, "Look, we've argued this out before. Administrations change. The Democrats will be back some day. Meanwhile, there's a job to do."

"But Internal Security?"

Newhouse smiled. "Your trouble is simple. You're too good! The Republicans want you where you can help *them*. Why not? It's their department."

Williams sipped his coffee and said quietly, "I liked it better in the Civil Rights Division. I don't mind compromises. Life is compromises. But I was *doing* something there."

His quiet voice did not fool Newhouse; Williams

18

could be close to rage but he would never show it. Newhouse said, "So what do you expect me to do at dinner. Encourage you to quit?"

"Why not?"

Newhouse took a bite of pecan pie. "I'd be too lonely, George," he said. "You're the only other fuzzy-headed liberal in the department."

— 6 —

Sarah Williams answered the front door. "Susan called," she said to Newhouse when they joined her in the living room. "She'll be a little delayed. She's taping Senator Buckley, and the senator was an hour late."

Susan Gray, Newhouse's current romance, was a girl known in Washington as a wit, with a television show in which she lanced egos with enthusiasm.

"Poor Buckley," said Newhouse. "She'll carve him up in fillets."

"But can you carve fillets out of ham?" asked Sarah as she led them out onto the patio.

Tonight was short on small talk. Newhouse was anxious to return to the subject he and George had discussed at lunch. He was convinced Williams should stay on at Justice. "After all, George," he said, "we're the last of the refugees from the Kennedy days. But we're all over government and we're needed more than ever now to keep the Nixon crowd from running wild."

By now Susan had arrived, an attractive auburn-haired girl with a rather sharp nose, hair that was too short, a pink dress that was decidedly too short, and tongue that was much too quick. Dinner was served and the evening was politics as usual. Not until one o'clock, when Newhouse and Susan were leaving, did George Williams see the envelope on a table in the foyer.

He took the letter into his den, poured himself a

19

brandy, and opened the envelope.

The letter was typed and unsigned. It said simply:

> November 22, 1973, is the tenth anniversary of our late President's death. For reasons which you will fully understand we will observe this anniversary with the death of the following:
> George Williams
> James Carson
> Thomas Medwick
> Everett Mellon
> Stephanie Spaulding
> Robert Warneky

Jesus! Williams' mind was in a turmoil. The letter was still open before him when his wife came to the door. Immediately she saw that he was upset. "What is it, George?"

He started to hand her the letter, then thought better of it. He returned it to the envelope and stuffed it back into his pocket. "Just some Justice Department business. But nasty."

"That doesn't sound right, George. We don't get Justice Department business at home."

"This time we did."

She looked at him probingly. "Well, if you're in this kind of a mood, I'd better get to bed before the storm breaks."

"It's one of those things, Sarah. I just can't talk to you about it."

"I understand. But don't take everything so *seriously*. No one is going to die."

Sarah walked down the green carpeted hall to their bedroom, a very worried wife. She knew George Williams. That look on his face had told her everything. Another crisis brewing, another period when she might as well be invisible.

She had married him on the rebound from that terrible Stephanie Spaulding affair eight years ago, surprised and pleased that such an attractive man as George Williams would marry a plain-looking woman two years older than himself. She had to be a letdown after the beauty of Stephanie, and she knew it. No contest. And yet, it seemed, he loved her. In his fashion.

That fashion, to her best knowledge, had been to be absolutely faithful to her but to keep her on the periphery of his life. Not only his mind but his heart was in his Justice Department work. And why not? Sarah had many friends among the Nixon people who had come to Washington in 1968. Time and again she had heard what a phenomenon her husband was at Justice; how meticulously prepared were his cases, how thorough his investigations, how successful his pleadings.

Time and again over the past eight years Sarah had seen her husband assigned to a new case, and then practically disappear in front of her eyes. Oh, he was there, all right, in the flesh, but his mind was miles away on other things, always probing, speculating. Often he stayed in town, or was traveling. When he came home, he spoke hardly a word.

Sarah was not without intelligence, and yet she was no lawyer either. What could she contribute during these periods? How could she help him? No way—he went alone. She was a wife who craved domestic tranquillity, quiet dinners with close friends—and instead she endured a never-ending series of crises.

Sometimes . . . a few times, like now . . . she wished she had left George to pine after that Stephanie bitch. Stephanie would not have stood for him sealing off his personal life from his work. She would have torn him out of that office, shattered that mental seclusion, and done whatever else was necessary—give Stephanie that much credit.

Sarah removed her dress and stockings. God, what she wanted was her husband in bed. But she knew there would be no chance of that tonight.

A few minutes later she was in the shower, water cascading down her body, a body she was proud of, full-breasted, slim-hipped, nothing to be ashamed of in that department, even when compared to Stephanie.

Damn Stephanie anyway. Why was she always thinking of her? And why was she so especially worried about George tonight? So it was another case. So George would be lost to her for a while. So what?

And then she remembered the look in George's eyes. Not just concentration this time but something else. What?

No one is going to die. One hour later George was still sitting rooted in his chair, and those words were going through his mind.

Today was October 22, 1973. If that letter was written by a Lee Oswald type, he had thirty days to live. And anyone in the Justice Department knew there were plenty of those insane bastards around in 1973. Plenty.

But the names—and the connection with Kennedy's death! That was what was driving him crazy. Why them? None of them was even important in the Kennedy administration; two of them, James Carson and Everett Mellon, he had never even heard of. And most puzzling of all, why was he, George Williams, on the list? He was as "minor" as everyone else in those days. He had never even *met* the President.

Williams went out on the patio. He had to figure this out or there would be no sleep for him tonight. High above, the moon rode through clouds, shedding a mellow buttery glow over the lawn. Williams sat on the edge of a chaise and looked at the illuminated water in the swimming pool and remembered when Bobby Kennedy had stopped by here that one and only time, a year after George went to work for him in the Justice Department. It was shortly after that famous party at Bobby's house when half the guests had jumped into a pool with their clothes on, creating not too favorable publicity—and on this occasion Bobby, ever a humorist, had nudged George on the edge of his own pool, then caught him before he tumbled in. "I've got to live up to my reputation," he had said with that soft voice which always seemed to contain so much hidden meaning.

Williams had acted as a liaison man in the trouble with Mississippi's Governor Ross Barnett, who refused to allow a Negro to attend the university, and had done so well that after it was all over Bobby had come over to the house to congratulate him personally, one of those characteristic gestures that endeared him to his workers.

Bobby gone, dead—but Bobby, much as George loved him, could never have replaced Jack. No one could.

A large bird clung to a tree close by. George saw its bright eyes briefly; then heard a flutter and there was only darkness. Somewhere a bullfrog croaked and a soft breeze sprang up, and sitting there, George Williams at last realized an awful truth about himself: he was playing out his time in this stupid century. Nothing had really mattered to him since that November day in 1963.

But there had been a time. Jack Kennedy had thousands of young people joining the Peace Corps, and thousands more coming in from all over the country to share the adventure of governing the country with a President who spoke their language and shared their hopes. It was a time when intelligent concerned young people set Washington bubbling with enthusiasm . . . a time when the Russians blinked an eyeball and were booted out of the Caribbean; when Negroes were about to earn that most essential right in America, the right to vote—and hell, who knows where we could have gone? Who knows?

Across ten years Williams found himself young

again, full of optimism again, remembering those exhilarating days when he really believed that the future belonged to the young, and the President of the United States stood on a snowswept inaugural stand and said it for them: "Let the word go forth from this time and place to friend and foe alike that the torch has been passed to a new generation of Americans . . . I do not shrink from this responsibility, I welcome it."

Robert Frost's hair blowing in the wind, a fire on the inaugural stand, Eisenhower looking straight ahead wondering what had hit the country, Chief Justice Warren holding a Bible in icy fingers, administering the oath of office to the tall young man——and snow swirling in young George Williams' eyes as he stood on the Capitol grounds and hoped to God he could help in some small way.

And after it all, the hope, the shock, the despair—this evil letter. This hateful poisonous letter saying that "for reasons which you will fully understand" he was in some way connected with the death of John F. Kennedy whom he idolized, and for that he must *die*. Whose idea of a sick joke was this?

But it was no joke. Thirteen years in the Justice Department had taught Williams that much.

In the end Williams had not slept that night. The next day he did some private checking at the Justice Department, called a friend at the FBI, and another at Internal Revenue, and soon had the current addresses of each of the other victims.

Had they received identical threats, or was he to be the messenger of fear? If so, he would soon have his first clue.

In New York Allen Lowell went to the Consolidated
Film rental office at 630 Ninth Avenue, a store-front
operation in a large office building. Allen pushed
open the door, a bell clanged and a woman in a blue
smock came out from the back.

"I called about the *Years of Lightning—Days of
Drums* film."

The woman was a pleasant pie-faced type with
rimless glasses. "There's no need to pay rental, you
know. You can contact USIA and get it free . . ."

"I haven't the time."

"What's your organization?" she asked.

"American Legion."

The woman pushed a form across the counter and
disappeared into the shelves. A few minutes later she
returned with a large film can which she placed on
the counter. "I can't tell you how many requests we
get for this," she said. "You'll have to return it tomorrow, you know. It's booked all weekend."

"I'll do that."

He paid the rental plus a security deposit, and then
went out by the back door into the lobby where he
waited for an elevator. A few minutes later he was
upstairs in the editing rooms of Audio Productions.
The president of Audio, a smiling Irishman named
Pete Mooney, had once fired him—but he was willing
to let bygones be bygones. "Take a moviola, Jeff," he
said. "Use it as long as you want."

Allen threaded the film, turned off the light, and
pressed a foot pedal.

He knew every frame of this film. But still he had
to make sure. The funeral came on, the black horse
tugging at its bridle, threatening to canter away, the
colorful flagdraped caisson, Jackie Kennedy in a

black veil, and then . . . there it was, the long shot of the Lincoln Memorial. Allen removed his foot from the pedal and the scene froze. He moved close to the screen until he saw what he was looking for.

Thirty minutes later he returned the film to the woman and walked down the street to the Avon coffee shop for a hamburger and a Coke. A pretty girl sat next to him at the counter, but he paid no attention to her. He was thinking of his plan.

By now Williams would have warned the other five. And Carson had had a double warning, if he ever slept in his own hotel room. Knowing Carson, that was debatable.

JAMES CARSON

From FBI files:

B-17743, an informant who has been reliable in the past, states that James Carson, while lecturing at UCLA in October 1964, told students that Communism has been treated in quote cartoon fashion unquote in American films and that a quote great unquote film showing the positive side of Communism is a quote epic waiting to be created unquote.

Jesus, Le Club was going crazy! New York hadn't seen a party like this in years. It started as the usual anniversary affair of the Stewart Model Agency, one hundred beautiful young girls as the draw—and the kooks kept pouring in. Hip boots, dungarees, microskirts, hot pants, see-through blouses, and flesh, flesh, flesh, and Jim Carson laughed and thought New York is too much. Too much. Three hours ago a complex legal discussion in a penthouse of the Chase Manhattan building in Wall Street—and now chaos and rock and grass and a five-foot-nine redhead dancing right in front of him in a microskirt and no panties, absolutely bare to the view.

After the record came to a halt, the redhead came over to his table, regally ignoring her date, a bald-headed veteran of the garment wars. "Mr. Carson, remember me?"

"Sure. You were in *Wild Man* at Universal."

"Yeah. Nothing happened after that."

"You should have looked me up."

From where he was sitting Carson was almost eye level with the redhead's waist, and when he looked up it was even worse. Too funny! He found himself laughing.

"How could I get in to see you? They don't let starlets into directors' offices any more, unless they're hookers."

"In that outfit, you'd have made it," said Carson.

The redhead laughed with him. "Where are you staying, Mr. Carson?"

At this her date, who had followed her, placed his hand on her hip. "Hey, Jade, remember me?"

"Cool it, Abe," said the redhead, shaking him off in one slight move. And Carson thought, what the hell. He stood and shook hands with Abe Weber, and then introduced his own table companion, who happened to be president of a major network. "Gee," said the redhead, "maybe I *should* have worn panties."

"Not on my account," said the man gallantly.

"I'm at the Waldorf," said Carson. "Room 1810."

"Hey look—" said Abe.

"Shut up, Abe," said the redhead, and they swept off.

And then the president of the network left and Jim found himself with a Hollywood actor of the Warren Beatty type, Buck Heming, and Buck was affecting that Texas accent that drove Jim up the wall, and saying, "Let's give a couple of these chicks a little hump at my place," and it was getting late now, two thirty, and Jim Carson had been smoking grass—and the two chicks idea didn't sound bad at all. "Which ones?" he asked.

"Pick any two," said Buck. "You know we can have any in the place."

Which was the truth. After all, Jim Carson was coming off two straight hits, still growing as a director—and Buck attracted girls, as he put it, "like a jar of vaginal jelly in a mosquito farm," and Jim smoked some more grass and laughed and they ended up with three girls, two models and a stewardess named Lynne Lippicott who refused to let go of Jim, and they went not to Buck's apartment but to P. J. Clarke's, smoky and full of noise, and ate hamburgers, and the stewardess, drunk, said to Jim, "You should have met me two years ago."

"Why?"

"That was the Year of the Cock!"

An adorable brunette, long hair over her eyes, really innocent-looking, really out of her depth with these people, but hanging on because she could tell everyone in the crew next morning that she had spent the night with Jim Carson.

And really, really, he should get to bed right now, he should hump these girls, but first they had to stop off at the back bar at the Hippopotamus to say hello to Olivier Coquelin, and the virginal-looking stewardess was hanging onto Jim Carson and the two models were all over Buck and the grass was flowing, the incense burning on the walls to remove the scent, and later that fool Buck was running up the middle of Park Avenue, shouting something, and the girls were chasing him, and Jim rode behind in the chauffeured limousine and watched the three of them tumble to the ground on the island and somehow, when they stood up, two of the girls were naked and everyone jumped into the limo and Carson said, "Now how are you going to get them into the building?"

"Easy," said Buck. "I tell the doorman they're two nuns from St. Mary's who bet on NYU," and everyone thought this was funny, hash-funny, grass-funny . . .

. . . and later that night in Buck's apartment the stewardess straddled Jim Carson joyously and exuberantly, and Jim had one of those marvelous erections that would never quit, would last forever, would end up in India as a monument, and he fell asleep with a blurry happy vision of an angelic young brunette in ecstasy, head to the side, lips open—

—but hell, he had seen it so many times before.

— 2 —

The next day Carson went straight from Buck's apartment to Wall Street, and a banker was saying, "The enterprise includes Candice Bergen and Donald Sutherland?"

"Under contract."

The banker took off his rimless glasses. "I am not familiar with Mr. Sutherland."

"M·A·S·H."

"The TV show?"

"The best movie of 1970. Sutherland was the star."

The man was not as unaware as Carson thought. "That was Elliot Gould," he said. Carson laughed. "Right on the button. Gould went to the moon and back. But Sutherland was the star—and he's a great talent. I used him in *Court-Martial*."

The banker gave a wan smile. "You don't mind my asking these questions, Mr. Carson. It's really so I can impress my teenage daughters that I have some inside knowledge. Of course, we rely on your judgment in these matters."

"Fine."

"Twentieth Century will distribute?"

"Yes." But Carson was thinking how simple it used to be five years ago. In those days, you had a package, you had a picture. MGM, Universal, Columbia just started you going, and hoped to God you'd stay in budget. Now the banks had to clear everything.

"You can tell Mr. Zifkind, unofficially, that we approve the enterprise," said the banker.

But as he was leaving, the man said, "Pardon me, Mr. Carson, but there's something I just have to ask you."

"What's that?"

"Haven't we met before someplace? The thing is, I've never been to Hollywood."

"I used to work in Washington ten years ago."

"Ah," said the banker.

"I was with USIA."

"Ah," said the banker.

"Were you in Washington then?"

The banker smiled that wan smile. "I'm afraid the late President was not one of my ideals," he said. "But I did attend the inaugural as a representative of the bank. The blizzard was hell."

"I was at the ball but it's unlikely we met in that mob."

"Now I've got it!" said the banker, delightedly.

31

"The ball. You were dancing with my niece. This is
. . . extraordinary. How ever did you get to Hollywood from *there?*"

"Somebody shot somebody," said Carson.

Suddenly, he couldn't stand being in the same
room with this happy little right-wing banker—but he
couldn't afford to blow the deal. "Well, I'm happy to
meet you again, although I doubt if I would remember your niece. I danced with fifty girls that night,
most of them strangers."

"Stephanie Spaulding?" said the banker.

Jesus!

— 3 —

Carson was anxious to forget about Stephanie
Spaulding, with whom he had once had a brief fling.
A typical Back Bay snob—that was all she had turned
out to be. Besides, it made him damn uncomfortable even to think back to those days in Washington
and he didn't even want to analyze why.

But today, apparently, he was not to be spared. He
returned to the Waldorf to find a telegram waiting for
him at the desk. He ripped it open and read:

> Would like interview with you at your conve-
> nience. Will contact you by telephone.
> George Williams
> Deputy Assistant Attorney General,
> US Justice Department

Justice Department! What was *that* all about?

Troubled, he went up to his suite. He hadn't slept
there last night and wilting in a vase were the flowers
from that press agent who was romancing him. The
guy would never give up.

But Carson wasn't thinking of press agents. His

mind was on that telegram. He threw his topcoat on a couch, ripped off his tie and tossed it on top, and went into the bedroom. There he saw something very strange. His passport, which he had brought along for his upcoming trip to Europe, was lying on his bed. In pieces! Somebody had cut his passport into shreds and scattered it all over the bed. What the hell was happening!

He found himself staring at a Kennedy half-dollar.

STEPHANIE SPAULDING

From FBI files:

K-30087, an informant who has been reliable in the past, states that Stephanie Spaulding Winthrop attended meeting of Wives Against Vietnam in Pound Ridge, N.Y., October 6, 1967. She contributed $500 to the organization, Cheque #32 on First National Bank, Pound Ridge, dated October 7, 1967.

No attendance at future meetings observed.

Stephanie Spaulding Winthrop tossed the tennis ball high, then smashed a serve hard enough to kick up chalk, and Bret O'Brien's racquet was knocked clean out of his hands. "You mad at somebody?" he called to her.

If he only knew, thought Stephanie, but she said nothing, crossed to the other serving side and smashed another ace. This time O'Brien was grinning. "I'm going to play with the boys."

And so the game went, with Stephanie putting everything into every serve and drive, trying to work out the tension she had felt since receiving that telegram from George Williams.

An hour later, the gray-haired man on the front steps of Stephanie's home in Pound Ridge watched the brunette in white tennis shorts walking toward him. She saw him, smiled, and swatted some fallen leaves with her racket. "Match point," she said.

"I just arrived and found the house empty."

"I was destroying our tennis pro," said Stephanie. "Sorry I'm late, Stan. But you're not my only problem today."

Stephanie went upstairs to shower and change while Stanley accepted a drink from a pretty Jamaican maid. He took in the original Miro and the small signed Picasso paintings on the wall, both of them splashes of blue in a green room . . . a long low-slung green sofa of the "Depression" period coming into vogue (Stephanie was always one year ahead of the vogue), see-through glass coffee tables, and square comfortable-looking arm chairs covered with light green silk and—how typical of Stephanie—a 1930s radio in a conversation setting across the room.

Stanley couldn't resist. He went over to the radio and turned it on—and then jumped. Franklin Roosevelt's voice rolled out: "I see one-third of a nation ill-fed, ill-clothed, ill-housed." Stanley smiled. The witch! He looked up to see Stephanie in a simple Pucci dress with a blue pattern, and leather thong sandals, laughing at him as she came into the room. "Bring back memories?"

"I have to admit I'm dated enough to remember the speech."

Stephanie settled herself at the end of the sofa, curling her legs under her loosely. Once again Stanley found himself marveling at her beauty, the green eyes, the intelligent face with the high cheekbones, the generous lips, the fine black hair which inundated her shoulders and licked against her bosom. He said, "Roosevelt's speech reminds me that some persons wouldn't mind seeing you ill-fed, ill-clothed, and ill-housed."

Stephanie smiled as the maid came in with some iced tea.

"The fam?"

"Your late husband's attorneys informed me today that the family is contesting the will."

Stephanie sipped her iced tea and said nothing. Stanley went on, "You were legally separated at the time of Mr. Winthrop's death."

"But he hadn't changed the will."

"No," the lawyer said, "but there's a legal shadow."

"Oh Christ, Stanley, come to the point."

There was no more conservative man than Stanley Harwell, but he was finding himself growing uncomfortable. That amazing client of his was deliberately—Stephanie did everything deliberately—sitting in such a way that he could not help looking deep into her curving thighs without pointedly turning away. It was damned disconcerting, especially from someone of her breeding. He was irritated with himself for his reaction and surreptitiously opened a button on his vest. "Do you mind?" he asked, when he saw her watching him.

"Take your trousers off for all I care," said Stephanie.

"But I—" he stopped as Stephanie laughed. She said, "You're such a darling. I apologize for that remark. Do tell me what horrors the fam has in mind." She tucked her legs under her decorously, and thought, these damn miniskirts, when will I learn to sit! Old Stanley's eyes were crossed.

The lawyer sipped his drink determinedly. He must remember never to call on Stephanie at home again. Finally he turned to her and said, "They're going to say you drove your husband to commit suicide, and that he was mentally incompetent when he drew up the will. There will be other charges."

"Including one from me!"

"I beg your pardon?"

"I tried to commit suicide first! It was a race."

Harwell was startled. "None of that is in the material you gave me."

"I didn't want those relatives of his to have the satisfaction. But Dr. Nelson can fill you in. I took twelve sleeping pills last May. The fatal dose is ten."

The lawyer reached into an expensive leather briefcase, brought out a notepad and a gold ballpoint pen and started scribbling. "I don't know where this will lead us—"

"Dr. Nelson is right here in Pound Ridge. You want me to call him?"

"Not just yet. I haven't sorted out the legal implications."

"Well, here's one legal implication. Bob Winthrop was a prick."

"Stephanie—"

"Everyone knows it including those sisters and brothers. They hated him, too."

Stanley lit a cigarette, inhaled, then watched the

smoke curl toward the ceiling. "So what?"

"So I didn't drive him to suicide. He drove *me*."

"But he died and you're alive." The lawyer suddenly leaned forward, elbows on his knees. "Stephanie, they know about the senator."

The maid came in and removed the glasses and the tray. Stephanie waited until she had left and said: "Poor Bucko. They're going to drag him into this, too? We had only one date and that was by accident."

"He's married. He's running for offiice. They figure he'll put pressure on you."

"For one date? When nothing happened?"

"It's hard to prove nothing happened, especially when you're a married man running in a tight race against someone unscrupulous who'll use anything he can find to discredit his opponent."

Stephanie thought for a while. "And suppose I say to hell with the relatives? Let them keep their blood money."

"Mr. Thomas at Banker's Trust tells me you will then be in debt thirty thousand dollars with no means of paying. You must fight it, Stephanie."

"But it isn't fair to Bucky."

"Senator Moore will have to worry about that himself. You can't sacrifice ten million dollars just to preserve his image. Frankly, the will looks unbreakable to me. The family is just going to make sure you suffer before you collect."

Stephanie suddenly smiled.

"In that case, exit Bucko," she said.

Harwell got the message. He'd better watch it or one of these days—exit Harwell. Lawyer or lover, you were never sure of yourself with Stephanie.

Thirty minutes after the attorney had left, Stephanie was pacing her living room. She was so angry she couldn't stand still. She picked up that strange telegram from George Williams and read it for the tenth time. So formal! Not even the slightest hint he knew her!

He must have realized when he sent the telegram what the very mention of his name would do to her.

She ripped the telegram in half, crumpled it in her fist, and hurled it at the picture window.

ROBERT WARNEKY

From FBI files:

PSI R-10675, an informant of unknown reliability, states that Robert Warneky appeared at a meeting of black militant students on the Ohio State campus on March 3, 1967, during student uprising, and stated his support of their demands. Warneky took an opposite position in public.

The pass went down the field, the ball glittering in the sunlight, and that colored kid went after it, the defending cornerback closing in, and up, up, the hands clawing and the boy had it, the cornerback going down, and he was away and Bob blew the whistle and the kid slowed up, grinning. He tossed the ball to the back, who gave him the Italian salute.

Bob Warneky smiled. That boy was going to be something. Only a sophomore but already six-two and with great hands. Just the wide receiver they needed.

He crossed the practice field of Xavier, a small high school in upper New York State. The team was in a huddle. The quarterback was saying, "This guy could catch a bucket of shit in a hurricane," when they saw Warneky. Bob outlined another play, then stepped back to the sidelines.

But instead of watching the play develop, he found his mind was suddenly hundreds of miles away. In Washington, where that telegram had come from. The name Williams meant nothing to him . . . it was the thought of the city that stirred Warneky.

Thirteen years ago and another telegram from Washington, this time from the President of the United States, the man Bob always called Lieutenant, and always noticed how it pleased him.

Bob had served in the PT squadron with Jack Kennedy in the Russell Islands, and after that had not seen him in years. A bos'n's mate from a poor family in Brooklyn didn't come in contact with people like the Kennedys in civilian life. But then that telegram had arrived, and just when Bob was desperate for a job.

And he had ended up on the President's Physical Fitness Program, and had actually gone to Moscow to talk with Communist leaders about a joint program. He, Robert Warneky, the Canarsie kid, in Moscow!

But he had done all right in the program, everyone agreed to that—and Jack had started giving him other little chores, some of a political nature, although always minor. Bob kept in the background, far from Lords Schlesinger, Sorenson, McNamara, *et al.* But every so often when Jack liked to reminisce about the old days in the Navy, he'd call Bob and they'd laugh it up over coffee in the Oval office.

Then, in one day, it had ended—so suddenly that Bob had never really adjusted to the change, could hardly believe to this day that the young President with the cool grin never again would call him from Washington.

After that it had been all downhill. Because of contacts he had made in Washington, he had landed a spot at a Big Ten college as an assistant coach—much to the irritation of the head coach. And then a vicious trick of fate had delivered Bob into his hands. A substitute halfback—angry that Bob had converted him to defense, even though Bob knew the kid just didn't have it for offense—decided to get even.

The next thing Bob knew the head coach called him in and said the halfback reported that Bob had "propositioned" him in the locker room. He, Robert Warneky, the All-American square! A frame-up so absurd and so vicious that Warneky couldn't believe it was happening.

But his denials were unavailing. The coach had told Bob that the "incident" would never be revealed but he would have to find another spot at the end of the season. Thanks to the grapevine, Bob never could find another college job. Now, here he was working for pennies at a high school. From the White House

Oval Room to a crummy little backwater job in ten years.

Christ, he had missed the play. He hadn't even seen it. Tears were in his eyes, and his boys were staring at him from the middle of the field.

THOMAS MEDWICK

From FBI files:

T-46782, an informant (reliable-protect) states that Thomas Medwick, Congressman, 14th District, Pennsylvania, received campaign contributions in cash from Anthony Caputo, vice-president of Philadelphia Electricians' Union. Transaction observed by informant from car parked in front of Belk Travel Lodge on Route 40 near Chester, Pa. Cash amount undetermined. Medwick's financial campaign report indicates no contribution from Electricians' Union.

Congressman Thomas Medwick opened his bottom desk drawer and brought out a bottle of J and B. From a tray on the small table next to his desk he took a glass and poured himself a drink. He needed it.

That fat-faced sneak working for Jack Anderson was after him again. Twice one of his legmen had been in to see Senator Murrow, and he knew why. But what had Anderson found out? Murrow said he had told him nothing.

Medwick was a stocky, broad-shouldered man with a rather short-sighted stare which, through thick glasses, turned his eyes into blue moons. Now that stare was directed at the ceiling as he tilted his chair back and thought, my god, it's all over now. An entire career wasted for one mistake. If Anderson dug deep enough on that International Dynamics deal—

There was a knock on the door and an attractive gray-haired woman entered his office. "I brought you the records you wanted," she said, depositing a thick pile of manila folders on his desk. Then she made a joke. "You don't want a shredder, do you?"

Medwick gave her a thin smile and she retired in some confusion. But a minute later she was back. "I forgot. This telegram came for you."

Medwick read it and his heart bumped. The Justice Department!

He told his secretary he would be in Senator Murrow's office and was on his way into the great echoing corridor of the House Office Building, passing the busts of statesmen, bypassing the tourists on their way to "drop in" on their representative, smiling at Congressman Dave Garth from New York, and descending to the little underground railway that would whisk him to the S.O.B. . . . the Senate Office Building.

Senator Murrow was a Republican from Texas, and one of the heirs to the Kinder Oil fortune. Perhaps the richest senator since Kerr from Oklahoma, and a man who had "adopted" Medwick from the moment he came to Congress. He was also the man who had got him into this sticky International Dynamics situation.

Medwick entered a little reception area to find a Texas girl with corn-yellow hair on the phone. "Look," she was saying, "I *know* he's married" . . . then broke off and looked up at Medwick. "Let me call you tonight," she said, hung up, and turned on a smile at him. "Hello, Mr. Medwick. The senator is expecting you."

Medwick went past her, his heart beating faster. This was turning out to be some kind of day. Why was the senator expecting him? Had the Justice Department called him too?

He passed a glass partition, behind which were young male assistants and attractive girl secretaries—no Women's Lib movement in this office—and smiled at a few who recognized him. The door to Murrow's office was partly open, and he pushed it the rest of the way and walked into the high-ceilinged room with a portrait of General Washington and a Texas flag behind the desk. Leaning against the desk front, the shirt-sleeved muscular Murrow finished off a pastrami sandwich while dictating to a secretary. "Make that the eleventh," he said to the girl. "Houston on the eleventh."

He waved the pastrami sandwich at Medwick. "The Jews do something good."

Medwick took a seat. "Is pastrami Jewish?"

"I get it from a kosher deli," said Murrow. "Every time I order I swing to the side of Israel. Thank God I don't eat all the time. I'd lose my constituency."

"Anything more?" asked the girl.

"An out," said the senator. "I need an out or that silly Livermore woman will expect me to stay the night. Let's try this. I must be in Dallas on the evening of the eleventh for conferences on the . . . on the . . ." He turned to Medwick. "What should I have conferences on?"

"The environment?"

"Perfect. Conferences on the environment. 'This gives me great sorrow because I always appreciate and look forward to the pleasures of the Livermore home. Best regards, etc.' "

The girl shut her book and disappeared into the outer office. "Great legs on that little girl," said the merry senator.

Medwick had never met anyone like Murrow. The man was a constant bubble of good cheer. Every other rich man Medwick had ever met was somber, always worried, suspicious and insecure. But Murrow was forever in a good mood, brightening everyone's life around him. The senator returned to his swivel chair behind his desk, leaned back and threw his feet up on some papers. "El pricko was in here again."

"Anderson?"

"His snoop. Fenton. I gave him nothing, of course."

"Why did your receptionist say you were expecting me?"

"Fenton just left—and knowing your radar, I figured you'd be over. You were a bit quicker than I expected."

Medwick tossed him the telegram from Williams. "What do you think this means?"

Murrow read it, then looked up. "You a traitor?"

"No."

"A spy?"

"Not lately."

"A long-haired rock-throwing radical college crazy?"

"Too old for that."

"Well, that's Internal Security," the senator said.

47

"And that's what Williams is. I know him." He paused. "I think this letter is on another subject, not mother Dynamics."

"But what?" asked Medwick.

"How the hell do I know? Call Williams and ask him. Stop worrying so much, Medwick! Your balls will start tightening."

Medwick went over to the window and sat down on the window seat. Outside, cars rolled lugubriously up Pennsylvania Avenue, people worrying about their bills or the next ball game or the high price of rib roast. And here he was, Tom Medwick, facing a possible jail sentence with a crazy millionaire senator who found the world a big laugh. "Anderson is so close I can hear him breathing," he said. "Doesn't this Dynamics situation worry you?"

"You were the one who signed the papers," said the senator.

And suddenly Medwick knew everything, knew why the senator had taken such a liking to him, knew he had been used—and knew he was at last about to be exposed. The senator wouldn't protect him. No siree.

White-faced, he went out of the office without saying a word, so preoccupied he bumped into desks, startling secretaries. He was remembering ten years ago when he worked for Fulbright, and this same senator had asked him for a favor and he had refused.

Those were the Kennedy days, and four years later, after Kennedy died, Senator Murrow had asked for another favor. By then Medwick was a Congressman, and he needed campaign funds, and Kennedy was dead, and this time he had agreed to the favor. And another. And then another.

Until now, there had never been a problem.

EVERETT MELLON

From FBI files:

H-19578, an informant who has been reliable in the past, states that Everett Mellon contributed two hundred dollars to a SNCC Negro vote drive. Cheque #14 drawn on Bankers Trust, Stonington, Massachusetts, dated September 3, 1966.

"An orgy! They had a bloody orgy on my boat!"

The crackling voice on the phone from New York was furious. "I could sue you!"

Everett Mellon tried not to show his worry, but he knew Jim Hartford had a point. The story had been all over the newspapers when a Coast Guard patrol boat, picking up a girl in the water, had found the *Tresca* filled with naked young boys and girls and enough hash to float Berkeley into the ocean. Now Mellon said, "You hired me to charter your boat and I did. *Playhouse* magazine wanted it for a sales conference-type thing. They lied to *me* so sue *them*."

"But you're responsible," said Hartford. "I'm checking with my lawyers and calling you back." He hung up.

Beautiful, thought Mellon. There goes the chartering business. Two years in Nassau, playing along with crooked white businessmen and crooked black politicians, and out of it all he had managed to set up a profitable yacht brokerage—and now this. And he deserved it!

Mellon knew that Hartford was right. He realized when he chartered the big yawl to Kellner that the magazine executive had something other than business in mind: most of the "sales executives" had turned out to be eighteen- and nineteen-year-old nymphets. But he had taken the risk. The deal had been too good— eight thousand for one week. No one paid that any more!

Just his luck one of those stupid kids had to fall overboard and wash him up on the front pages and out of the business. Mellon, you really get the breaks!

He went out on the dock and looked at the *Tresca,* a beautiful yawl with the trim lines of a Newport racer. Boats like this had been the reason he had gone into this business. Outside of that brief episode in Washington, sailing always had been his life.

His black man, Rafael, was scrubbing the deck of the ship. "Very bad," he was muttering. "Very bad."

"What's bad?"

"Cigarette burns all over ship. Mistah Hartford angry when he sees."

"And the other damage?"

The black smiled, showing blinding white and dazzling gold teeth. "Broken chairs, glasses, torn mattresses . . . real good party I think, yes!"

"That party is going to throw both you and me out of work," snapped Mellon. He went up the gangway and stepped gingerly on the deck, then ducked into the entranceway leading down into the cabin area. The bar was in back with high stools bolted to the floor, and aluminum deck chairs with bright red cushions scattered around. It didn't look too bad. Rafael had done his work well, as usual.

But my God they must have smoked! The smell of hash still hung in the air three days after the party. The furniture was soaked in it. He went behind the bar and saw cardboard cartons filled with broken dishes and glasses, then stepped into the passageway and straightaway tripped over some shattered furniture Rafael had stacked up. A long ugly scar gashed the paint on the wall. What had those idiots done?

He couldn't take any more today. Tomorrow he would total the damage and fire a letter to Kellner. Kellner would write a check in a minute, considering the bad publicity.

But it was over for him in Nassau. Trying to make a quick buck at the risk of someone's boat just wasn't done by yacht brokers who wanted to stay in business.

He went back topside, patted Rafael on the back, and walked ashore. A little black girl came running to him. She was the daughter of his secretary. "Telly-gram," she said.

Two minutes later he was calling George Williams, long distance. The man from the Justice Department said he would fly down to see him. Then he asked something strange. "Have you gotten an anonymous letter lately?"

Mellon said, "My creditors all sign their names."

"Your name is mentioned on a death threat," said Williams.

"Me? A death threat? Why would anyone want to kill me? I'm just a yacht broker, for God's sake."

"You worked for the Kennedy administration?"

Mellon was almost too puzzled to reply. He said, "Work isn't quite the word. I was a Senate page for all of three months, that's the nearest I came to Kennedy."

— 2 —

Excerpt from Allen Lowell's diary . . . entry October 23, 1973:

. . . How these six will be surprised when they see *me!* I who know them better than anyone.

In some ways I have grown to love them . . . as the hunter loves the duck that lands in the water near his decoy and is blasted into feathers and blood by his shotgun. I love them that way. Head for head, blood for blood, six for Tommy.

BOOK II

THE DEATH OF
THOMAS MEDWICK

— 1 —

The Metroliner to Washington waited in the station, steam and compressed air wreathing its wheels. Allen Lowell carried suitcase and briefcase aboard, taking a seat in the second car front. He placed his briefcase carefully on the seat next to him, keeping his hand on it; but it was Friday afternoon and the train was nearly filled and a tall black in a dashiki asked to sit down.

Allen moved the briefcase between his feet.

The train lurched, then started, and soon was clicking along rapidly, and Allen stared bleakly at the passing New Jersey countryside, the swamps stretching to the horizon. Ahead a plane zoomed gently from Newark airport.

Peaceful—but Allen had something else on his mind. That black.

Taking his briefcase, he slid by to the aisle. Back through the weary, half-slumbering faces of businessmen, college girls, to the end of the car with its push-button door. A touch on a pad and the door slid open and he went through. He made his way to the little bar where a few men clutched drinks and sandwiches, trying to keep their balance in the tiny swaying cubicle.

He would have to remain here the whole trip—or find another seat. But he had seen the train was completely filled.

He ordered a Scotch on the rocks which he didn't want, and went over to the window away from the pushing crowd at the bar. He drank his Scotch slowly, pondering. FBI! He had to be. On his way to jail some unsuspecting kids, setting them up, big funny goddamn joke.

The FBI, Fucking Bad Investigators, according to some of his friends. But Allen Lowell knew better. He really knew better!

An hour later he was back in his car again, and from the door saw that the black man was gone. He went back to his seat, and found the note:

WHITEY IS SHIT.

Of course the note didn't fool him at all.

He kept his hand on his briefcase.

— 2 —

When a man has received an anonymous threat, every crowd becomes a danger, every high building a multiple opportunity for death. But George Williams thought nothing of this; he was convinced that the man behind the threat was intelligent, that he was playing some kind of murderous game, that he would not be satisfied with a simple shooting. The reason was the reference to the Kennedy assassination. For some reason, perhaps political, perhaps something else, the killer put them right in there with the Kennedy circle, or the Kennedy enemies, or what?

After he received the letter Williams had taken the day off to track down the addresses of the other victims and send them telegrams. But the first telephone call had confirmed his suspicion: he had been the only victim to receive the threat.

Why? Either the letter writer knew a top official in the Justice Department could immediately locate the others, or he had special plans for Williams.

Whatever, he had to see Harley Connors. This thing was bound to leak in the wake of those five telegrams he had sent yesterday. Williams would have preferred to lone wolf it—one lone wolf against another—in a silent struggle of wit he'd take his chance. But Connors, he knew, would have none of it. And Connors was his superior.

On Friday morning Williams parked his car in the garage of the modest office building on 9th Street which housed the Internal Security Division along with a profusion of other government divisions that had overflowed their headquarters. Internal Security and the Civil Rights Division were both billeted in this building far from the Justice Department proper.

Williams stopped by his office, checked the mail, then headed down the corridor to the big corner office of his chief. "Has he got time?" he asked the secretary.

She looked at her calendar. "He has to be at the Barn at ten, but now he's free. I'll buzz him."

Two minutes later Williams was talking to Harley Connors. "Take a look at this," he said, handing him the anonymous note. Connors, a big florid man with quick intelligent eyes behind hornrimmed glasses, studied the note professionally. "A crazy?"

"That remains to be seen," said Williams.

"These other five your pals?"

Williams took out a cigarette and lit it. "I've met the girl, that's all."

"Strange," said Connors. "The names don't make sense."

"That was the first thought that occurred to me."

Connors studied the note again as if trying to find some clue he had overlooked. "Where the hell is Salinger, Sorenson, O'Brien, O'Donnell? If you're going to make a grandstand play why not go for the headliners? Why you?"

"I never met Kennedy in my life. I think we'll find the same thing with most of the others."

"Strange," said Connors again, and pursed his lips. "But not so strange that I don't believe it."

He put down the note. "The trouble is we can't afford to put a three-shift guard on six people on the strength of a note. We get a hundred of these a day from the White House."

Williams leaned back in his chair. "I know that, of course. That's why I'm warning them myself."

Connors looked at Williams. "Knowing you, I expect you to do a *little* more than that." He smiled, almost to himself. "Jesus. He made one big mistake in this little package. Five nobodies OK. But George Williams? Doesn't he know about you?"

Williams said nothing. Then: "I might ask you for leave now and then in the next thirty days."

Connors said, "I'll bet. Well, George, I want to tell you something straight. I broke every ball in the White House bringing you into my division, but I told them I need you and I can handle you. Whether that's true or not, one thing is straight. I don't want to lose you to some psychotic maniac with ten rifles up his ass."

"I can take care of myself. It's the others I'm concerned about."

"You contact them already?"

"Telegrams."

Connors said, "Let me think about this for a while. The fact he has you on the list might give the department jurisdiction. Assault on a federal officer is covered, I know. If it doesn't spell out threat we can get at it under conspiracy."

Williams stood up. "I can handle it. I don't think we have to make it department business."

Connors stood up with him, looking surprised. "Quasi-official, George. No big thing. But we do want the bureau's help, don't we? Now let me get Jim over there on the phone, and get off a supporting letter, and you and I will talk later today.

"Oh," Connors said. "One more thing. Can you leave me that note?"

"No."

The two men stared at each other, and Connors finally gave him a nod and Williams left. Connors looked at that door for a long time after it closed. He was tough, some said ruthless—but Williams was something else.

He flicked on a switch and in a minute their previous conversation was coming out of the speaker of the tape recorder. "I don't think we have to make it department business," Williams was saying from the machine.

Why? Was he afraid of something?

— 3 —

The black man in the dashiki got off the train at Union Station in Washington and waited in the shadows until he saw Allen Lowell coming through. He knew that mother. And he didn't want no part of him. No part.

That time they had fought their way into Lon San, taking fire all the way, and the gooks behind them trailing as usual instead of covering; the black had come around a hut and found three Green Berets holding a crowd of Charlies prisoner. The Berets must have been infiltrated in before, and now they held submachine guns loosely while the battle raged beyond them.

The Negro did not like the Berets. They went too far. They cut balls, collected ears, and blasted out brains like it was nothing. And this one Beret, a slim guy with sloping shoulders and gray eyes, this Beret whom the black had just recognized on the Metroliner, suddenly started firing his machine gun into the crowd of unarmed prisoners. Right in front of him! Screams and faces flowering into blood and some trying to run, and this cat mowed them down. Sadistic! No reason!

He had never forgotten those gray eyes and now there he was, Mr. College Boy again in a blazer, snappily getting into a taxi.

WHITEY IS SHIT he had written on the card he left on the seat. And this is one time he meant it.

4

Hundreds of miles north of Washington, the first input to the FBI's National Crime Information Center on Allen Lowell was about to take place. It began with a man sweating.

Joe Ignelli, Chief of Security at US Steel's Largo Falls plant, was chewing out Harry Andrews. "Harry, you screwed up but good!"

Andrews wiped his forehead with a green kerchief. "I knew the kid was acting weird. I should have been on my guard."

"When do you think he took them?"

Andrews thought. "It could have been any time—but my guess is when he threw one of the cartridges a mile high in the air and I was waiting to see who caught it."

"Takes two off the back of the truck and flips them away—then returns later while you're drinking martinis at home?"

Andrews stood up. "I'm going out there again. There's still a chance someone misplaced them. Nobody knew what he was doing out there."

Ignelli called for his secretary by simply yelling, "Hey, Mary!" She came into the room, and Ignelli told her, "You and I are going to be busy." To Andrews he said, "Harry, comb every inch of that damn desert. Spend a week if you have to. But every inch!"

5

October 23, 1973

From: Chief Security Division, US Steel, Largo Falls

To: Director, Industrial Explosives Division
Subject: Missing explosives

1. Inventory shows that two chemite "sticks" were not accounted for after motion picture demonstration by Coleman company on October 22, 1973. Harry Andrews, the man assigned to the project, did not notice the missing "sticks" at the time. Claims general confusion of shooting and unfamiliarity with motion picture procedures.

2. Five "sticks" were "blown" in the demonstration out of twelve brought to the location. Five were returned to inventory.

3. A film editor with the company, described as a "free-lance," that is, a man not permanently employed by subject company, disappeared the evening of the demonstration. It is assumed that he found a means to obtain and conceal the sticks until his disappearance.

4. The man's name is Jeffrey Bolton. Address listed as 1340 Marlton Avenue, Baltimore, Maryland.

5. The president of Coleman Productions, Leonard Coleman, hired this man for the particular film. He informs me that he is contacting Bolton immediately.

6. Further steps will be taken as soon as Mr. Coleman speaks to Bolton.

                              Joseph Ignelli
                              Chief, Security Division

Telephone call on October 23, 1973, from Martin Harvester, US Steel, Largo Falls, to Agent 12, Syracuse Field Office FBI, taped after warning to caller:

HARVESTER: As per routine, we're reporting the disappearance of two explosives. Product is chemite.

AGENT 12: Chemite?

HARVESTER: Yes.

AGENT 12: Any distinguishing marks on the package?

HARVESTER: Yes, hold it a minute. I have one here. Red letters: Reynold's Chemite, that's all. White package, incidentally.

AGENT 12: What were the circumstances of the disappearance? Could it be just an inventory error? Or misplacement?

HARVESTER: A motion picture company was using live stuff for a PR film. The editor disappeared on the same day as the explosives. That's what's got us worried.

AGENT 12: Name and address. Do you have it?

HARVESTER: Jeffrey Bolton, 1340 Marlton Avenue, Baltimore, Maryland.

TWX Syracuse Field Office FBI to National Crime Information Center, FBI Headquarters, Washington:

SUBJECT JEFFREY BOLTON ADDRESS 1340 MARLTON AVENUE BALTIMORE MARYLAND SUSPECTED OF EXPROPRIATING TWO STICKS OF EXPLOSIVE FROM US STEEL PLANT IN LARGO FALLS NY. CHECK REQUESTED ON NAME.

TWX NCIC Washington to Syracuse Office FBI:

AGE AND PHYSICAL CHARACTERISTICS OF SUSPECT?

TWX Syracuse Office FBI to NCIC Washington:

AGE IN TWENTIES SIX FOOT SLIM GRAY EYES NO DISTINGUISHING MARKS OBSERVED WEARS HAIR FAIRLY SHORT DESCRIBED AS QUOTE ALL AMERICAN TYPE UNQUOTE THAT IS, NO HIPPIE.

October 25, 1973

Joseph Ignelli
Chief Security Division
US Steel, Largo Falls, N.Y.

Dear Mr. Ignelli:

I telephoned Jeffrey Bolton at the number which

we have used before in working with this man. The telephone was disconnected. A visit to his address revealed a rooming house in which he rented second floor front room. His landlady, Mrs. Margaret Smith, said that Bolton had paid his rent in advance and moved out last Thursday with no forwarding address.

I am at a loss to understand the situation. We have used Bolton on two industrial films and found him a fine film editor. We can show you his two films as proof.

Nevertheless I understand from the director that his conduct was peculiar at the location site, and his disappearance seems to confirm that something unusual is involved here.

I can only offer my extreme apologies and promise you every form of cooperation in locating this person. I have contacted the Film Editors' Union in New York, but he is not a member, and they can offer no help. Irving Miller, the union president, states that he never heard the name.

Please contact me immediately with instructions.

> Regards,
> Leonard Coleman, President
> Coleman Productions

TWX NCIC Washington to Syracuse Office FBI:

JEFFREY BOLTON OF 1308 MAPLE STREET, PROVIDENCE, RHODE ISLAND, CHARGED MARCH 8, 1968, WITH THEFT OF CAR LICENSE NRB-50083, 1968 FORD MUSTANG, FROM OWLSLEY REPEAT OWLSLEY MOTORS, 1600 MAIN STREET. CHARGES DROPPED.

NO OTHER JEFFREY BOLTONS INCLUDED IN NCIC FILES. JEFFREY BOLTON OF 1308 MAPLE STREET, PROVIDENCE, RHODE ISLAND, IS A NEGRO.

SUSPECT JEFFREY BOLTON 1340 MARLTON AVENUE, BALTIMORE, MARYLAND, HAS LEFT THAT ADDRESS LEAVING NO FORWARDING ADDRESS. COMPUTER SEARCH BEING INSTITUTED THROUGH SOCIAL

SECURITY, INTERNAL REVENUE, AND DEFENSE DE-
PARTMENT IDENTIFYING NUMBERS.

October 25, 1973

From: Chief Security Division, US Steel, Largo Falls
To: Director, Industrial Explosives Division
Subject: Missing explosives

1. Rest easy. The two missing chemite sticks have
   been found.
2. Harry Andrews made one last search of the location site and reported the two sticks were half
   buried in the sand about fifty feet from the camera
   location.
3. Personnel unfamiliar with explosives were handling same during the filming and someone apparently placed them down and forgot them.
4. I await instructions on reprimand or fine for
   Harry Andrews. This lapse is serious enough to
   justify dismissal. But the circumstances of a motion picture demonstration are unique to his experience, and perhaps he is justified in his claim
   of confusion.

                              Joseph Ignelli
                              Chief, Security Division
                              US Steel, Largo Falls

TWX Syracuse Office FBI to NCIC, Washington:
    CANCEL ALL. MISSING EXPLOSIVES HAVE BEEN
    FOUND.

— 6 —

The young man in the green windbreaker was waiting
at the appointed spot, in front of the Riggs Bank at
Du Pont Circle. When he saw Allen he headed
toward 19th and N, where he took a right turn. Allen

followed a few feet behind until they came to a blue Volkswagen. Both of them got in.

The young man had a beard and a slightly pockmarked face. As soon as the car had started he reached into his pocket and handed Allen an envelope.

Allen opened it and read:

> You are stalling us. Why?
> Did you get the white stuff?
> All contacts through man at Riggs, 9 A.M. Tuesdays and Fridays as scheduled. He knows you as Stan Harker, deserter, St. Louis.
> He and his group will provide you with weapons and assistance while in Washington.
> Call him Alix.

Allen settled in the corner of the car. Alix said. "Did you get the powder?"

"Two sticks," said Allen. "That should be enough."

"Dynamite?"

"Something new called chemite. Here's the check." He handed him a baggage check from Union Station. "It's in a briefcase. Store it in a cool spot."

"Dig," said Alix. "Man, you come through."

They drove to a Hot Shoppe on Connecticut Avenue and had a cup of coffee. Allen told him, "I'll let you know when we're ready to go. Meanwhile I need something from you."

"What?"

"A twenty-year-old girl who's willing to spend a night in jail. Also a pen gun with mace. She'll have to use it."

The bearded boy looked at him, eyes sparkling. "I've got just the chick. She'll flip over a chance to help."

Allen arranged to meet the girl at an address on K Street at five o'clock, then asked to be driven to Dumbarton Street in Georgetown. The bearded kid let him off, and Allen waited until he had driven off before starting for his destination. He walked up to P Street, and a few minutes later was knocking on the door of an apartment. A girl called through the door, "Who is it?"

"Jeff," said Allen.

The door opened with a cry of delight as the girl, a brunette in jeans and an orange halter, threw herself at Allen and hugged him. "Where have you been? God."

Allen disengaged himself. "I just got back from San Francisco on a job," he said.

"Don't tell me you're working," said the girl as she led him into her apartment. He saw a gray functional couch and a few bright yellow chairs and a stereo with record album covers lying around and a banyan tree in a vase. "The living room is a front," said Peggy Barton. "Come to the real me," and she led him around the corner and to a room absolutely empty except for a tiny statue of Buddha on a dais six inches high against one wall. "This is where I think."

But Allen did not care where Peggy thought. He said, "I brought you something from Tommy."

She was stunned. "You did?"

Allen opened a little cardboard box, and there was a gold link bracelet with a St. Christopher's medal. "He bought the bracelet for you," Allen said. "I've been looking for you ever since. I didn't know you went off to Europe."

Peggy started to tear up. She went back to the living room and sat down on the couch, the box in her hand. "God, I can't bear it," she said.

Allen was standing stiffly in the center of the room. "Sit down, for God's sake," she said to him, half crying. "Can't you show some . . . sympathy?"

Allen said nothing but sat down. Peggy dipped into her handbag and came up with a small glassine bag. "I know you don't like this, Jeff, but I have to. I'm all torn up."

She crumbled some hash into a little white pipe, lit it, and inhaled deeply, then put her head back on the cushion and let the blue smoke spiral into the air. After a moment she was more composed. "I'll never understand you and Tommy being so close," she said, turning her head on the cushion to look at him. "You don't smoke, you hate to drink, you're so . . . straight. You used to drive Tommy to the wall."

"Peggy, I have to go."

But hash or memory was driving Peggy now. She thrust the little pipe at Allen, with an unreal smile. "Do me a favor, Jeff—for Tommy. Take one puff. Just to prove you're *human*."

Allen knocked the pipe out of her hands. Burning embers sprayed all over the carpet and Peggy was on her knees trying to sweep them up as Allen went to the door. He said tightly, "I'm straight—and Tommy's dead."

And now Peggy was looking at him with glittering eyes. "Tell me something I *don't* know, you bastard."

An hour later Allen was back in his modest hotel at 14th and K, lying on his bed in shirtsleeves, thinking. Spaulding in Pound Ridge, Carson in Manhattan, Mellon in Nassau, Warneky in Ithaca.

It was important to Allen Lowell that he begin in Washington, so Medwick drew the straw. Williams he would keep on hot coals.

Of course, Williams knew something about death. Oh yes, he did. But even George Williams would be astonished at the method of Medwick's violent passing. There were ways to kill and ways to kill. A piano wire and sneakers, the classic Special Forces technique? Too bloody easy.

Medwick deserved something better.

— 7 —

In J. Edgar Hoover's day the anteroom of his office was a nostalgic trip into the exciting past. In a glass case on one side a plaster facsimile of John Dillinger's death mask, the straw hat he was wearing when gunned down, even the Corona-Belvedere cigar from his shirt pocket; in a corner a revolving rack of newspaper cartoons extolling the exploits of the G-men over the years; and in another a roll of FBI martyrs killed in action, over twenty since 1924. And covering the walls hundreds of scrolls and plaques from organizations and schools praising the great Director.

Now most of them were gone, although the Dillinger exhibit remained, and even that would not survive the move to the new FBI building going up across the street. Today the FBI was computers, scientific instruments, electronic devices.

Fred Jarvis, one of the old boys, went through the anteroom and into the director's office, and across thirty-five feet of deep-pile carpet noticed that even with a new director, the great mahogany desk still sported the two small American flags furled on either side and a small replica of the FBI seal at the center. The arrangement was repeated on the rear wall with two large American flags with gold eagle standards, and a large replica of the FBI seal in the center. You still got that Mussolini feeling, thought Jarvis.

The director watched Jarvis approach, a tall, tweedy man with graying hair who walked with a permanent stoop, with eyes under scraggly eyebrows that always seemed to be looking up with a disbelieving expression. Jarvis dropped in a chair, as if weary from the effort. "You rang the alarm?"

The director smiled. When he had entered the bureau he had found Jarvis down the list and had upped

68

him over the fast-vanishing gangbusters crowd. He relied on Jarvis for common sense, and relished the man's refreshing irony. He said, "We have a funny one. George Williams has got a death threat."

"From the White House?"

The director laughed. "It's anonymous. Maybe they should have looked at the return address."

The two men smiled, and the director went on. "Some freak has sent a note saying six people will die on the tenth anniversary of Kennedy's death."

"Whoopee," said Jarvis, but he wasn't smiling.

"Connors takes it seriously."

"So do I," said Jarvis.

"We've got six names to put through the chopper, including Williams. The only other one I've heard of is Congressman Medwick."

The two men looked at each other. "And that name, as you know, is another funny one."

Jarvis said nothing. The director went on. "We have to find an anonymous killer in an attic somewhere on the whole continent. And we start out knowing it's impossible."

"But this is different," Jarvis said quickly. "This time he sent a note. It's not in the pattern."

The FBI director swiveled his chair and stared out of his office window at the new FBI building going up across the street. Jarvis said, "It comes down to this. If you find exactly *why* he sent that note, why he warned them when he didn't need to, you might find your man."

But then the director was swiveling back and leaning on his desk. "That is exactly what makes this so confusing. Question: why does he send a note to Williams? Question: why does he name all six? Question: why does he mention the Kennedy assassination? Damn it, it can't be anything to do with Dallas. Those bones have been picked clean!"

"Question number four," said Jarvis. "Why *these* six?"

The director slapped his palm on the desk with a crack. "Some maniac wants to kill six people to observe the Kennedy assassination—and all but one of them didn't even know Kennedy. Incredible! It doesn't make sense!"

But Jarvis once again said quickly, "It makes sense to him."

The director nodded. Then he said, "Connors seems to be off on another trail. He asked me to make a special check on Williams."

Jarvis was shaking his head. "Only an insane man wrote that note, whether he knows he's insane or not. Williams is definitely sane."

"But still it could be a red herring. One of the other five might be involved in some way."

Jarvis shrugged. "It's one line to follow, I suppose." He stood up and stretched. "My mother always told me to excuse myself when I did that." He waved the list of names. "Somewhere there's a connection among these six names, a job, a girl, a club. Something. I'll plug them into the gray machines and see what spills."

— 8 —

Night on the Capitol grounds. Searchlights blazed on white stone, two security men patrolled the grounds and another stood guard at the door.

Suddenly a carload of teenagers roared up to the broad steps leading to the Capitol door and stooped with a screech of brakes. "Here we go," said one of the security men, heading toward the car.

A young blonde climbed out of the car in a microskirt, and ran up the steps, as the car barreled off. She reached the guard at the door and said, "I'm looking for my father."

"Cut the clowning, miss."

The girl suddenly plucked two buttons and her

blouse came off in front of the guard's amazed eyes. She was bare beneath. Then, before he could say another word, she got him with a pen gun filled with mace. "Ah Christ," he yelled, bending over, rubbing his eyes. The girl turned and ran down the steps. "He tore my blouse," she shouted to the guards who were pounding up the steps toward her. And indeed the blouse was torn; Allen and she had torn it an hour before in her room. "He wouldn't let me in and then he ripped off my blouse!"

The two guards weren't even listening. They grabbed the insane teenybopper and half-carried her to a car below. "You're going to spend a night on a floor, stupid," said one.

Allen Lowell slipped by the blinded guard at the door.

In Medwick's office, Allen donned infra-red glasses. With the infra-red flashlight, he determined the file cabinets were locked, but the shears from his kit did the job quickly. He riffled through folders until he came to one marked simply "Taxes." He pulled that file. Then he looked for International Dynamics, but no go. He settled for two bulging files marked "Personal."

That was all he needed. It was damned unlikely a crook like Medwick would leave about memos on a deal like Dynamics.

Allen took the personal and tax files to a desk and sat down and started typing a note.

An hour later he was back in his room writing in his diary when he suddenly stopped. That letter to Williams!

When he had traded those stolen FBI papers through an intermediary to Jack Anderson he had forgotten one little fact.

Not that they could trace him, anyway. It was impossible. But still—

The next day George Williams took the letter across Pennsylvania Avenue and into the FBI building. He went to the fifth floor where Bill Orenburg, head of the Anonymous Documents Division, sat in a long glassed office. Bill said, "I understand we're handling this on a quasi-official basis, whatever the hell that means."

George smiled. Behind him one of J. Edgar Hoover's great PR ideas mushroomed into view; a tourist group was passing through the corridor, led by an agent, peering in through the glass. They couldn't believe they were looking into an actual working office. But they could see men and women looking into microscopes, pulling files, and watching meters on obscure machines. On a table under a strong light near Williams a woman threw down an old brown hat, turned it inside out, then proceeded to brush it briskly. Why was she doing that? "She's removing hair for examination," spieled the agent to the tourists. "The agency has classified three hundred types of hair, and one strand can tell us things like the sex of the suspect, the age, the race, sometimes even the nationality. Also, if there's any grease we can classify it, too . . ."

The tourists must go, thought Williams. He said to Orenburg, "How do you like working in a zoo?"

"We get used to it . . . gradually."

"I want you to run this letter through," said Williams, handing him the note. But Orenburg drew back. "Whoa there," he said, "Fingerprints first. You check it?"

"Of course. Not a smudge. The kid is a pro."

Orenburg settled himself on a high stool in front of a lab table with microscopes and other equipment. "Why do you say 'kid'?"

"Just an instinct. I could be wrong. It could be a whole organization."

"Yeah," said Oreburg. He held the paper to the light. "Well, this should be no problem."

"Why not?"

"He used a typewriter. And what's worse, he used *one* typewriter. Your kid will never make it as an anonymous killer."

"If that typewriter is a Royal portable we have two million suspects."

"Only one typewriter typed this note," said Orenburg. He had fitted stereoscopic glasses to his eyes, and was studying the note. "The 'm,'" he said. "Take a look." He removed the glasses and strapped them around Williams' eyes. Williams saw magnified letters like hills, and the 'm' had a worn left serif which smudged the ink miscroscopically. He handed back the glasses. "I see it."

"Let me have the envelope," Orenburg said. "Most of the time they don't like to put it through the platen, so they write the address in block letters. When they do that, we have them. They forget that ninety percent of the forms they fill out they use block lettering."

Williams was smiling; he and Orenburg had worked together before. Williams handed him the envelope and said, "You're out of luck. He typed the envelope address too." Orenburg picked up a magnifying glass and studied the envelope flap. "First thing we look for, lipstick. But you have a man here—or a chick that's cool." He laughed. "Well, let me put the letter and the envelope through my monster machines and start narrowing this down a bit." All the while he was talking he was holding the envelope upside down and shaking it. "You never know what they leave in these things by mistake . . . a fiber, a hair, sometimes even a return address."

Williams stood up. "I don't expect miracles, Bill.

We've been there before. But one thing I want to know as soon as possible."

"Yes?"

"Was it typed on a government typewriter?"

Sharp! Orenburg looked up and once again marveled at George Williams. He still remembered that civil rights murder case when Williams had prodded the FBI into scraping mud from the inside of a fender of a car found abandoned sixteen hundred miles from the scene of a murder. The computer boys with the soil samples had identified it immediately as soil peculiar to only one region in the US, the area where the murder had been committed. And the owner of the car had been found—confessed—and the legend of George Williams grown larger.

And now Williams was scenting a government civil servant, Orenburg realized, and by God his monster machines could tell him that. And if it was a civil servant, on file in a hundred places, the search would be homing to the source in hours. Orenburg said, "I'll give you the typewriter class, the name of the manufacturer, and the year of the manufacture, and we'll know if it's government issue. Then I'll analyze the paper and the envelope which might also be government issue. And for a bonus, if we're lucky, the type and year of the typewriter ribbon to see if that's GI. Also, any other goodies I pick up, such as the off-chance that your friend used this sheet of paper as a back-up sheet before and left any impressions. Enough?"

"I'll settle for half," said Williams with a smile. "Give me a call when you're through."

Orenburg said, "One more thing. If I have trouble with the paper, can I burn a fragment for the spectograph?"

"One corner," said Williams, and left.

Orenburg placed the letter flat on a glass plate and lighted a two-hundred watt bulb beneath it. He was surrounded by computers, microscopes, X-ray diffraction powder cameras, electropheris and chromatography and spectrograph and infra-red and ultra-violet equipment, all of which he used constantly. But what he relied on most was his "flair." Often his first examination with a simple magnifying glass told him more secrets than all the complex apparatus at his disposal. Right off, for example, he noticed something funny. The last name on the list of victims had been typed at a later time than the previous five. The quality of the ink impression was different, but more important the horizontal alignment was a fraction off. A measuring microscope confirmed this fact immediately. The writer had apparently taken the letter out, then rerolled it through the platen to type the last name. He had been almost perfect. Almost.

Orenburg followed that up like a shot. He placed the envelope flap under an ultra-violet light, and the adhesive glue glowed blue-white, and over the blue-white a smudge of fluorescent yellow. Done.

Orenburg made a note. The writer had steamed open the envelope and needed a trace of glue to reseal it. Reason? Obviously, the writer had forgotten to include the last name . . . or had only decided to include it later. Why?

Not much to Orenburg but it was clues like that which sent Williams racing. He studied the last name.

Robert Warneky.

An hour later Orenburg had photographed and enlarged the typescript on the note. The type he knew from sight was pica, ten characters to the inch. And it was from a manual typewriter, not an electric, with its easily recognized proportionate spacing with each letter allotted two to five units of space, each unit 1/32 or 1/36 of an inch.

He also knew from the uneven impressions that the typist was an amateur.

He was puzzled: the typescript looked vaguely familiar. He placed the enlarged photograph on a scanner of the computer which contained in its memory core samples of every known typescript in the country. Then he pressed the keys for the character search. He began this search with the letters "a," "g," "t," "r," "s," and "m" because their design varied widely in different makes of machines.

In a few minutes, after the half-dozen characters were compared, the number of possible machines had been reduced to a limited number of keyboards—five typewriters. Photographs of these typescripts clacked out of the computer storage.

Orenburg picked up his magnifying glass again. As usual Williams had been right on target! Three of the five possible typewriters were government issue. He placed the anonymous letter beside one of the samples and bent over. A thousand to one, he was thinking. A thousand to one. But you never knew.

— 10 —

A crisp lovely day on Pennsylvania Avenue; a blonde in a Jaguar laughing; the breeze scurrying golden leaves along the pavement beneath great granite buildings; and all the world sparkling, feeling the pulsing freshness of October, the cool air that set the blood racing, and you felt suddenly alive, sharp, eager.

George Williams noted these things as he had not noted them for a long time because of an anonymous letter that sounded like a joke but was not; that should not have made sense but did.

Someone must die, Williams knew that. There was no way to forestall an anonymous attack. Presidents and candidates with platoons of secret servicemen on every side had been killed or wounded. Here were six people on the streets every day with no guards!

George Williams crossed Pennsylvania Avenue and did not see a slim young man watching him.

Williams had an appointment with the FBI director, whom he liked. The director told him Fred Jarvis would be his liaison man.

At the present time, the director said, Jarvis was checking the files on each of the persons on the list, and on an off-chance the NCIC computer tapes. This first search, Williams was told, must be made confidentially. For one thing, the director had once said, the FBI had no files.

But Williams was not to be put off with a joke. "You can keep my file confidential, but I have to see the others. The connection must be there."

"That's what we're looking for," said the director. "Give us at least a day."

"And if someone dies tonight?"

"You think it's that close?"

Williams looked at him. "That is a threat with no ransom, no blackmail. That means it is triply dangerous. The man who wrote it did so for one reason only."

"What?"

"He *wants* to kill!"

— 11 —

August 13, 1945. Okinawa. The officers of LST 848 were angry. All day they had been tied alongside the *Pennsylvania,* a battleship that had been hit by a kamikaze the night before, and now showed only a foot of freeboard above the water. But the damage had been contained, and the LST had been assigned to take off the ammunition aboard to forestall the danger of an explosion.

LST 848 was one of the great bastard ships of the amphibious fleet in World War II. It had gone into Okinawa last April as an LST (H), a designation meaning it was a casualty evacuation ship. A team of Navy, Marine, and Army doctors was aboard along with scores of pharmacists' mates, with a mission to evacuate the most severely injured from the beach, and operate on them here, on improvised tables in the crew's quarters.

Along with this medical team the LST had the following: two barges, strapped like carbuncles to port and starboard; an LCT sitting on top of the main deck; a tank deck full of amphibious tanks called LVTs, and officers and men of the Marine First Division.

When the invasion of Okinawa had started at Blue Beach last April 1, the LVTs had driven off the lowered tank deck door, sinking first in the water dangerously, then churning up white water, barely afloat until finally they were strung out heading toward shore. The barges lashed to the sides of the ship had been cut loose, disappearing with a mighty splash before bobbing to the surface. A Seabee team from the LST got aboard and soon the barges were ferrying supplies to the beach. Then the LST shifted the ballast in its tanks until it was at a forty-five-degree angle to starboard. The cables on the LCT were cut and the ship slid awkwardly into the sea to become another component of the amphibious fleet.

Approximately half an hour later the first casualties started coming aboard. The next month was a blur of wounded men, a hundred and more at a time strapped to tables on the tank deck, while in the crew's quarters the young doctors worked steadily, professionally, performing desperate operations on the spot.

What did Lt. (jg) Pete Schovajsa remember? He remembered a husky man lying on a table, with white flesh pitted with shrapnel from an exploding land mine and with sightless eyes. Lt. Schovajsa just happened to be there when the man said, "Doctor, I can't see. I know it's dark but am I going to be able to see?" Panic was in his face. A passing doctor said, "Of course. It's just shock."

"Thank God," said the man. But catching up to the

doctor, Schovajsa found that it was a lie. And he couldn't bear to look at the wounded man again, white chest exposed, blank eyes staring hopefully, heart no doubt beating wildly with panic thinking that doctor was lying, knowing he was lying, hoping to God he was not. He couldn't be blind!

He had never forgotten the face of that man nor of the boy whose breathing was shallow, a boy who looked younger than the rest, and Lieutenant Schovajsa had stopped by his table, his alone out of the scores of wounded men on the tables on the tank deck of an LST off an island in nowhere. And the lieutenant had whispered to another doctor: "How's he doing, Doc?"

"Oh him?" the doctor said in a loud voice. "He's got only a few minutes to live."

Tone it down! He'll hear you! Pete Schovajsa wanted to shout. But the doctor was gone and Schovajsa was left with the man lying there, doomed to die in a few minutes right before his eyes. He watched him breathing. Was it possible? He was alive, his lungs operating. He wasn't even in pain. His profile, young and peaceful, as he looked at the ceiling. It was a grim joke, Schovajsa thought, one many doctors pulled on the crew to keep themselves from going insane.

Then the young man died. Just like that. He stopped breathing. No cough. No convulsion. No last cry. He was in front of Schovajsa, near enough to touch, still warm.

Why did this one death out of so many affect him? Perhaps he was beginning to crack up. Months on a ship with wounded, dying men in every corner had brought him to the edge of insanity.

Later it was over and the LST was officially transformed into an ammunition ship assigned to sail to Guam and bring back tons of small arms ammunition. The Japanese were battling stubbornly near Naha. The doctors and pharmacists' mates departed, the tank deck was scrubbed and painted, and off they went to Guam to fly the red flag Baker—warning all ships away—knowing that any slight mischance, a dropped box of ammo, a sudden little fire, a tracer shell from another ship, a lucky kamikaze, would transform them into fragments.

They had done the job and now on August 13 they were ready for a rest. Atomic bombs had hit Hiroshima and Nagasaki; the Japanese were negotiating for peace through the Swiss Embassy, the war was over. Last night had to be the end, the last Japanese fanatic had hurled himself to fiery death on the deck of the *Pennsylvania*.

What burned the officers of the LST was the order to cast off from the *Pennsylvania* and move half a mile to a station near the entrance to Buckner Bay. As usual, an ammunition ship was a leper that must be quarantined from the rest of the fleet.

It took them an hour to set special sea detail, warm the engines, start out to the new anchorage, and finally let go the anchor near the entrance buoys. Needless work. The war was over. Diplomats were working on the wording of the surrender cable at this very moment.

Around dusk, the tired officers gathered in the wardroom for dinner and were just settling down when a violent explosion was heard.

To those who serve on an ammunition ship the sound of an explosion tears the heart. In seconds they were hurtling up ladders toward the bridge; general quarters was being sounded, and Schovajsa emerged on deck to see that an AKA transport ship apparently had just arrived and anchored next to them on the starboard. A kamikaze had dived straight down through the bridge, straight through the officers' quarters, its bombs exploding and setting off a fire that was now raging on the ship.

Beautiful! Then Lt. Pete Schovajsa heard another sound which made his heart stop. Above to his left the washing machine Charlie sound of another kamikaze. It was moving along the port side of the LST preparatory to circling around for a dive. To finish off the AKA? Or to hit the next ship in line, the LST? If the kamikaze pilot recognized that red Baker flag he would surely go for the ammunition ship.

Over the head telephones Schovajsa heard the gunnery officer shouting to the forward 40 mm gun crew. But they were too late! They didn't have time to aim! Down roared the kamikaze toward them, a wild veering line of tracers from the ship missing him by yards. Two hundred feet away and coming strong; a single engine monoplane thundering toward an ammunition ship. One hundred feet and coming, and still the gun crew couldn't hit!

And then the pilot did something unexplained; he veered off and crashed to his death into the water between the LST and the burning AKA. Why? He wasn't hit. What made him decide not to strike?

Later Schovajsa was sent with a small boat to the AKA to offer assistance, if needed. The fire was under control. The lieutenant went into the stricken officers' country, accompanied by an officer from the AKA who was half crying: "He killed eleven officers. Eleven! With the fucking war over!"

The Japanese pilot's body had been removed; it had ended up with the cowling of the plane in the engine room. Lieutenant Schovajsa went through the charred officers' quarters and there, in a little room, he could not help it—he read a half-finished letter. The officer had been writing to his wife when the suicide plane crushed him to death.

The letter congratulated her on the birth of Allen Lowell, and pleaded with her to send pictures of him as soon as she could. The officer had written: "I have great plans for that boy."

12

Excerpt from Allen Lowell's diary . . . entry October 26, 1973:

It is five P.M. Seven hours to go.

Have spent the last hour rereading JFK's favorite poem:

It may be he shall take my hand
And lead me into his dark land
And close my eyes and quench my breath . . .

But I've a rendezvous with Death
At midnight in some flaming town . . .
And I to my pledged word am true,
I shall not fail that rendezvous.

I will call Medwick exactly at midnight. In two hours he will be dead, but in such a way that Williams will be confused.

I now make the sign of the Cross. And I swear before God that what I intend to do is not evil.

I swear before God that what I intend to do is not evil.

I swear before God that what I intend to do is not evil.

But they must pay.

13

Thomas Medwick looked at the tall lean man in a conservative, well-tailored blue suit and vest. This was George Williams; Justice Department written all over the clothes. But the blue eyes were not Justice Department, dulled by a thousand briefs. Those eyes, set deep beneath heavy brows, were more like blue laser beams, and they pierced right through Medwick, as he sat in his living room in his colonial-style home in McLean, Virginia, and tried to bluff it out. Those missing files were driving him crazy!

"I'm no enemy agent, Mr. Williams," he said.

"This is not internal security business," said Williams. "I want to know if you've received any kind of anonymous note lately."

Medwick paused. International Dynamics? It had to be! "With all the mail I get from my constituents some of them must be anonymous."

"This note you would remember. A death threat."

Medwick relaxed for the first time that day. Holy Jesus Christ. Was this all? He smiled. "I get *those* every day, too, Mr. Williams."

"I'm afraid you don't realize the seriousness of what I'm saying. You are mentioned in an anonymous death threat. The Justice Department is convinced it's authentic."

"Oh?" Medwick said. "What's it about?"

"The note says it concerns the tenth anniversary of President Kennedy's death."

"But I didn't even know Kennedy!"

The blue eyes never wavered as Williams said, "Did you know any of the following people: Jim Carson, Stephanie Spaulding, Robert Warneky, Everett Mellon?"

Medwick's wife came into the room, a pretty blonde in tight yellow pants and a green pullover sweater. "Hi boys," she said.

Medwick introduced her. "You look so somber, Mr. Williams," she said. "How about a drink? The Medwick bar is famous."

Williams smiled. "A Scotch and soda would unsomber me."

Mrs. Medwick turned to her husband. "Where

have you been hiding *him?* He's gorgeous."

"Stop working, Marie," said Medwick. "He's not a potential vote."

She laughed and was soon back with the drinks. She deposited a tray with the bottle and a bucket of ice and soda on the table in front of them. "We can't afford a live-in maid because Thomas won't steal," she said. "I keep begging him to join the crowd."

Christ! thought Medwick, she sure picks the right time to talk clever. He hurried her out of the room.

"It's remarks like that," said Medwick, returning, "that will put an end to women's lib. Back to the scullery on their knees, I say."

Williams said, "What about the names?"

"I've been thinking. I don't remember any of them—except the name Stephanie Spaulding. But even she doesn't really come back to me."

Williams sipped his drink quietly. One thing he knew for certain. Medwick was a crook. But that must be saved for another time. He said, "All of them—plus myself—are mentioned in the death threat."

"Oh, come on."

"Here's a Xerox of the note." He handed it to Medwick, who studied it for minutes. Finally the Congressman handed it back. "It's incredible. It doesn't make sense. What do I have to do with the Kennedys?"

"Well, let's talk about it."

"But what—"

"Mr. Medwick, somewhere there's a connection among the six of us. The names are specific; a check shows that every one of the victims did work for the Kennedy administration, but only in the most minor capacities. None was important in any sense. But still . . ."

"What do you want me to do?"

"Tell me what you did for Kennedy in your own words; who brought you into the government; why did you come into politics; anything you can remem-

ber that would have any bearing on a death threat
morè than a decade later. Help me find the connection . . ."

— 14 —

"Well, I was one of the originals," Medwick said.
"One of the hot eyes."

"What does that mean?"

"Some reporter—I think it was Merriman
Smith—called the people who came to Washington in
1961 the . . . wait a minute, see if I can remember
. . . the 'hot-eyed, curious, yeasty with shocking ideas.'
Something like that. I lived in Georgetown with three
other Harvards, and we used to call ourselves that.
Liked the sound of it."

"Who brought you to Washington?"

"Nobody. I came. I was all afire, to tell you the
truth. I did have hot eyes. A friend of my father's
knew somebody at State—"

"Who?"

Medwick stood up, glad for an opportunity to re-
lieve the tension. "Mind if I refresh my drink? What
about yours?" He made them two more drinks while
he tried to maintain his composure. He sat down
again and picked up the story. "George Ball. I never
saw him. Just some staff guy. I told him I wanted to
take the Foreign Service exam. I had some hazy idea
of serving in an African country, or some emerging
nation, as Kennedy was always calling them. I wanted
to contribute something, the key word in those days."
Medwick smiled at the memory. "Contribute. We all
wanted to contribute."

"So?"

"So I flunked the exam."

Medwick sipped his drink in silence. Then he went
on, "So I was ready to leave Washington when one of

my housemates, Joe Forester, arranged for an interview at CIA. They were looking for guys fluent in Spanish. My major at Harvard. I was hired."

The sudden surprise in Williams' face made Medwick say, "I thought you *knew* that. Haven't you seen the files?"

"Not yet," said Williams, but the revelation had disturbing implications. He would have to see the files on *all* of the suspects immediately. If all five had worked at one time for CIA—and it was possible— the dimension of this threat was increased thirty ways. Palestinians, Cubans, Israelis, South Americans, our own ex-agents, disaffected military men . . . "How long did you work there?"

"Seven months," said Medwick. "Started as a Grade Seven analyst, and then I got some 'spook' training. The usual. Don't think I should go into that too much, do you?"

But Williams did not bother to answer at once. He was realizing again how impossible it was to track down an anonymous killer until you had the motive.

"Look," he said, "when we're finished, I'd like you to write down the names and addresses of every significant person you met or dealt with in Washington, beginning with your three roommates and including everyone you worked closely with. And now I want you to tell me particularly of your CIA job."

"I worked for two years *after* CIA as an assistant to Senator Fulbright," said Medwick.

"First, let's hear about CIA."

"But that was only seven months, and except for one week I just shuffled papers, and did some Spanish translation."

"Involving Cuba?"

"Yes."

"Tell me about that one week," said Williams.

Handwritten letter delivered by officer messenger from White House to Deputy Director, South American Division, CIA:

THE WHITE HOUSE
WASHINGTON
February 10, 1961

Dear Bill,

All systems go, although JFK is upset about the situation. Feels Ike put him in a bag with a knot. The brasshats are in here every day telling him it will only be a three-day operation—no sweat—but the people here all think they're playing with themselves, as usual.

The Pres. has asked me to contact someone in the Dirty Tricks Department of your outfit, and I told him I could trust you. It involves a trip to our friends in Guatemala. Soonest. Can do?

George Latham,
Special Assistant

February 13, 1961. Thomas Medwick, called into the office of his chief, William Kerrwood, found a slight, intellectual-looking man with thinning hair and glasses. The man with him Kerrwood introduced as George Latham, a White House assistant.

Kerrwood said, "Your supervisor says you speak Spanish?"

"I majored in it. My father was in South American imports, and I was supposed to take over the business."

Kerrwood was ex-colonel to the bone. He could afford to ask one more question, even though he couldn't care less about this errand boy's background.

"Why are you working with us instead of the business?"

"My father made some bad decisions, and the business went up in smoke."

"OK, to the present. You settling in down the hall?"

"Yes, sir."

"But you're still in training? You're not actually on an assignment?"

Medwick was confused but he kept his answers straight, and military. Always military around CIA. "I'm still in training, sir. But I'm getting the hang of it."

"I'm sure I'm not making myself clear," said Kerrwood. "What I really want to know is, can you be spared for a little trip? We need an interpreter for one week in all. Now we can't take away any of the regular interpreters—they're three weeks behind as it is, so—"

"I'd very much like to go," said Medwick. Jesus Christ! he was thinking. Were they going to drop him behind the lines somewhere? After only three weeks and no special agent training? Perhaps Kerrwood saw the look on his face, for he smiled. "You're going with us, Medwick. A little diplomatic mission, that's all. To Guatemala."

"What's down there?" Medwick blurted out.

Kerrwood and Latham looked at each other and laughed. "Well, George," said Kerrwood, "at least you can't complain about our security procedures."

Latham spoke for the first time. "We're training Cuban exiles down there. For the invasion of Cuba. Only there may not be an invasion."

Medwick said nothing, but the look on his face told them everything. Latham turned to Kerrwood. "I think Mr. Medwick will be the *perfect* interpreter. No bias, fore or aft, because no information. Let's keep it that way."

* * *

An Air Force sergeant was shaking Medwick's shoulder. "We're landing, sir." Medwick sat up, blinking. The C-47 military aircraft was chilly, dark. Ahead in one of the seats under an overhead pin light Latham was reading dispatches.

Medwick still couldn't get over the fact that he, Kerrwood, and Latham were the only passengers on the huge aircraft. Medwick again felt the thrill of adventure as he stretched, then looked out the small porthole window at dark clouds and a luminous moon and, far ahead, the twinkling lights that must be Guatemala City.

The roar of the engines beat at his ears, the aircraft circled slowly and began a long sloping descent, and suddenly he saw the green and red lights of a runway. But it was far from the lights of the city; in fact they had vanished from the horizon as the plane came in low and the wheels touched jarringly, the tires screeching. Then a higher roar as the engines were thrown into reverse to slow the momentum. Someone was standing next to Medwick. "Get some sleep?" It was Kerrwood. He looked gaunt in the half-light inside the taxiing plane. Medwick nodded. "Good," said Kerrwood, "it might be your last for three days."

The plane stopped in the middle of nowhere. As far as Medwick could see, no buildings, no control tower; how had they landed this huge aircraft? He unbuckled his seat belt, grabbed his suitcase from the floor rack, and made his way forward. The co-pilot held him at the door. After a few minutes the pilot turned in his seat and said, "OK."

The signal must have come in over the earphones, but Medwick was beginning to realize he was in a world where everything was planned, and of which he was to know nothing. The co-pilot opened the door and said to Kerrwood, "Good luck, sir."

"Thank you, Captain," and the three men went down the folding ladder single file, Medwick last.

The airstrip was in the middle of a forest which closed in on all sides. To the right was a small building Medwick had been unable to see in the complete dark, but that must be the control tower, all right. Kerrwood and Latham were heading in that direction when suddenly Medwick heard gunfire. He almost panicked, but Kerrwood and Latham went on, unconcerned. As they approached, he could see rotating above the building a huge dish radar. Kerrwood motioned to them to stay outside, and knocked on a door. It opened, revealing a dull red light inside as Kerrwood entered.

Five minutes later he was out again. Gunfire crackled from the forest not half a mile away. Kerrwood still paid no attention, said only, "Usual snafu. They're on their way. We wait here."

The C-47 was now taxiing off and in a minute was airborne. Kerrwood had lighted a cigarette so Medwick thought it was all right to do the same. He leaned against the wall of the building, looking up at the yellow moon, and trying to remember every detail so he could tell his children some day. Then he saw illuminated in the light of the moon a body in the air! "Mr. Kerrwood, look!"

Savage gunfire erupted even closer, and a parachutist descended, swaying, toward the strip. What was going on? Behind him there suddenly appeared other parachutists, drifting down in clusters, and now the first was hitting the strip, rolling, coming up fast and getting rid of the parachute, and Kerrwood was saying, "Looks good. Looks good!" And then the twin headlights of a car suddenly appeared and the car pulled up and Medwick was watching the parachutists come racing toward them, and they jumped into the back seat of the car and no one shot at them.

"The trouble with that," Kerrwood was saying, "is it's so easy in Guatemala. In Cuba, they shoot."

Medwick's heart was beating fast. It had looked

like a goddamned realistic exercise to *him*. In fact, he
still wasn't sure it was an exercise. For the first time
the dimensions of his adventure became apparent to
him. War! Those people weren't playing. They *were*
going to invade Cuba. They *were* going to be shot
at—perhaps killed!

"You picked a hell of a night to arrive," a man in
a sports shirt and green slacks was telling them. They
sat having coffee in a bunkhouse, each of them on a
different lower bunk. The man, Kevin O'Shea, looked
completely unmilitary to Medwick. He was a bit
paunchy, graying, with the weary look of an ex-newspaperman.

"Every day counts," said Kerrwood. "The President hasn't given the final OK yet."

This seemed to make O'Shea angry. "Why the
stall? For Christ's sake, we're all set!"

"Not everybody agrees," said Kerrwood, and nursed
his coffee, while O'Shea stormed about the room.
"So that's it," said O'Shea, angrily. "Routine trip
bull!"

Kerrwood stood up and for the first time Medwick
noticed the authority in the man. "You're just one
small soldier, O'Shea. Keep it calm."

O'Shea sat down, again angrily. "You're going to
kill it, right? Say it and let's get it over with."

"We are doing what you were informed we are
doing . . . fact finding. Now when this exercise is
over I want to speak to the Cuban colonels, and to
Dave Griffin. Where is Griffin?"

"Guatemala City, seeing El Presidente. He should
be back any minute."

"What's he doing?"

O'Shea looked at him with an ironic half-smile.
"You kidding? He's bringing him another present."

"OK," said Kerrwood. He lay back on the bunk,
his hands behind his head. "What a sweet mess.
When this thing is over Drew Pearson will write four

thousand columns and still have ammunition for more."

"At the risk of blowing your top again," said O'Shea, "I'll remind you that *you* were in on the planning."

"Yes—before I found out those Cuban exiles were telling us lies and we were swallowing them. 'The people are just waiting for this invasion. They'll rise up in the streets and revolt against Castro. All we have to do is land on a beach somewhere!' Bull dickey, brother, and you know it. We sent our own men in there and got the real story, and you've got it too. But you and Griffin and the rest are still beating a dead horse."

Quiet menace in the room. Medwick looked at O'Shea and saw that no longer did he look like a weary newspaperman. He looked like an assassin. Maybe it was the light that made his small eyes seem to glitter in pouches. Maybe it was because he said nothing but just glared at Kerrwood.

Latham broke the silence. "The thing is, O'Shea, no matter which of you is right, the President is in a bind. If he goes, and those boys get slaughtered, he'll get slaughtered. If he calls it off, and thousands of Cuban exiles come back to America after training and say it would have been a success, he'll have no way of proving they're wrong. And Castro will be strengthened. So it's a Hobson's choice."

"Fuck Hobson," said O'Shea. "We have trained men who want revenge. We have ships. We have air support. The worst happens, we take them off the beach. The President can't lose, I'm telling you. And if he wins, he gets all the glory, not us poor bastards who have been sweating and screaming in the jungle for two months."

O'Shea went out to start rounding up the people for the meeting. About an hour later they came in, four Cuban officers and three other CIA men. The three all looked military, tough. The oldest was a heavy-set baldheaded man in a khaki field jacket and pants, with binoculars hanging on a strap. He was retired General Frederick Sharpe, in charge of the operation. David Griffin was lean, wiry, in a Marine officer's uniform with no bars or insignia. The youngest was a hard-jawed, blue-eyed man named Carl Richardson, no doubt just a spear carrier.

After some small talk, they made room for themselves on the bunks and Kerrwood started to query the Cubans through Medwick. What was the state of morale? Did they have enough supplies? Enough ammunition? What was missing? What were the complaints? What was still needed to ensure the success of the mission?

The answers came in volleys of Spanish which Medwick interpreted for Kerrwood, who took notes on a pad as he talked. Routine military briefing as far as Medwick could tell. But then Kerrwood threw in a shocker. "What would be the reaction of you and your men if for some reason the President was forced to cancel the mission?"

There was a silence. The Cuban colonel being questioned was one of the most dangerous-looking men Medwick had ever seen. Small, taut-muscled, with flashing black eyes and a perpetually angry look, his answers had been barked with a mixture of military precision and contempt. No doubt O'Shea had warned them of Kerrwood's real intent.

"We shall go in anyway," the Cuban replied. "And those that remain behind will tell the story to the people of the world. How your great President Kennedy said he would drive Castro out of this hemisphere, and how he is a coward and a liar."

The tension and bitterness cracked in the room. But Kerrwood was smiling. "It is the answer I would expect you to give, Colonel. You are a brave man."

The answer startled the Cuban. For the first time he looked at Kerrwood with respect—but still wary. Kerrwood turned to the retired general and told him that would be all he would need to say to the Cubans for the present. The Cubans left, abruptly.

After the door closed, Kerrwood leaned against a wall, smoking quietly. "The thing is, the man was right. In those TV debates with Nixon, Kennedy did say he would drive out Castro. All America heard him."

"Yes," said the White House assistant, Latham. "But he's willing to say he was wrong and take the consequences. That's the way Kennedy is."

"But it's now or never," said the ex-general. "In six months Castro will be so entrenched we'll never get him out."

Latham stood up and took command of the meeting. "Now at last we come to the real reason for this trip, gentlemen. You all must be crazy, the way you've been attacking Kerrwood. You don't think he'd waste his time coming down here trying to talk *you* out of the mission. Not you Olympians!"

And that was the first time Medwick had heard mention of the Olympians.

Latham was continuing, "What we need is your on-the-spot information. Can you succeed on this invasion without air support?"

Everyone was on their feet shouting. "Suicide! Impossible! Traitors!" Kerrwood stood and held up a hand. "Gentlemen," he said, "the decision is out of everyone's hands, including the President's. If American planes are shot down over Cuba, if American personnel are found to be involved in this play, we lose the whole value of the operation. *Without* us, it's the Cubans winning back their homeland. *With* us and our planes, it's a huge bad Yankee power clobbering a tiny island. It won't work."

Silence.

"So what we want to find out here is your evaluation. Is it impossible without air support? If it is impossible, we call it off here and now and take the consequences. If it's possible to succeed some way, we'll let you go ahead but only under those ground rules. No overt American support."

"Christ on a bicycle," said the general.

Griffin turned to him. "We better put our heads together on this, General." To Kerrwood he said, "How much time do we have to analyze it?"

"We have to know by tomorrow. Every bloody day is a loss," said Kerrwood.

"We'll see you in the morning," said the general. "And now, men, have a good sleep."

The three CIA men left the room, and Kerrwood stood for a moment looking at the closed door. Then he turned to Latham. "You were out of line with that Olympians crack."

"I just wanted them to know we were on to them at the White House," said Latham.

"Still . . . we want their honest advice. We won't get it now."

"Why not?"

"If they are Olympians, as you say, they can do nothing but win if this invasion goes through. Even if it's a disaster they win. All they do is scream that Kennedy withdrew air support and slaughtered his own freedom-loving exiles, and the Olympians take over CIA—and I'll be out."

"Like that, eh?"

"Like that."

Latham lay down on the bed and looked at the ceiling. "I don't like CIA," he said. "Neither does Kennedy."

"Someone has to do the dirty work," said Kerrwood.

— 16 —

Early the next morning the exiles had left for their exercises again and Medwick, with nothing to do, strolled around the encampment. World-War-II-style Quonset huts in a clearing in the rough jungle, jeeps on dirt roads, and gray bunkhouses behind, and the chirping of wild birds in the forest, and deep in the mountains the intermittent crackle of gunfire.

The air was soft, thin. Medwick walked down the dirt road, his city shoes sliding off sharp little rocks, until he came to a barbed-wire fence and a gate where a Cuban guard sat on a canvas chair, smoking, a machine gun across his lap. Medwick turned without saying anything to him and started back up the road. An all-day conference was underway in the general's quarters with Kerrwood, Latham, and the CIAs—the Cubans weren't even invited—so Medwick's part in this mission was over. Suddenly a jeep came to a stop before him in a flurry of dust. The driver called, "Medwick!" It was Carl Richardson, the youngest of the CIA types he had met last night.

"Just taking a walk," Medwick said, almost apologetically.

"Want to take a ride instead?" asked Richardson. "I've got to take a message to someone in the field."

"Great idea." Medwick climbed into the little seat next to the driver, the gear shift was shoved backward and then forward, and they roared down toward the guard who sent them through with a wave.

The Guatemalan jungle stretched out to either side of the bumpy dirt road. Thick oak trees waved over them—and underneath dense underbrush as high as a man's head.

"How do they fight in that stuff?" asked Medwick. "How do they even see each other?"

"It took us a month to clear the area we needed," said Richardson. "But we did it. And now you can see good enough to kill."

Medwick laughed, but then he noticed something odd. Richardson was serious. He said, "Nobody *kills* each other here, do they?"

"We've had some . . . accidents," said Richardson, "Cuban family feuds, that sort of thing. They wait till they get here and then one bullet in the back and the feud is over."

"Tell everyone I'm not Cuban," said Medwick, hoping to get a rise out of the driver. But none came. This was one serious boy.

They drove on in silence for a while, and then Richardson said quietly, "What did Latham mean about that Olympians remark?"

"Mr. Richardson, let me tell you something right now. I've only been with the agency three weeks. I don't know anything. I didn't even know we were in Guatemala. And the Olympians is a code word as far as I'm concerned."

"Well, you're driving with one," said Richardson.

"And you're not going to tell me what an Olympian is, of course."

Richardson's knuckles tightened on the wheel as the jeep chewed through the jungle road.

"You'll find out soon enough, everyone will," he said, as if talking to himself. "There are patriots in the agency. And there are soft heads left over from the early days." He turned sidewise and must have seen Medwick's startled look because he said, "Don't look so surprised. We were infiltrated too, you know."

"You mean there are Communists in the . . . CIA?" It seemed impossible to Medwick.

"Of course," said Richardson. And the expression on his face seemed to say: what kind of wetfoots are they recruiting lately?

"And what side is Kerrwood?" asked Medwick.

"He's against the invasion," said Richardson. "So draw your own conclusion."

The Bay of Pigs was a moment in history; the preparation took a year. What might be called the flower of Cuba's rich youth was involved; brave and bitter young men who had suddenly been ousted from a life of ease and exiled to a strange country, with no money, no connections, no influence. They would die to get back their home. And die they did.

Medwick saw them that day in a clearing in the

forest, taking a break, while an American explained the .105 mm gun to a small group. The rest sat on the ground, elbows on knees, smoking and chatting and making rough jokes in Spanish.

Medwick saw them and knew from the conversation he had heard last night that they were doomed. Without air support they had no chance. And their naive belief, fostered by their own optimism that the Cuban people would revolt when they hit the beaches, sealed that doom.

Suddenly Medwick had a wild impulse to tell them—to say they must call this disaster off, they must save their lives. But then a whistle was shrilling, and the Cubans in green fatigue suits were jumping to their feet and forming up, and the moment was over.

But still the impulse was in his mind. On the way back to the encampment in Richardson's jeep, Medwick turned to him and said, "Kerrwood's right, and you're wrong."

Richardson's jaw tensed slightly, but he said nothing. Medwick said, "If you send them in there without air support they'll be annihilated."

That was when Richardson gave him the real insight. "Too fucking bad," he said.

"I don't like you, Richardson," said Medwick, and neither one spoke for the rest of the trip. But when Medwick got out at the barracks Richardson said something very strange, "Watch out or you'll be on somebody's list."

Three days later Medwick was back in Washington, and one week after that the whole Guatemalan trip seemed like a dream, an impossible imaginary bizarre experience that really hadn't happened, and three weeks later he was reading about Cuban exiles going onto a beach, and Castro's aircraft sweeping down on them unopposed, bombing and strafing, and seeing pictures of corpses and of young men condemned to prison for life, and remembering the gay rich youths in a Guatemalan jungle clearing in a moment of a cold war that would never really end.

— 17 —

"How old was Richardson?" asked Williams.

"Late twenties, I'd say."

"And he said, 'Watch out, you might end up on somebody's list'?"

"That's right. But it was just a figure of speech. I'm sure as hell it doesn't refer to a list like this twelve years later."

Williams was not quite so sure, but he asked, "Did you ever hear what became of him?"

Medwick puffed on a cigarette. "As a matter of fact I did. I'm on the House Military Affairs Committee, and some years ago his name came up in one of the documents we were studying. He was then a major with the Green Berets—at least, that was his cover."

"What was the document about?"

"What else with Richardson? A massacre."

Williams thought for a minute. "Did you make any of the so-called Olympians angry for any reason?"

"Just what I said."

Williams stood up. "The age is wrong. He'd be in his late thirties now, and I have a feeling our man is younger. Still—the Olympians. Look at Watergate?"

"What about it?"

"I got involved with them there. When you put right-wing CIA types and Cuban exiles together, anything can happen—including this threat." He was moving to the door and Medwick accompanied him. Williams said, "We don't have much time. Write down all the names you can remember—and anything during your days with Fulbright. Meanwhile, I'll check Richardson."

Then he was gone and Medwick was left with his

memories. In some ways Guatemala had been the high point of his life, and he still admired himself for standing up to that maniac Richardson. After that, everything had changed. Everything had gone downhill. His work for Fulbright was routine—and then Kennedy had died and with help from Fulbright he had won a congressional seat, and without help from Fulbright he had discovered you could make some illegal money as a United States representative in Congress, and had started to make it, lots of it, and the lean idealistic boy who had gone to Washington as one of the hot-eyes and had challenged a right-wing CIA man in a Guatemalan jungle had died beneath fat, beneath ease, beneath greed.

Would any of that have happened if Kennedy had lived? Medwick didn't know, because he didn't want to think about it.

— 18 —

At midnight Medwick's phone rang. He answered it and a low voice said, "Congressman Medwick?"

Medwick knew immediately who it was. "Yes."

"I have the files that were stolen from your office."

"Then you have nothing. I don't keep my confidential papers in that file."

That was a lie but Medwick hoped to God it would work. But the voice was saying. "What about International Dynamic's contract Number 100478?"

Medwick said nothing. He was hooked.

The voice said, "You can have them back—for a price."

"Name it."

"Five hundred dollars."

Medwick could hardly restrain the joy in his voice. After a second he said quietly. "I'll pay it. Where and when?"

"Right now. I'm parked in the shopping center off Virginia Road, at Route 138."

Medwick said, "I could call the police and have you picked up for breaking into a congressman's office."

"Do that," said the voice, and Medwick knew it had been a foolish move. An empty threat would only guarantee that the contents of that file would become public.

"I'll be right over. How will I know your car?"

"Park—and I'll come to yours."

Click, and Medwick was holding a silent phone and trembling. Then he stood up, slipped into his coat and started for the door. Marie came to the head of the stairs. "Who was that, Tom?"

"I can't tell you," said Medwick. "It's some confidential business."

"At midnight?"

"It's nothing to worry about. I'll be back in half an hour."

"Tom—" but Medwick was out of the door. He was so upset it wasn't until he was halfway to the shopping center that he realized he had forgotten the money! Should he go back? He slowed down the car and then thought he'd better get there right now and talk to the man. He could always get the money. He had ten thousand in cash in his private safe in the house, gifts from his friends in industry.

Allen Lowell waited in the darkened shopping center lot. It wasn't long before headlights speared the darkness and a car turned in, then stopped uncertainly. There were a few other cars and some trucks in the lot. Taking the files and a .38 police positive, Lowell pulled on a pair of black leather gloves and walked over to the driver's side of the car and looked into the frightened face of Thomas Medwick.

"Turn the lights off," Allen said.

The man's hand was trembling as he reached for

the dash-board. Then all was dark. Medwick peered at him through the blackness. "Do I know you?" he asked. "I think we've met."

"No chance," said Allen. He thrust the two bulky files and the pistol inside the window. The pistol landed on Medwick's lap and fell to the floor. "What's that for?" asked Medwick, his voice rising in fear.

"I'm going to leave," Allen said. "There's a note on the first page of one of the files. Read it after I'm gone."

He got into his car and pulled away, blue Ford license plate VA 17089, Medwick noted quickly. He was more frightened than he had ever been in his life. No money had been asked. No five hundred dollars. And a pistol thrown into his lap! What the hell—

He turned on the overhead light and found an envelope. Inside was a typed letter:

> For the past three years I have been taking money from International Dynamics in exchange for my services in helping them to receive certain contracts. Now someone is about to make this information public.
>
> My family must not bear the shame for this. But in expiation of my guilt, I have decided to take my life.
>
> To my wife Marie and my two sons Tom, Jr., and Bill, I beg you to consider your father as a man who did his best for a long time, but then made a few mistakes and feels he must pay for them. My love to you is the last gift I can give.

THE NOTE WAS SIGNED IN HIS HAND-WRITING!

Medwick looked around wildly. The parking lot was silent. The .38 still lay on the floor of the car. He picked it up and held it for a moment, thinking. Unbelievable! That kid actually thought he would kill himself! Just like that. Was he crazy?

Or was he not so crazy? Suddenly he remembered what Williams had told him about the death threat. He had been so concerned with his missing files that he hadn't put two and two together. Of course! He was on the list. And that young fellow was the killer!

He looked at the letter and then at the envelope. For the first time he noticed it still contained something. Hard, bulky. He spread it apart and a Kennedy half-dollar dropped into his lap.

He had to get to a phone immediately and call Williams. Wildly, he drove around the lot looking for an outside telephone booth. He was afraid to move without Williams—and yet he couldn't call the police. They might start asking questions. What should he do?

Home. Get home. No phone booths here. Maybe he'd find one on the road. He started the car and raced out of the lot, turning on two wheels and heading onto the road that paralleled the Potomac—and then he saw it. A phone booth.

A minute later he was holding the dead instrument in his hand. The wire had been cut. Oh God!

Back in the car and racing now. Forget the phone booths. Get home in one piece. Watch for sudden obstructions on the road, a car pulled over to block, anything could happen.

The armor-piercing bullet hit his left front tire when he was taking a sharp turn along a cliff at seventy miles an hour. The car slued violently, tires screaming, and Medwick fighting, fighting, and then he was sailing into space over the lip of the cliff.

— 19 —

Detective Division Unusual Occurence Report

Det. Sqd.	Date & Day	Time	Crime/Condition
2	10-30-73 Fri.	0800	(Brief & Concise) Apparent Suicide

Details:

1. On Route 138, one mile south of Virginia Road intersection, a white male tentatively identified as Thomas Medwick, of 1707 Harper's Road, McLean, Va., congressman from Pennsylvania, was found DOA.

2. Dr. Alfred Zeser from coroner's office tentatively places time of death at approximately midnight of 10/29/73.

3. Car a green Chrysler sedan, License VA 70555, went off the road at high speed. Victim apparently died in the crash.

4. A .38 police positive revolver was found in front seat, along with personal and tax files. A letter signed by Medwick states intention to commit suicide.

5. Revolver has been turned over to Homicide Division for fingerprint tests.

Sergeant Al Tenney and Captain Gordon Masterman of the Alexandria, Virginia, Homicide Division pulled up at the scene of the crash. The body had been removed, fingerprint men had done their work, photographs been taken, as they carefully made their way around the pancaked sedan with its two front wheels resting in the water of the Potomac.

"Suicide, your ass," said Tenney.

"Exactly what I was thinking," said Masterman.

The two men conversed in low tones, probing the car, looking for anything unusual. "Suicides like to kill themselves as quickly and easily as possible—a sleeping pill, a bullet through the brain," the captain said. "No, Al, there's something else here."

"I think it was set up somehow. It's a hit."

"Did you ever think it could be just what it looks like? An accident? Man decides to kill himself, loses his nerve as they almost always do, then drives home upset, preoccupied, and starts to skid. Same result. No suicide."

"Here's why he skidded," said Tenney. He was crouching next to the left front tire. It was ripped open. "A goddamn flat tire. That was it. And the poor bastard dies with a suicide note in disgrace."

The two men made one last search through the wrecked car. Under the jammed front seat, they found some loose change, a key ring, and a St. Christopher's medal.

"The medal didn't help," said Masterman. He put the medal and the change, including a Kennedy half-dollar, into a small paper bag and sealed it.

They climbed up the hill and when they got to the top a car had driven up with two FBI agents.

Allen Lowell was on his way to New York City by car that same morning. He arrived at the Holiday Inn and checked in again. After filling out the registration, he went across the lobby to the newsstand. No story on the front page. Why?

As soon as he had parked his bag in the room he went downstairs and bought the *Post* and read it through. No story at all. The police were obviously holding it up.

Allen smiled thinly. The reason was obvious. They didn't know what the *hell* had happened! Accident? Suicide? Homicide?

He wondered what Major Carl Richardson would have said if he had seen him take that tire from thirty yards away. The results had been spectacular, more than even he bargained for. If the car merely had been stopped, Allen was prepared to finish Medwick off with the rifle. But his plan had worked as it should against a bastard like Medwick. A crook getting fat wasn't worth a spare round.

He took a subway downtown to the discount electronic stores, and bought a large tape recorder used for FBI bugging, an electronic filter, some jump wires. Then he stopped in at a music store and bought a tuning fork.

Carson would be tough; no doubt he would be guarded well after news of Medwick's death. But Allen had one glass ampule left. It had been Carl Richardson's last gift.

THE DEATH
OF
JAMES CARSON

The morning after Medwick's death, George Williams went straight to the Pentagon. He had not yet heard of the incident on Route 138.

He entered Room 301, US Army Personnel, an enormous file room, and told the receptionist he wanted to see Colonel Larma. The girl spoke into the intercom and a lieutenant appeared who brought Williams to the colonel, a jovial fellow with a paunch and a white mustache. "What brings the Justice Department into our dull midst?" he said.

Williams smiled, took a seat in a wooden hard-backed chair, and placed his briefcase on the floor beside him. "A follow-up," he said, "on Major Carl Richardson."

Colonel Larma did not change expression, but he watched Williams intently. "Carl Richardson isn't that unusual a name. Which one do you have in mind, in case there are several?"

"I think you know the Richardson I mean," said Williams. "A Green Beret. Involved in a massacre incident in Vietnam."

The colonel sighed. "That would be Lieutenant Colonel Carl Richardson. I know the one. You want to look at his file?"

"Yes."

"Why?"

"I want to interview him—on another matter. Not the massacre."

The white-mustached colonel leaned back in his chair. "That might be difficult even for a Justice Department lawyer," he said. "Lieutenant Colonel Carl Richardson died in a helicopter crash in 'Nam in 1968."

"Confirmed?"

"Confirmed."

Williams said, "I still want to see his file."

And now the colonel was staring at him. "But he's dead! That file is buried. It would take us a day to dig it up, and for what?"

And then the phone on his desk was ringing and the colonel answered. "It's for you," he said with new respect, handing Williams the phone. "The FBI director."

Williams took the phone and heard the director say: "Thomas Medwick died in an accident last night."

— 2 —

"After last night the director gave me permission to show you the files on everyone," Jarvis was saying. Williams had come right over to the FBI when Fred called.

"It's a little late for Medwick," said Williams.

"I'm sorry, George. The thing is we took it seriously here, but not seriously enough."

"What happened last night?"

Jarvis told him the details, as far as were known. Williams listened stonily. When Fred finished he had some questions. "Had the pistol been fired?"

"No."

"Registration of the pistol?"

"Serial number filed off. The wife says Medwick didn't own a gun of any sort."

"But that doesn't mean Medwick didn't have one," said Williams.

The two men sat thinking until Williams said, "It's open and shut murder except for one thing. The corruption bit is authentic, I take it."

"We were closing in on International Dynamics," said Jarvis.

Williams stood up and swung his hands together, fist against palm. "Fred, did you ever hear of the Olympians?"

Jarvis's eyes wavered. He said nothing.

Williams went on. "Medwick had a run-in with one of them in 1961——"

"1961?"

Williams had paced across the room, now he turned back. "That's what we're talking about, Fred. 1961. The note refers to Kennedy."

"But this is . . . weird. It's mythology. Nobody waits twelve years for revenge!"

Williams came back and sat down. "It's even weirder than that," he said. "Number one, it was a mild run-in, just a few words exchanged. Number two, the man who Medwick had a run-in with died in 1968 in a helicopter crash in Vietnam."

"Then what the hell are you talking about?"

"I don't know," said Williams. "I'm just following any lead I can find." He gathered the files on Fred's desk. "Everybody here?"

"Everybody, including Stephanie Spaulding and a six-foot-two Yugoslav named Drndov, photographed coming out of the Yugoslav Embassy on Massachusetts Avenue at two in the morning. She's holding her shoes in her hand. Want to drive out and see Medwick's car?"

"Why bother? Either way, he's dead."

Jarvis's voice lashed out. "But he wasn't killed! We checked, I tell you!"

"Which way was the car traveling?"

"East."

"He shot the left front tire," said Williams.

Jarvis was after him like a tiger. "I said nothing about the tire. How could you know the left front tire was shredded?"

"Figure it out," said Williams.

Jarvis stared at his retreating back. A shredded tire? And then it came to him, as Williams knew it would. Tacks or glass on the road would have turned up in the *other* tires. Jarvis phoned the director. "It was murder. Someone shot Medwick's left front tire."

"How do you know?"

"Figure it out," said Jarvis.

— 3 —

Bill Orenburg of the Anonymous Documents Division glared at Williams across his lab table. "OK," he said, "1961 Underwood Standard." He looked down at a paper. "Purchased that year by the following departments. You're lucky——" he stopped.

"Why?"

"No Defense Department. That cuts it in half right there." He read from the list. "HEW, USIA, Commerce, and one other."

"The FBI," said Williams.

"There goes my surprise."

Williams spoke over Orenburg's disappointment. "Mustn't be many 1961 typewriters still in use. Have you checked?"

"Memo to every agency, but so far no one's reported back. It's a bit of a chore, I take it. But we'll find it if it's there."

"You don't seem too hopeful," said Williams.

"Well, it is a bit of a wild goose chase, isn't it? I mean, it's great if your man is a government employee, but what if he isn't?"

Williams said only: "While you're at it, check whether any 1961 typewriters disappeared from inventory in the last ten years. That should be easy."

"Everything's easy to you," said Orenburg.

Williams smiled and said, "At any rate, we have one break. He typed another note, a suicide note for Medwick."

But Orenburg was holding a Xerox of the suicide note in front of him. "Got it this morning," he said.

"And it's no help. It's another typewriter. Furthermore, we know whose typewriter it was. Medwick's."

"He typed that note in Medwick's office?"

"That's what the type says. 1971 IBM. Look." He held up another version of the same note. "This was typed on Medwick's 1971 machine. Identical."

"Forget that one then," said Williams. For the first time he read the forged suicide note in its entirety. "Why would Medwick leave his house last night after I had warned him? Our man must have known something specific, something he got from Medwick's contract. How could he have got that?"

"Easy, if he worked for the FBI," said Orenburg.

Williams was excited. He leaned over and grabbed Orenburg's arm so hard it hurt. "Or if he had access to FBI files! Media, Bill. Those kids who stole the files from the Media office! They stole the typewriters too. How fast can we round up samples of those files?"

And Orenburg's heart was beating fast. He was caught up in Williams' excitement. Media! He knew he had recognized that type!

— 4 —

FBI OFFICE AT MEDIA, PA.
Broken Into: Files Removed

Washington.

March 14, 1971. The Federal Bureau of Investigation announced today that the Media, Pennsylvania, Field Office was broken into last night and looted of its files. The announcement came on the heels of disclosure by several newspapers that copies of the documents had been sent to them anonymously.

The FBI acknowledged the authenticity of the

documents which revealed that the agency is engaged in active surveillance of student, Negro, and peace groups.

Williams was on the phone to Fred Jarvis. "Sorry, George," Jarvis said, "this time you picked the wrong operation."

"What do you mean?"

"I personally handled that Media break-in, and we never got anywhere. All we know it was done by eighteen- to twenty-one-year-old kids, new leftists."

"My man *must* have been in Washington in 1963 to know these people on the list," Williams said. "That would make him at least twenty-eight now. I don't get it. What was he doing at Media with the kids?"

"Hold on," said Jarvis. In a few minutes he was back and in spite of his mumbling Williams could detect the note of triumph in his voice. "I got a file eight inches thick but I know what I'm looking—ah, here it is."

From FBI files:

PSI 187965, an informant (reliable-protect), states that he heard two students talking about the Media break-in on the University of Pennsylvania campus, March 13, 1971. Overheard one of them say that he distrusted quote that so-called Beret who executed the break-in unquote. He went on to say that he was sure quote the crewcut is an FBI plant unquote.

— 5 —

A Green Beret! It made sense to Williams. The shooting of a tire at high speed had to be done by a marksman, that was no amateur shot. And although Williams had instinctively thought of the killer as a "kid" in the Bremer vein, he knew also that this "kid" most likely had known all the intended victims in 1963, so he was probably in his late twenties—and could have served in Vietnam.

The suicide note gambit also indicated that this was no wild young militant flailing blindly out at society. He was a cunning and experienced killer.

Now it was more important then ever to look at Carl Richardson's file. The possibility the letter writer was an ex-GI was intriguing. Besides, it was the only lead he had. He knew the Media trail was cold right now, but Williams was pretty sure it would tie in eventually.

But he didn't have time to wait. Right now a killer might be planning his next victim. That night Williams put in a call to everyone on the list and told them about the death threat and Medwick's murder. Robert Warneky didn't take it seriously, Medwick or no. Who would want to kill him? A high school football coach! Everett Mellon said he would start carrying a gun, but he had a special idea about why his own name was on the list. It was obviously a case of mistaken identity. Carson was out of his hotel room as usual. Then Williams was left with the call he had put off to last—Stephanie Spaulding.

George Williams' first year in Washington had been spent chasing the most beautiful girl he had ever seen. A year later Stephanie had suddenly announced she was in love with him, moved into his flat in Georgetown, and started making little gourmet dinners for two—she was an extraordinary cook. Williams couldn't believe his luck, couldn't believe that someone so sophisticated could be in love with someone as square as he was, that someone so desirable and elusive would turn up to spend every night with him.

Sure enough, one evening he came home and she was gone, just like that. No note, no explanation, until a card came from Acapulco with the inscription Williams never forgot: "Too boring, darling." At first he thought the comment applied to Acapulco, but later he ran into her at a party—she had a tall, muscular Yugoslav's arm draped around her shoulders possessively—and she told him with her sweetest smile that she was referring to their life together. And told him she was sorry.

That meeting took place a year after she walked out, and three months after he had met Sarah. He said, "In that case, will you pick up your clothes?" and Stephanie said, "Those old things. Throw them away!" Williams had tossed everything in the trash—Guccis and Puccis and Galanos' and Balmains, a $10,000 gift for a sanitation man—and three days later Stephanie stopped by and turned white. "I was just *saying* that. You are so bloody stupid!" That had been their total communication except for a letter from her in New York saying, "I still love you. I always will. But you really were so quaint!" George had showed it to Sarah who laughed at it— and that was the end of it. Except for one thing—Stephanie still had the power to excite him.

He was not proud of it, but it was true, it was happening now, as he called her.

Stephanie came to the phone right away. "I've got something very important to tell you, Stephanie."

Silence. He imagined those luminous green eyes, the fair skin, the perfect cheek bones . . . she was saying, "Why are you so . . . formal, George. That telegram sounded like a Justice Department summons."

Williams told her why. They were both mentioned in a death threat, along with four others. "The threat mentions the Kennedy assassination."

"You're kidding . . . what a fantastic—"

Williams said, "One of the people on the list, Congressman Medwick, was murdered last night."

There was a sharp intake of breath on the line. "Oh George, I'm frightened. What shall I do?"

"Can you go to Europe for a month till we get this straightened out? Just disappear?"

"I have to be in court next week," Stephanie said after a pause. "The relatives are contesting my husband's will. But under the circumstances, maybe I can get a postponement."

"I'd advise it very strongly," said George.

Neither of them said anything, until Stephanie spoke. "How is Sarah?"

"Fine."

"Too bad," said Stephanie, and George had to smile. You could accuse Stephanie of many things, but not hypocrisy. Stephanie talked over his silence. "Shall I call you tomorrow after I speak to my lawyer? In case he can't get a postponement?"

"Yes, of course. But Stephanie—"

"Yes."

"There was a murder last night. No one knows what's happening. So be careful. Have a friend over tonight. Or sleep somewhere else."

"Any suggestions, darling?"

"This is serious, Stephanie. I spoke to Medwick last night just like this and two hours later he was dead."

Williams spent the rest of the evening reviewing the victims' files. Which one would be next? Warneky? Orenburg told him that Warneky's name had been added to the list after the envelope was sealed. It was reopened and the name typed on. Williams interpreted that to mean Warneky was the least likely target, that perhaps even the killer himself had doubts.

Mellon? He was in Nassau. Logistics alone might rule him out.

Stephanie? A definite possibility.

Williams? A very definite possibility.

Williams called Carson in New York. This time he was in. "Jesus, buddy, I've been waiting to hear from you. What's up?"

Williams explained and then was stunned to hear Carson say, "I came up to my room three days ago and found my passport had been cut to fragments."

Williams thought fast. "You mean you're planning to leave the country and the killer knows it?"

"As soon as I get a new passport. A couple of days, they tell me."

Williams tried not to show his concern. He said, "Mr. Carson, one of the people on the list was murdered last night. The fact that the killer knows you are leaving the country means he knows he has to hurry with you. You're next—"

"But what's going on! Who the hell knew Kennedy? Jesus, that reminds me. The kid left a Kennedy half-dollar on the bed."

"Mr. Carson, get lost tonight," said Williams. "And keep a sharp lookout. I can guarantee that the man who intends to kill you is in New York right now."

"Why don't I call the police?"

"They won't help. They can't. They can't play babysitter to everyone who receives a threat."

"I'll disappear. Right now."

Williams said, "I'll be in New York tomorrow night. I'll check in at the Ambassador Hotel, Room 2103. You meet me there at eight o'clock."

"How do you know what room you'll be in?"

Williams said, "That's the FBI room, the room the hotel uses to put up labor leaders, embezzlers, hoods. The bugging equipment is next door."

"I'll be there."

Carson next. It had to be. But tonight if Carson took precautions—and the sound of the fright in his voice indicated he would—he might be safe. And meanwhile there was a bulging FBI file on Carson.

FBI NARRATIVE FILE

CLASSIFIED SECRET
NOT TO BE OPENED UNDER ANY
CIRCUMSTANCE
WITHOUT AUHORITY OF DIRECTOR

James Carson
3190 Mulholland Drive,
Beverly Hills, California

Carson Background

1. Born 10-29-1938 at 433 Collings Avenue, Evanston, Illinois. Father a surgeon at Chicago Mid-City Hospital. Attended Evanston junior schools, then four years Hill Preparatory school. Enrolled Northwestern 1956, Liberal Arts: Major, English; Minor, Drama. Graduated 1960.

Subject applied for position as film editor, USIA, 2-22-1961. Accepted, Grade 10, Salary $6200 per annum. Received promotion in three months to director/producer, Grade 12, $9600 per annum.

Personnel file at USIA shows commendations from USIA Director Edward R. Murrow.

Subject directed ten USIA films. List is appended. Screening shows no Communist bias in films, although *Bay of Sorrow,* the film about invasion of Cuba by patriotic exiles, does show strong anti-American flavor. Film was never distributed because of objections of CIA, plus many congressmen, particularly Senator George Harrison, Texas, who spoke in Senate session against showing "anti-American propaganda" around the world.

After this incident, phase three surveillance was begun on subject.

Subject left government employment 2-4-1964 professing disillusionment with USIA after President Kennedy's death.

4-15-1964 obtained employment as director at Cascade Films, 2300 Sunset Blvd., Hollywood, California. Engaged in directing television commercials and industrial public relations films.

10-18-1966 was engaged to direct a feature film called *Crackback,* an independent film production. Financing was not fulfilled, and picture not completed.

11-8-1967 was engaged to direct one-hour television drama for DuPont Drama Hour on CBS, entitled *Three to Get Ready.* The TV drama won the "Emmy" award, highest award for television drama.

Carson's career took major step forward after that award. Signed by talent agency William Morris as a client. Directed a feature film for MGM 3-10-1968 in Berlin entitled *Last Parade* which won an Academy Award nomination. 1969 directed *Sun Dance* for Columbia which was a financial failure. But in 1970 directed *Spy on a New York Street* which is termed one of the greatest financial successes in motion picture history. Followed this with *Heritage,* still in distribution. Another financial success.

CURRENT:

Engaged to direct motion picture in Spain by Twentieth Century Fox, title not yet known. Will leave country 10-24-1973.

2. Summary of unevaluated information following shows a persistent anti-American bias. Subject is also obsessed with opinion that President Kennedy was the victim of a conspiracy, and that Lee Oswald was not a lone killer.

3. Screening of his feature films shows no anti-American bias.

4. Subject's record at USIA, and unevaluated information since, shows anti-American bias. Remarks made to college groups are particularly noted. Yet

subject has never transferred these opinions to his feature films.

5. It is recommended that surveillance be downgraded. All feature films directed by him nevertheless should be screened, despite downgrading of status.

Forwarded from Central Intelligence Agency 6-7-62

On 6-6-62 subject engaged in violent quarrel with agent sent to question him re *Bay of Sorrow* film. Spoke malignly of this agency, referring to it as "nest of kill-crazy maniacs."

Also stated that President Kennedy intends to "wipe out" the agency as soon as it is politically feasible.

Forward from Central Intelligence Agency 10-17-1965:

An agent whose cover is a motion picture director overheard subject at party in home of Mrs. Edward Morrison, 3102 Palmyra Road, Beverly Hills, California, state that "CIA was behind the Kennedy assassination."

Forwarded from Narcotics Bureau, Treasury Dept. 1-12-70:

Subject is known user of marijuana. Buys from Hal Casko, unemployed actor, 1030 Las Palmas Avenue, Hollywood, California.

Forwarded from Internal Revenue Service 3-14-1973:

List of charitable deductions for 1972 includes Vietnam Veterans Against the War, $300, and Senator George McGovern's campaign. Deduction for Vietnam Veterans disallowed.

In New York Carson hung up the phone and thought a moment. He wanted protection. Whenever someone passed his hotel door he jumped. He considered calling the Pinkertons—for peanuts he could hire full-time bodyguards—but then he had a better idea. He picked up the phone again.

"Sam, this is Jim Carson. Remember?"

"Sure. You gave Stella a job in *Last Parade*. I owe you a favor."

The voice was quiet, heavily Brooklynese, but the mind was sharp. Sam was no stranger to unexpected phone calls at night. Carson said, "Some kook is threatening to kill me. In fact he's got six on the list, and one of them was killed last night."

"Where you calling from?"

"The Waldorf, Room 1101."

"In ten minutes you get a knock at the door. Their names are Mac and Angie. Big one is Mac. Tell 'em your problem."

Carson was feeling better already. "I appreciate—"

But Sam interrupted him. "When my boys come in, you walk out of the room with them—stay between!—take the elevator and go out of the lobby just as if you're going out for a night on the town. But you don't go back. You go to 134 East 35th Street, Apartment 14E . . . write that down."

Carson did so.

Sam said, "You stay there till this thing blows over. Tomorrow I'll have one of the boys pick up your things at the hotel. You want a chick?"

Carson was smiling. "Not tonight," he said. He felt safer than the President. These boys were maniac-proof.

Allen Lowell entered the Ambassador Hotel with a briefcase, but this time he didn't escape the sharp-eyed attention of one of the hotel detectives as he had once before. This time he was followed.

The detective was surprised therefore when Lowell headed for the registration desk and checked in. But not surprised enough to forget to send a maid up to Lowell's room thirty minutes later. The maid let herself in and heard Lowell in the shower. She pretended to straighten up the room, edging closer and closer to the briefcase when Lowell walked out, naked.

"Night service," said the maid quickly.

Lowell had ducked back and gotten a towel which he now wrapped around his waist. "The room's OK," he said. "I'm just going to sleep." He started to pull back the bedcovers.

"I'm sorry, sir," said the maid, blushing, and went out. Downstairs she reported that he looked all right to her. A jewel thief would have been through three rooms by the time she got there, anyway.

Allen slept until 3 A.M., then got up noiselessly, dressed, and stepped into the hall with his briefcase. He climbed three flights to the twenty-first floor, and then used his tools to pick the lock of Room 2103, the FBI room in which Williams would be staying tomorrow.

He worked inside that room for quite some time. Then he let himself into the room next door.

— 9 —

Excerpt from Allen Lowell's diary . . . entry October 31, 1973:

> . . . I have killed my first victim, and the odd thing is I feel nothing. Medwick made my skin crawl when I saw him.
>
> Carson is different. Carson, it will hurt. The thing is I *like* Carson. He is what he is. A phony.

— 10 —

Williams had no luck at the Pentagon the next morning. He had intended to spend the day going through the file on Carl Richardson. But Colonel Larma apologized. "There is no file on Richardson," he said. "I had three men in the dungeons all day looking. Then I woke up."

"CIA?"

"That's it."

"But still he'd be carried in your records."

The colonel stroked his white mustache. "Here's the pink slip," he said. And Williams read, "Transferred to Central Intelligence Agency September 12, 1969, by authority of Colonel William Atwell, Chief of Personnel, USA."

Williams nodded. "Actually, I'm not as interested in Richardson as in the men who fought with him."

The colonel looked perturbed. "Goddamn," he said, "you're getting into ticklish stuff here. First of all, who's kidding who? He was no Lieutenant Colonel. So he didn't have a battalion or anything. He floated. He went where he was needed."

"How do you know so much about him?"

"Hell, we had a hundred of those characters in there—and that's what they all did. And all we got to show for it is a hundred pink slips."

But Williams was unfazed. The colonel took in the stern eyes peering at him across the desk; he wouldn't want to be against *him* in court. "Then we attack it another way," Williams said quietly.

"Hold it," said the colonel. "Hell, you know the FBI director. One call from him and CIA shows you the Richardson file."

"Not since Watergate," said Williams.

"But still—"

"Besides, you've forgotten one thing," said Williams. "Richardson was involved in a massacre. If you'll call your Military Justice head—"

The colonel was already reaching for the phone. "Smart fellow. The pre-trial investigation will tell you everything."

Fifteen minutes later Williams faced a tall, pleasant captain named Joe Ross. "Richardson, sure," Ross was saying. "But he wasn't court-martialed, you know. The boys down the river quashed it."

"But there was an investigation?"

"Of course. At the time we thought he *was* a major. Let me make a call and see where that stuff is."

He talked on the phone for a minute, then hung up. "Just what I thought," he said. "It's in Rockville, Maryland."

"What's out there?"

"Our records, along with eight million tons of other government papers." He gave Williams the address. "Big windowless warehouse place. Give this note to Jim Kalick, he's the supervisor out there."

Williams drove through the Maryland countryside, green suburbia dotted with little towns that had suddenly swelled as the federal payroll grew and the white civil servants fanned out from D.C. to avoid the Negroes in the city. An old story now, but somehow ironic in Washington, town of the Emancipation Proclamation. Many of these fleeing white workers toiled in federal agencies to make sure Negroes got equal housing elsewhere in America.

But Williams had little mind for social phenomena today. In New York Carson's life was on the line. And here in Washington he was following a far-out trail because of one incident in Medwick's life. Wasted time, almost certainly. A long, long shot. But as he had told Jarvis earlier, he was taking what he could get.

He entered a two-story brown building with a discreet sign beside the entrance: "Archives, Rockville County Division." Inside was a large reception room, and a guard at the desk. Williams showed him the note from Colonel Larma, and in a few minutes the door to the lobby opened, and a thin little man in a white smock said, "Come in, please, Mr. Williams."

Williams was taken to a library-type desk, where he sat for twenty minutes before a trolley with cardboard cartons rolled up. The top carton was removed and placed on his desk. He looked inside and saw thick legal documents in stiff binders.

A note on top said: "Pre-Trial Investigation of Sergeant Greenwood, in re Richardson."

Greenwood? Williams opened it and read the first page, a letter from the Defense Department: "For reasons of national security, the charges against Sgt. T/5 Charles Greenwood are voided. No notation to be placed in his record. No further action by this department to be taken."

It was signed, Robert McNamara.

Williams was puzzled. Something was wrong. These papers should be classified. When visiting Military Justice headquarters today he had anticipated some wire-pulling would be necessary before he could obtain the confidential investigator's report, but here it was available to anyone. Then he turned to the next page and saw the reason. "Hearings before the U.S. Senate Judiciary Committee, October 3 to October 8, 1967, *in camera.*"

Beautiful! Somewhere along the line the old Army filing system had slipped a cog. Instead of the Army investigator's report, a congressional hearing had ended up in the files. Or maybe someone had purposely removed the Army report.

Whatever, Williams was not too disturbed. He knew from experience that congressional hearings behind closed doors often surfaced more information than a rigidly limited Army investigation.

— 11 —

*Transcript of US Senate Judiciary Committee,
March 7, 1969, hearing in Room 103, Senate
Office Building*

Present: US Senators Temple, Benson, Carmichael,
Jensen.
First witness: Sgt. T/5 Charles Greenwood, USA.

TEMPLE: "I want to open this season by telling the witness that the committee realizes that national security is involved here. But these proceedings are secret. So the witness must realize that and make his own judgment as to response. Now I'll begin with the statement of facts that the Army has given us."

WITNESS: "I know the facts, sir."

TEMPLE: (Holding the paper) "Have you read the investigator's report?"

WITNESS: "Yes, sir."

TEMPLE: "Well, why don't you tell the committee in your own words the facts as you remember them."

WITNESS: "Well, it began when we caught that double
    agent, Hu Ling. Major Richardson—"

TEMPLE: "Carl Richardson?"

WITNESS: "Yes, sir. Major Richardson gave him a
    lie detector test. We was in our headquarters
    near Chu Lai, and someone from Army Intelli-
    gence gave the test. Ling must have flunked it."

TEMPLE: "So?"

WITNESS: "So we had a problem."

TEMPLE: "And what was that? Keep talking, Sergeant."

WITNESS: "That night Ling escaped. Walked right out
    of camp after knifing a guard. Old Major Richard-
    son went after him. He was a tiger."

TEMPLE: "Before you go on, Sergeant, will you answer
    this question. Did you know Major Richardson
    was a CIA agent?"

WITNESS: "I didn't know anything about that, sir.
    As far as I was concerned he was attached to the
    Berets for special missions. Just another intelli-
    gence officer. And from time to time he would
    take some of us on those missions."

TEMPLE: "Did you ever find Ling?"

WITNESS: "No, sir, and the major . . . he was damn
    mad, I can tell you. He had us up all night."

TEMPLE: "All right, what happened the next morn-
    ing?"

WITNESS: "Well, first off we slept. We was bushed.
    But around noon the major says he's taking us
    on a patrol. And instead of that, he marches us
    to a helicopter, and we fly north of Chu Lai and
    there's a battle going on beneath us, and the
    chopper puts us down outside a village. Now
    this makes no sense. We're behind enemy lines,
    the Charlies are retreating right toward us, and
    who knows how many of them are hiding in the
    village. And it was at this time, Senator, that I
    began to think Major Richardson had flipped
    out."

BENSON: "He was acting crazy?"

WITNESS: "Yes, sir. I mean, he wasn't taking any

precautions. Nothing. He just motioned to us
and started running toward the village. We
couldn't do nothing but follow."

TEMPLE: "And were there Charlies in the village?"

WITNESS: "Lucky for us, no. Nothing but old men
and women and babies. The colonel had us start
rounding them up in the center of the village
and I mean I felt naked. Any minute I expect a
platoon of VC to come charging in and there
five of us are standing all alone in the middle of
a square."

TEMPLE: "Please continue. Do you want a glass of
water, Sergeant?"

WITNESS: "No, sir. But the next part's kind of . . .
hard. (Pause) Yes, sir, I'll have that water."

TEMPLE: "Have the Master at Arms bring the witness
a pitcher and a glass. Sorry we can't offer martinis,
Sergeant. (Laughter) Are you all right now?"

WITNESS: "Yes, sir. Well, there we are and the gunfire
from the South is getting closer and then Richardson says to me, quick as a cat, 'Hold them, Greenwood, I'm taking the others back.' "

TEMPLE: "What did he mean by that?"

WITNESS: "I didn't know what he meant. I thought he
was gonna leave me and take off. But then I seen
him and Bolton . . ."

TEMPLE: "Sergeant Jeffrey Bolton?"

WITNESS: "Yes, sir. Bolton, and Sergeant Marconi
. . . Joe Marconi . . . and . . . and two pri-
vates . . . they took off for the edge of the village and they drop in the grass. And by God
here come some VCs breaking out of the woods
retreating and firing as they go and not even
looking back and Major Richardson captures the
whole bunch. Must of been twenty of them or
more. And one of them is Ling, the double
agent. You want to know the truth? I thought
right then Richardson was the greatest officer I
ever saw. I still think so. Only he was crazy."

TEMPLE: "What happened next?"

WITNESS: "The grunts come charging through the village and they are really shook when they see a few of us already in town holding all the prisoners. But right then Jeff Bolton . . . I don't know why . . . he just goes ape, I guess. Bolton opens up and starts slaughtering everybody. Richardson had to stop him."

TEMPLE: "It seems to me Bolton was the crazy one, not Richardson."

WITNESS: "That was what I couldn't understand. Bolton was a terrific soldier in a way, he knew all the tricks, but he wasn't . . . sadistic like that. If Bolton shot somebody, he had to."

TEMPLE: "Aren't you forgetting the testimony in the investigator's report? Sergeant Marconi says that Richardson *ordered* Bolton to shoot."

WITNESS: "Yes, and Richardson killed Bolton later."

BENSON: "I must caution you, young man. That has not been proven."

WITNESS: "Yes, well he *did! I saw him do it.*"

TEMPLE: "Tell us what you saw."

WITNESS: "Well, to begin with, when we got back to camp the division commander, Colonel Barston, didn't like what had happened at all. There were all kinds of news people floating around, and this little story wouldn't do the Berets any good at all. We was always being written about as killers and all that. Well, the colonel dragged Richardson on the carpet but Richardson didn't tell him anything I guess. But the next day Bolton and me and the rest were going out on a patrol with Richardson and we run right into an ambush. I mean a big one. We get reinforcements in a hurry, and gunships come in, and we're all laying flat and then running back and laying flat again, firing all the time, and Bolton is behind a tree firing, and Richardson is behind him and there's a machine gun burst and Bolton goes down. Richardson takes off but I seen him with the gun, all right. And I'll say what I seen in a court of law, even if I am a sergeant—"

TEMPLE: "Go right ahead, sergeant."

WITNESS: "Well, I got mine about five minutes later. Shot through the shoulder and the thigh. The stretcher boys got me back to the village and saved my life. The next day Marconi comes in to see me, and he's crying. 'They buried Bolton,' he said. Bolton was Marconi's best friend. Marconi said, 'And that' . . . excuse me, sir, this is the word he used . . . 'that prick Richardson didn't even show.' " (Sound of sobbing)

TEMPLE: "If the witness would like a recess . . ."

WITNESS: "No, sir, that's all right. Anyways, I told the investigators what I know . . . Richardson killed Ling. But Bolton killed the others. Now Marconi says Richardson ordered Bolton to do it and then Richardson killed Bolton. As if Richardson didn't want Bolton to testify, in case something came out."

End of Section One of Transcript

— 12 —

Williams finished reading the transcript, taking detailed notes of names. Then he leaned back and saw a welcome sign on the wall: Smoking Permitted.

He lighted a cigarette and pondered some questions: One, why so much fuss over a tiny massacre? CIA's Special Operations Division had made such massacres a specialty.

Two, why had Richardson killed Bolton? Not just to stop his testimony. Others such as Greenwood and Marconi were still alive and could corroborate what had happened.

Three, something about Greenwood's testimony bothered him.

An hour later he was back in Colonel Larma's office in the Pentagon, and this time he met with success. After some phone calls Larma managed to get the death certificate of Sergeant Jeffrey Bolton. His body had been transshipped to the USA in 1966, and buried after a Catholic ceremony in the Christ the King cemetery in Webster Groves, Missouri, October 12, 1966.

Then Larma got him the records on Greenwood, Marconi, and the rest. All except Marconi were still in the Army. Marconi had been dishonorably discharged in 1967 after assaulting an officer in Fort Benning. Marconi had heard Richardson order Bolton to shoot; Marconi was out of the Army; Marconi was the man Williams wanted next.

He thanked the colonel and went home. Sarah was out, so he left her a note, packed his bag, and headed for the airport.

By seven o'clock he was in Room 2103 of the Ambassador waiting for James Carson.

— 13 —

"We got us a fucking sex maniac," Big Mac said.

"How long has he been in there with the chick?" asked Little Angie.

"Two hours, and me with a hard on."

Inside the bedroom in the apartment on East 35th Street a redhead named Michelle McCourt was being given the ball of her life by James Carson. He just couldn't seem to get enough of her. You'd think it was his last time on earth.

But he was good-looking; he was fun; and he was a big movie producer who could get her into that picture in Spain. This was the last thing she thought before she started to respond again, and found her legs over Carson's shoulders, and ecstasy starting to build.

Ten minutes later she lay there serenely, feeling

great all over, when there was a knock on the door. She scurried into the bathroom to get dressed. "Just a minute," Carson called out.

Big Mac was waiting for him, looking impassive as ever. Angie was slumped in a chair in the corner, reading an old *Playboy* magazine. "It's after seven," Mac said. "You gotta be there at eight."

"Sure, listen," Carson felt he ought to explain. "You guys must be suffering."

"We don't mind," said Mac.

"The thing is, right now I'm a condemned man—"

"And you just ate your last meal."

Carson laughed, and Mac gave him a slap on the shoulder. "Knock off that condemned man crap. Nobody touches you while we're around, so just relax."

They waited a few minutes and then Michelle appeared in a green silk miniskirt and knee-high white boots, flouncing her long red hair. Mac looked hungrily at her and asked the classic hood's question: "How'd you like to make $300 for ten minutes?"

Michelle was shocked. "Really, Jim, that's not nice," she said to Carson. But Mac was unfazed. "Think about it," he said, and handed her his card. It read:

> Mac Vendotti
> Vice-President
> Simonpure Realty Co.
> 435 Madison Ave., N.Y.

Michelle read it and had to laugh. Mac said, "The Feds love that name."

— 14 —

In Room 2101 of the Ambassador, Allen Lowell waited with a .38 in his lap. The room was filled with electronic recording equipment including a zoom microphone, wall plugs, recorders which started automatically at the sound of a voice—all covered with dust; apparently the FBI had not used the room for some time.

Allen was obsessed by the thought that Williams was on the other side of the wall. All Williams had to do—and knowing Williams, it was always possible—was to check the room next door and that was it. Williams would go down right then, and the plan would be finished.

I don't want it to end that way, Allen was thinking, when suddenly he tensed. Someone had put a key in the door.

Allen faded into the bedroom quickly, slipped into a closet, and cocked his gun. So be it. He should have known Williams was too smart. He had predicted it!

Then he heard the voices of *three* men, and Williams was saying, "Thought it might be a good idea for you to give this room a rundown before we hold our meeting next door."

Another man spoke, "We're not technicians, Mr. Williams. All we do is take the stuff on tape."

"Check if everything seems in order," Williams said quietly. "You must know the equipment well enough to see whether it's been tampered with."

"Well, hell, of course."

The third man spoke. "How long do you want us?"

"My meeting is at eight. If you can stay until that ends—and keep your pistols ready."

"Like that?"

"It's possible," said Williams. "All set?"

"OK."

Williams went out, Allen heard the door slam, and then the two men, obviously relaxing in chairs, talking quietly. One of them was saying, "So that's the legendary Williams."

"He didn't impress me," said the other.

"No?" said the first. "You notice he didn't miss a trick. He covers his flanks."

There was a silence, then one of them said, "Think we should look in the bedroom?"

"We better or Williams will have our ass."

Allen Lowell tensed in the dark closet as footsteps came into the room, voices getting closer, and approached the closet, and Allen, for no reason, found himself thinking of his mother and father and that was all the time he had before the door opened.

— 15 —

On September 19, 1960, the Democratic presidential candidate came to Steubenville, Ohio. Kennedy would later say that he never saw such crowds as on that swing through Ohio. Women cried and tore at him, hoping for a piece of his clothes, a button, anything. Men surged through police ranks trying to shake his hands and shouting encouragement. And the young screamed from limbs of trees, from tops of cars, some holding each other up, a young high school girl suspended in the air and waving a Kennedy banner.

One of the young men beside her was Allen Lowell, fifteen years old, taking pictures one after the other. He was experiencing for the first time a feeling that almost frightened him. Steubenville had been a closed world; Wheeling Steel across the river had been his destiny; but look at Jack Kennedy. Handsome . . . rich . . . been around the world . . . war hero, and still *young!*

Presidential candidates may not realize the implications of their hurried sweeps through backwater towns and cities around the country. Television, it is said, has brought the world into everyone's living room so American youths in rural areas should feel no sudden strange emotion when a presidential entourage roars into town bound for the nearest airport. But how many Allen Lowells are there today who can still remember the first time they saw in the flesh

their first real creatures from out there . . . beyond
the limits of town, and their young horizons.

The limousines and motorcycles roared off, the
crowd subsided as if after an orgasm, and then the
girl, Peggy Goldthorpe, was dropping to the pavement, and she and Allen Lowell retrieved their bikes
from behind Leary's store.

Steubenville was not a bike town. In fact, it was
not like any other town in America. To the south it
cradled dingy brick buildings pressed against the bosom of the Ohio River. Climbing north the main
street of the city passed the conventional eight-story
hotel, a railroad station, and a shabby rundown business area.

This was the area referred to by Pennsylvanians as
the red light district of Pittsburgh, a city fifty miles
away. This was the section that ran its own gambling
school, turning out croupiers and dealers and card
sharps with diplomas, no less. A tough, tough city,
Steubenville, steeped in smoke from steel mills, dedi-
cated to the illegal dollar, a mixture perhaps unique
in America of steelworkers and hoods in $200 suits.

But once past this shabby central city you climbed
sharply up a long winding hill and soon came to
pleasant homes and tree-shaded streets and station
wagons in driveways . . . not one mile from the
teeming city below. Allen Lowell had grown up here
since his stepfather, Pete Schovajsa, had decided to
take the job at Wheeling. Lieutenant Schovajsa had
followed up on that letter he'd found aboard ship in
World War II. He'd tracked it down to Allen's
mother, and he liked what he found and married her.

Peggy Goldthorpe's father was rich in Steubenville
terms. He was a vice-president of Wheeling and—
more important to Allen—he owned the only swimming pool in town.

Peggy, Allen, and his friend Bob Crowley huffed
and puffed going up that steep road to Peggy's home.
That hill was actually a mountain; time and again the

big trailer trucks roaring south from Pittsburgh would careen around the bend at the top of the hill, their brakes jammed, and they'd jack-knife, hurtling down the road demolishing cars until they tilted over or crashed into a house or just plain stopped somehow. No amount of signs at the curve above could halt them. Allen had seen it happen dozens of times in his years in Steubenville.

A few minutes later they were sitting around the pool and Peggy was inside the house changing into a bathing suit. Mrs. Goldthorpe brought the boys Cokes. "You see Mr. Kennedy?" she asked.

"Yes, ma'am," said Lowell.

Mrs. Goldthorpe had been an amateur golfer. She was still tanned and somewhat muscular. She looked down at Allen and said, "What do your mother and father think of him?"

"Even split," said Allen with a smile. "My mother is for Kennedy and my father for Nixon."

"Of course *she's* Catholic," said Mrs. Goldthorpe, smiling brightly. Allen didn't like that smile. He said, "I'm for him, too."

"Thank heavens fifteen-year-olds don't vote. We'd have only Presidents who play touch football."

"Why do we have to have crummy old politicians all the time?" said Allen, and now Mrs. Goldthorpe looked at him more closely. "You do get steamed up," she said. "But just take it easy. There's precious little you're going to have to do with who's President, even when you grow up. Steubenville doesn't pack that much weight."

"*If* I stay in Steubenville," said Allen—but at that moment Peggy came out of the screen door onto the lawn and Mrs. Goldthorpe saw Allen look admiringly at her daughter, very precocious in a one-piece red bathing suit, and took her leave with one last remark, "I'll see you on *Meet the Press*."

Peggy overheard the remark. "What was *that* all about?"

"Your mother doesn't like Kennedy," said Bob.

"He's Catholic and a Democrat," said Peggy. "What do you expect?"

But Bob had apparently forgotten politics in favor of more immediate fascinations. He said, "Hey, Peggy, you're growing."

Peggy blushed. "I know it," she said. "It just happened all of a sudden."

The two boys laughed. The air was cool up here, not really for swimming, and they had intended to just stop off and then pedal home. But when Peggy dived into the water they had second thoughts. Allen said, "I'll call Tommy and ask him to bring my suit around. What about you?"

"I'll go get mine," said Bob. Allen walked across the lawn to the screen door and rapped. Mrs. Goldthorpe appeared. "Can I use your phone, ma'am?"

"Certainly, Allen."

Tommy Schovajsa was in the basement as usual when the phone rang. He was making a model airplane. He did this day and night. His father complained he would turn into a mole. But Tommy was the quiet one of the family; shy and introverted. Only alone in the privacy of the basement, with an overhead light flooding the precise miniature parts of a German Fokker or a Spad or a Hurricane or a gullbacked Corsair, did Tommy feel secure and confident.

"Allen wants you to bring his bathing suit over to the Goldthorpes' house," his mother called from the top of the stairs. "Do you mind?"

Tommy didn't mind. He loved his half-brother who was five years older than he. Allen was an end on the Steubenville High football team, too short for the position, but could he catch! Last year in the crucial game against Wheeling High he had caught three touchdown passes, one of them one-handed a foot off the ground as he lunged between two defenders.

A few minutes later the ten-year-old pulled into the Goldthorpes' driveway carrying the suit in the basket. He parked the bike and went into the back yard, and there saw a sight he hated: his brother kissing that girl. He watched as they broke apart and Peggy said to Allen, "I'm getting you all wet." Tommy noted with even more dismay that his brother seemed flushed and kind of breathless. Then they both saw him at the same time.

"Tommy!" said Peggy. They both saw his expression and started laughing. Tommy didn't know what was funny but he smiled too and brought the suit over to Allen, who knocked him playfully on the ear. "How you doing, old buddy? How's the Fokker?"

"The what?" asked Peggy, and this started them laughing again and Tommy was embarrassed. "A Corsair," he said to stop them. "The one with the crooked wings."

"I'll see it when I get home," said Allen, and Tommy realized he was being dismissed. "I'll have it finished in an hour," he said, and then started running back to his bike. "See ya," he shouted and pedaled off.

"I do think we shocked your little brother," said Peggy. "He should have seen us last night."

"Nothing happened last night," said Allen.

"It was a lot," said Peggy. "That's as close as I'm going to get."

Allen patted her on her cute behind and went inside and changed in one of the bedrooms, and came out and dived into the cold water, and later Bob arrived with a pretty brunette named Polly Stennett who had eyes for Allen and it was an altogether glorious day, this day that a future President came to town and opened for one boy at least a vision he had never had before. And that night, to top it off, he made real love for the first time in his life on the grass in the shadow of dark empty bleachers of the Little League ball park. Peggy went ape with worry for a month until she found out she wasn't pregnant. And Allen, who was just not tall or big enough for football, kept making miraculous catches, was elected president of his class, drank his first glass of whiskey and didn't like it, was seduced by Polly Stennett at a cabin party, and somehow managed to get straight A's through a year of lighthearted fun while President Kennedy took office and young people started flooding into Washington, and Allen was debating between college and the Peace Corps when his mother and father, sailing smoothly up the steep road from the city in a blue Chevrolet one night, heard a roar and saw twisting headlights and a cascading idiotic trailer truck veering out of control down the mountain road, and too late, too late, and the blinding fatal crash put Allen and his brother in Chicago with an aunt who hated them.

— 16 —

Now Allen Lowell waited in the darkened closet, pressing himself against the wall as the door opened. The FBI agent saw the man in a ski mask and jumped back but Allen had the gun on them.

"Not a sound," he said softly, and gestured at the bed. "You," he said to the one on the right, "take one of those sheets and tie up your partner."

When he had done so, Allen hit him with the side of his palm above the ear. He went over like a tree. Allen gagged him.

Allen examined the tape recorder which was connected to the telephone in the next room and made some adjustments of the wires. He then stripped the insulation from two wires and attached them to the power transformer in the corner of the room. Through the open door, the FBI man on the bed saw what he was doing and struggled with his bindings.

Allen didn't want to do it, particularly, but there was
no choice. He hit him above the bridge of the nose
with an upper chop that blacked him out completely.

Allen went to the door and put his eyes to the
crack. Two big men were just entering the room next
door with Carson. Allen calmly went to the desk, removed a tape cassette from his briefcase, put it on
the recorder, and picked up the phone. He asked for
Room 2103 and then put the phone down softly.

Williams heard the ring and was startled. He hadn't
told anyone, not even his office, where he was. Carson
and his two bodyguards watched as he answered
it.

A metallic voice, obviously filtered, said, "This is
the man who sent the threatening note. I'm ready to
do business. Meet me at the lobby newsstand in five
minutes. I'll approach you." Click. The phone went
dead.

A recording! An obvious attempt to get him out of
the room. Williams told the others what had been
said. But Carson said, "Well, take a chance. What's
five minutes?"

"Time enough," said Williams.

Mac said, "You're forgetting us."

Williams considered for a moment. Two FBI men
next door, Mac and Angie here—and there was always the one in a hundred chance the kid would be
at the newsstand. If so, he couldn't afford to let the
chance pass.

He said, "Mac, you stand outside. Nobody gets
near the room. If a hotel detective bothers you, show
him this card and tell him it's Justice Department
business. He'll understand. He knows this room."

He directed Angie to sit in a chair between the
door and Carson. The hoods thought he was crazy;
no one but no one was going to get by them, anyhow.

In the next room Lowell changed back the tape
cassette. Out in the hall Williams was passing by the

room next door when he heard voices through the door. One was saying, "So that's the legendary Williams?"

And the other was answering. "He didn't impress me."

Williams smiled and went down to the elevator.

In Room 2103 the telephone rang. Carson was sitting at the desk and Mac said, "Don't answer it."

"Why not?" asked Carson. The ringing went on.

"In these kinds of things you don't answer phones," said Mac.

But Carson had had enough of this charade, and besides the ringing was driving him crazy. He picked up the telephone, the hood yelled, "DON'T," and then, eyes wide, watched as Carson stiffened and dropped the phone, clawing at his throat, his head rolling back. "Holy Jesus!" yelled Mac. "Angie! Angie!"

Angie burst in the door and saw Carson, his head lolling forward now, and Mac next to him, slapping his face. "What the fuck happened?"

"The goddamn phone was booby-trapped. I told him not to pick it up. Jeez, he's dead. Right in front of my face. Sam will take me out for this!"

Outside Allen Lowell hurried down the emergency stairs to the eighteenth floor, where he took an elevator and disappeared into the busy lobby.

Two for Tommy Schovajsa.

— 17 —

A few minutes later Williams was back in the room with hotel and homicide people. The hoods had disappeared. He watched as the police went through the routine but he was as mystified as anyone. He had returned to the room to find the hoods gone and Carson sitting back with his head slumped forward, dead. The phone was on the floor.

Williams was despondent. *He* had killed Carson when he left that room against his better judgment. When he went next door to see why the FBI agents hadn't reported what happened, he found two bound and gagged men lying on the floor, eyes staring, and he cursed his fate, cursed himself, cursed everything he had ever been taught.

A cop helped him untie the agents and they got shakily to their feet. One of them said, "I saw him rig the wiring. He had four hundred amps going through there."

"Funny thing, too," said the other one. "He puts on a tape and I heard a whistle like I never heard!"

A tape with a whistling noise? Williams went back into the other room with the agents who were promptly corralled by a homicide captain named Pat McGrady, a big bluff fellow who had one of his men take down their story. Suddenly there was an interruption. A newsman had somehow managed to get through the cordon of police in the hallway. "Get lost, buddy," said McGrady.

"It's my job," said the newsman.

He was being taken by an elbow and ushered roughly outside when Williams went up to him. "I'll give you the whole story as soon as I can. But I don't want it exclusive."

"Shit!" said the newsman.

Williams was thinking he had to do it. Break this story on every television network and every newspaper he could; turn the hunter into the hunted. His department wouldn't like it; the FBI would think it a slap in the face; but there was no other way to stop this man. He was too skilled. He said to the newsman, "What's your name?"

"Phil Keller, *Daily News*."

"I'll call you later."

* * *

Back in the room a doctor was saying, "No external bruises."

McGrady told him, "There were two FBI types next door. They say the phone was rigged."

The doctor looked at the phone. "That's not my field, but isn't that phone insulated?"

"Not against four hundred amperes," said the captain.

The phone had not been touched as yet. It lay there on the floor and Williams dropped a metal letter opener on it. No sparks. He picked up the instrument in two fingers although he knew there was no chance of finding fingerprints. He did it by habit. He turned to McGrady, "Let's open this thing up."

The captain unscrewed the mouthpiece and looked inside. Nothing there. Then he unscrewed the earpiece and shattered fragments of glass dropped on the carpet. McGrady looked at Williams.

— 18 —

November 1, 1973

FILM DIRECTOR SLAIN IN ROOM AT AMBASSADOR

Justice Dept. Official Tells Story

Death Threat Involves Kennedy

James Carson, 34, director of such films as *Last Parade* and *Spy on a New York Street,* was found dead in Room 2103 of the Ambassador Hotel at approximately 8:05 P.M. yesterday.

George Williams, Deputy As-

sistant Attorney General, US Justice Department, told reporters in a hurried press conference an hour later that the murder of Carson, and the death last week of Thomas Medwick, congressman from Pennsylvania, were both the work of one man.

The case took a bizarre turn when Williams said that he and five others, including the two victims, were mentioned in a death threat which implied a connection with the "tenth anniversary" of President John F. Kennedy's death.

The others had been warned, he said. At the time of his murder Carson himself was under guard.

The others mentioned in the death threat are Mrs. Stephanie Spaulding Winthrop of Pound Ridge, New York; Mr. Robert Warneky of Ithaca, New York; and Mr. Everett Mellon, Nassau, the Bahamas.

The press conference was in pandemonium after the announcement. Williams refused to answer questions about the Kennedy angle, except to say that none of the victims—with the exception of Mr. Warneky—had ever met President Kennedy. However, he did say that all six of them had worked in what he termed "fringe" jobs in the Kennedy administration. For example, Mr. Mellon, he stated, had been a Senate page for only three months.

High police officials were still not certain of cause of death, although the first hypothesis was electrocution by a specially rigged telephone. New evidence has cast doubt on this theory.

Williams said that a nationwide manhunt, led by the FBI, is under way to find the anonymous killer. No clues to his identity have as yet been uncovered.

Following is the text of the death threat, as received by Williams, and released to the press last night:

"November 22, 1973, is the tenth anniversary of our late President's death. For reasons which you will fully understand we will observe this anniversary with the death of the following:

George Williams
James Carson
Thomas Medwick
Everett Mellon
Stephanie Spaulding
Robert Warneky."

— 19 —

Excerpt from Transcript of CBS Evening News November 1, 1973:

NEWSCASTER: In the studio with us today is Dr. Kenneth Langhart, who was one of President Kennedy's close advisers from 1960 to 1963. Mr. Langhart's field was international relations, assisting McGeorge Bundy. Tell us, Mr. Langhart, what's going on?

LANGHART: I've been asked that a hundred times today, John. I'm afraid I can't give you an answer. It's so . . . puzzling.

NEWSCASTER: Do you believe it's another conspiracy

theory on the assassination?

LANGHART: I don't believe that enters the picture at all.

NEWSCASTER: Why not?

LANGHART: The people involved. I know two of them, George Williams and Mrs. Winthrop. They're hardly likely to be assassins. Furthermore, both of them are Kennedy loyalists. I once accused Mrs. Winthrop of believing the world ended when the President was assassinated. She said, "The good part of it did." And everyone in Washington knows that George Williams' job was in real jeopardy when the Republicans took over the Justice Department. The conservatives didn't like having a Kennedy Democrat in their midst.

NEWSCASTER: Tell us something about George Williams. I was talking to our Washington staff today and I'm told he's considered a top man there.

LANGHART: Well, I would say if George Williams is involved in the investigation, this maniac, whoever he is, is in *some* kind of trouble.

NEWSCASTER: But if the killings are not connected with Kennedy, and if the victims didn't even know the President, what possible reason could this murderer have for mentioning Kennedy and saying "for reasons which you will fully understand"?

LANGHART: I would venture to say, John, that in some room, somewhere, a mentally twisted man has his reasons. But what they can be absolutely confounds me.

NEWSCASTER: Excuse me, Mr. Langhart. This just in . . . from the Associated Press . . . Police officials in New York City stated today that the cause of death in the James Carson case was cyanide gas. The gas was secreted in the earpiece of the telephone in a glass ampule which was shattered by an unknown remote control.

This is the gas which first became known when East Berlin agents attacked and killed members of the West German government some years ago. A Defense Department spokesman today denied that this nation has stockpiled this gas, and went on to say that all chemical warfare stocks are being destroyed under presidential order.

"Well, one thing is certain," said the newscaster after the broadcast, "this is no Bremer or Oswald type. We're up against a professional killer who has studied and maybe even practiced exotic modes of death. And he can place his hands on chemicals the Defense Department claims it doesn't even have. That leaves only one possibility. CIA. It's got to be."

Langhart said nothing.

"Who else has cyanide gas? No one."

But Langhart was sipping his coffee and thinking. "Your theory has one major flaw, John. Espionage agents in America or Russia or anywhere don't write *warning notes* to their victims."

— 20 —

Excerpt from Allen Lowell's diary . . .
        entry November 1, 1973:

. . . Williams is breaking. I don't believe he realized what he is up against.

Tonight ends the first phase of my project, and it ends exactly as I had predicted to myself—in a wave of publicity which is exactly what I want. Everyone is wondering why, why? Why those six?

I will let them know at the proper time.

And now for a confession. I hate what I'm doing. I hated to kill Carson. He gave me my first job.

BOOK IV

THE DEATH OF EVERETT MELLON

Everett Mellon lay warming in the sun on the beach in front of the Paradise Island hotel in Nassau. Two pretty girls in bikinis walked over to him and stopped.

"That's him," said one.

"You sure?"

"His picture was in the paper today. I recognize him."

A Bahamian in white ducks suddenly came up behind them. "Move along, ladies," he said.

"You see!" said the first girl. "He has guards! I'm right."

Everett Mellon sat up and regarded the scene with amusement. This was the damnedest thing! One of the girls, a blonde with her hair in a pigtail, gave him a heavy flirtatious look that caused him to laugh out loud. He was a celebrity!

And he was going to be a millionaire. His office phone had been busy all day with richies from New York suddenly wanting him to charter their yachts and asking—just by the way, old boy—anything new on that crazy Kennedy plot?

Mellon told them all what was the truth: he didn't know anything.

This morning a representative of the Nassau police had informed him that as long as he remained in Nassau he would have around-the-clock protection. Someone named Fred Jarvis from the FBI in Washington had called to say that when and if he returned to the United States he would also have a full-time guard.

In the furor resulting from Williams' press conference, the FBI had gone all out to protect the victims.

Jarvis made one further comment: Don't open any mail, don't receive any strange visitors, don't go out at night alone, even with the guard.

Madness, Everett Mellon thought. Madness. Three months with a bunch of kids as a page in the US Senate, and ten years later this happens.

While there was no doubt in his mind that the threat was real, he knew there could be only one explanation for his inclusion on the list. It was a mistake. The would-be killer had him confused with someone else.

— 2 —

In New York, George Williams waited outside Captain McGrady's office. He had no illusions about the FBI's offer of full-time protection. Anyone who could pull off last night's stunt in the Ambassador would not be deterred by guards. But the public attention was something else. The remaining victims now were under the scrutiny of thousands of eyes: it had to be a problem for the killer.

And this was a killer you wanted to give as many problems as possible. In his whole history in the Justice Department, Williams had never met a more resourceful killer. Or more *prepared!* This fantastic plot against six people had obviously been planned to the smallest detail for months—the fake suicide note with Medwick, the "poisoned" phone with Carson. What was next? And who would be the next victim?

Williams had every computer in the FBI and Justice and local police departments to work with. He had scientific laboratories eager to pounce on any scrap of evidence; analyze it, follow it to hell and gone. But what shred of evidence did the killer leave behind? A broken glass ampule in the earpiece of a phone, a bullet in a shredded left front tire—that was all.

Meanwhile the routine leads must be followed up. They now had a physical description of the killer from the FBI agents who had been in the room. He was about six feet tall, slight in size, and in his late twenties.

And his use of a classified chemical warfare gas pointed to a man with a specialized military background, as did his knowledge of karate.

Williams went in to see Captain McGrady, and found McGrady upset. "The newspapers are killing us," he said. "And it wasn't even my men—the goddam FBI squareheads blew it."

"Something has occurred to me," said Williams, leaning forward slightly in his chair. "There's another man in the hotel who not only saw the killer, but spoke to him."

McGrady sat up and looked at Williams. "An innocent bystander? You're dreaming."

"The killer knew the room," said Williams.

"What?"

"The killer knew the room where I was staying."

Silence in the office . . . then the captain slapped his palm on the desk. "Of course. He knew the FBI room, too! Half the people in the hotel never heard of it!"

"Somebody on the hotel staff talked to the killer and gave him that information."

The captain stood up quickly, the movement of his heavy body sending his chair back cracking against the wall. "Son of a bitch! We've got him! We'll find that staff guy in twenty-four hours!"

— 3 —

Six A.M. Toronto. The previous night's snow had ceased, and already Toronto's well-drilled clean-up crews were at work. Snowplows groaned down quiet streets; one of them passed the Bon Soir tailor shop throwing a cloud of snow in a continuing mist along the curb.

Allen Lowell cruised down the street, his eyes on the parked cars. The snow was his ally. If someone was watching the shop, the motor of his car would be running to provide heat, the windows would be clear.

But the cars were all lifeless mounds of snow. Allen drifted along and then stopped. In a car across the street he saw a splotch of red against the window.

He slogged across the newly swept road and over to the side window. The red blotch turned out to be a ski cap; someone was asleep inside. Allen knocked on the window loudly. The red cap moved. Allen turned the ice-crusted door handle and opened the door. The man inside was about twenty-four. His teeth were chattering. "Christ, I fell asleep." he said. "I could have frozen."

The young man looked up at Allen. "You're not Les Randolph," he said. "What's up?"

"Les can't make it so I'm relieving you," said Allen. "And I'm going to do you a favor and not tell Mike Gorgio you were asleep."

The man started the car engine. "Oh man, am I cold. You saved my life." He looked at a clock on the dashboard. "What the hell," he said. "It's only six. I don't get relieved until eight."

"Mike took pity on you," said Allen. "Get home and into a warm bed."

But the man seemed doubtful. "What's your name?"

"John Thompson," said Allen, looking carefully at the man. "Ever hear of me?"

"Nah," said the guy. "But as far as I'm concerned you're Jesus Christ." He turned on the heater, but apparently got only cold air. His face was blue. "OK," he said. "Take over. Where's your car?"

"Back about a hundred feet," said Allen. "You move out and I'll take your spot."

A minute later the car was edging out into the snow, wheels spinning and then gripping, and then the car was inching slowly down the street, and Allen was thinking, eight o'clock before the relief. He had two hours.

He crossed the snowy street and pressed the doorbell of the Bon Soir shop. He kept his finger on the button until a white-faced teenager in pajamas stared through the glass and then, seeing who it was, opened the door wide.

"Allo, Jeff," said the boy. Allen slapped him on the back. "Tell your father that Jeff Bolton is here."

"He will be angry," said the boy, smiling. "But not surprised. Always it happens this way. Doorbells early in the morning. Come upstairs."

A few minutes later a tiny baldheaded man appeared tying the ends of a belt across a worn red bathrobe. "Jeff," he said, "I was expecting you later."

They walked through a room; Robere pushed a spot on the wall and a panel slid open. Behind it was a tiny room filled with presses and inks and copying machines. "Gorgio has a watch on this place," Allen said, "so I had to come earlier."

"Why is Mike doing that?" asked the little man.

"He must have heard I'm in trouble with the police."

"Mon Dieu," said Robere.

"I need a new set of papers in less than two hours. Can you do it?"

"For you I make the mountain jump." The little man took a passport from a stack, alongside which were piles of snapshots and Army ID cards, and sat down at a table in the middle of the room. Allen idly thumbed through the Army ID cards and when he saw Robere had his back to him, he slipped into his pocket the ID card and passport of T/Sgt Harold Daub. Robere was saying, "I was preparing a set in the name of Jim Adams, 135 Oak Street, Seattle, Washington. I will give these to you and make a new set for the other man. Give me your passport."

Allen handed him the Bolton passport. Robere took

a knife, pried loose the snapshot, and affixed it to the inside pages of a loose passport cover he had prepared. While he stapled it together, Allen said, "The police will be all over you soon."

Robere only smiled. He inserted the passport in a small envelope. "Voilà!" he said. "A new man is born. You are now M'sieu Adams. And here is your Social Security card, a Gulf Oil credit card which you most definitely must not use, a voter's registration card, and a membership in a Seattle sailing club."

Allen smiled, "Where did you get all that?"

"I exchange! When I make new papers I take what the boys have and then, with a little magic, different people walk out of my place."

Allen took the passport, put the cards in his wallet, and handed him the Bolton papers. "These I will burn," said Robere. He looked up at the tense face watching him. "Something tells me you are in real trouble now. Is it so?"

"Yes."

"Can I do anything to help the friend of my son?"

"You can somehow avoid telling the police my new name until November twenty-second."

Robere said, "I do not understand the date. Why then?"

"I don't want to implicate you any more than necessary, Robere. The American FBI will be putting pressure on the Canadian police."

"If it is only until November twenty-second I can hold them off. I will give them a different name which will keep them busy chasing around for two weeks, and in the third week, my wife and I are scheduled for a trip to the home country. So you are safe until then."

Allen was thinking. He said, "If Mike Gorgio asks you what name you used to make false papers for me, tell him Joe Marconi, any address."

Robere wrote down the name, making sure he spelled it correctly. He said, "I owe my son's life to you. And nothing you could do would make me forget that."

Two hours later Mike Gorgio was ringing the Bon Soir doorbell. By then a man bearing the passport and ID cards of James Adams, 135 Oak Street, Seattle, Washington, was settling in his seat on the eight A.M. businessman's flight to New York.

In another pocket he carried the ID card and passport of T/Sgt Harold Daub. Let Williams trace that!

— 4 —

Billy Farran was a small scrawny little fellow in a blue shirt and jeans. He, McGrady, and Williams sat in a small conference room with a goose-neck lamp and a tape recorder on the table. The recorder was going as McGrady said, "OK. Here we go. Did you tell anyone that George Williams was going to check into room 2103?"

"I told you one hundred times no. I told nobody."

"Then why were you poking through the reservation slips? The desk clerks saw you!"

Farran said nothing, and McGrady dropped his voice to a confidential tone. "Listen, kid, if you cooperate you go free. Free. If you don't, we hold you as an accessory to murder."

"But I did nothing!"

"You gave some killer the information he needed, and because of that information Carson was killed."

Farran looked around wildly at Williams, then turned back to McGrady. "A lawyer, I want a lawyer. You got no right—"

"Oh for Christ's sake," said McGrady.

Williams spoke up for the first time. "Let me question Farran, if you please, Captain." He turned to Farran, "*I'm* a lawyer, Billy. And I tell you what I think. You don't need a lawyer."

"You're just trying to—"

157

"Because I know you're innocent, Billy. Someone's made a sucker of you."

"You can say that again," said Farran bitterly.

"Paydirt," said McGrady to Williams, but Williams was going on. "Somebody whom you trust asked you to do a favor for them, to find out where I was staying—"

"Now I didn't say that—"

Williams sat back patiently. "Let's start at the top, Billy, I'm here to prove you're innocent, so pay attention. A man named Carson was murdered, and you never even *heard* of him. Right?"

"Right."

"In fact, as far as you were concerned I was going to use the room."

Farran was beginning to perspire. He suspected a trick, but he couldn't figure out Williams' angle. He said, "But I had nothing against you, either—"

"I know, Billy," said Williams. "Now, when this young man who told you he was hiding from the FBI asked for that information you just logically thought it had something to do with the FBI, right?"

This time Farran thought for a few minutes before answering. "OK, right. I didn't trust that character, anyway. Son of a bitch. Hey, is that on tape?"

Williams smiled. "Nobody will hear it but us, Billy. We'll talk to the DA in the morning, and you'll be clear. Just answer some questions. What did he look like?"

"I'd say he was just under six feet tall, kind of slim and wiry. Gray eyes. A square."

"Crew-cut hair?"

"Not that bad. But short hair. Looked like a jock on TV commercials, if you know what I mean. All-American type, fair complexion."

McGrady said, "Any moles, scars, or birthmarks?"

"None that I could see."

"Who introduced him to you, Billy?"

This time there was a long, long pause. "Is that a problem?" asked Williams.

"Yes," said Farran, "because they didn't know about this, either. The murder thing threw them."

"Who are they, Billy? We can't find them if we don't know."

Farran said, "It isn't fair to them, I tell you. I talked to them today."

Williams' voice was suddenly sharp. "You talked to them at three o'clock this morning in Toronto, telephone number KI 8-3748, a man named Mike Gorgio. Right, Billy?"

Billy was looking white. Finally, he shrugged. "If you know his name and number you'll track him down anyway. But I swear Mike Gorgio didn't know about this. He almost fainted when I told him on the phone."

"But what's his connection with the murderer then?"

"How do I know?" said Farran. "We just got word from Mike to help this guy who's been working for the deserters for years. Listen, any of those kids I can help I will. I didn't believe in that fucking Vietnam war and you can put that on tape and—"

But Williams was holding his hand up. "OK, Billy. Just relax. We're almost through with you. How did Mike Gorgio get word to you and your friends?"

"About a month ago the word went up and down the coast. They had some kind of a deal going, but you can bet it wasn't murder. They aren't that stupid—they're in enough trouble already up there."

"What was the deal?"

"Some kind of robbery, I think. This guy told Gorgio he would rob an armored truck, and with the money the deserters could get out of Canada under false papers and set up somewhere else. Gorgio fell for it."

"Who are you—your group, I mean?" asked Williams.

"SDS. We help deserters. There's no secret about it."

Williams said, "So this murderer cons the deserters

and the SDS into helping him, and he double-crosses them and uses the SDS for his own ends. I get it Billy. Do you?"

"Hell, yes," said Farran. "We've been shafted! And look at the spot I'm in."

"Well, I'll go up to Toronto to speak to Gorgio, but if it will make you feel any better I won't take any action against him. I want his help."

For the first time Farran smiled. "Good. Don't get Mike in trouble because of me."

"OK, Billy," said Williams, "now what name did the murderer give you?"

"Jeff Bolton."

Williams just looked at Farran strangely until McGrady said, "What's the matter, George?"

"I'm thinking," said Williams. "Jeff Bolton. I just saw his death certificate. He was a Green Beret who was killed in Vietnam by Carl Richardson who knew Tom Medwick."

"What the hell is *that* all about?" said McGrady.

Williams said, "Material, Captain. Material." He turned to Farran. "Billy, thanks for your cooperation. I'll help you all the way. Captain, Jeff Bolton is a lead I've been following and every minute counts so if you'll continue the questioning—"

"Sure. Sure," said McGrady. "But you said you saw Bolton's death certificate. He obviously just took the name so what's so hot?"

"It's more than that, Captain. But I have to be going. Let me see the transcript when you finish." He stood up, shook hands with McGrady and said good-bye to Farran. Farran watched the door after it was closed. "Jesus," he said, "that name shook him up. And he doesn't shake too easy. Well, I don't blame him."

"Why not?"

"There's one thing more I didn't tell you about Jeff Bolton," Farran said.

"What?"

160

"You're never going to catch him."

McGrady said, "We'll have him in five—"

"The papers all say that man is crazy," said Farran. "He looked like he knew what he was doing to me."

— 5 —

The Library of Congress is one of the most beautiful buildings in Washington. A visitor climbs marble steps and enters a soaring lobby flanked by curving staircases with busts of statesmen; under great chandeliers hanging from the ceiling, purposeful scholars make their way into the largest collection of books in the world.

But the Library of Congress is not only a repository for literature. It also provides offices for lawyers, researchers, document scientists all engaged in a single endeavor: to assist Congress in the formulation of legislation. More than fifty attorneys devote their efforts to this task; every proposed statute must be researched, buttressed with references to past legislation on the same subject, court decisions, potential litigation.

And among these experts sat a tall, spinsterish gray-haired lady who was not an attorney, had no legal training, but was a legend in the field. Clara Abbott was her name. Grade 10 Administrative Assistant was her title. Instant memory had made her into legend. Only the hard-pressed lawyers in the library knew how many hours of research she had saved them by her spontaneous recall of the date of past statutes, past court opinions.

Today, as every day, the visitors poured into the library's lobby, craned their necks at the domed ceiling, then hushed as they walked through an arch into the main reading room, in the center of which clerks sat at the circular desk, surrounded by curved tables with green-shaded reading lights and scholars bent over books.

The second floor was Clara Abbott's domain. She was working at her desk outside her chief's office when the phone rang, and was truly delighted when she recognized the voice on the other end. "George, how nice to hear from you again."

George Williams was calling from New York. He said, "Do you remember the Senate hearings on a massacre in Vietnam? Carl Richardson——"

"Secret," said Clara, promptly.

"Weren't there House hearings, too, in addition to the Senate?"

"Yes. Both Senate and House secret. Senate's took place in October 1967, I recall. Chief witness, Sergeant Charles Greenwood."

"Fantastic, Clara. Incredible. You always surprise me."

Clara smiled. "Nobody surprises *you*. So stop buttering me up, you old flirt. The House hearing was in November of the same year, I believe, and a Sergeant Joe Martoni——"

"Marconi."

"See, I'm not perfect. Joe Marconi appeared there along with Greenwood. But George, I can't help you. Those hearings are in the classified room. Need-to-know basis."

"Clara, there's a connection between those hearings and the two murders last week, the ones associated with Jack Kennedy."

Clara picked up a pencil and began drawing precise doodles as Williams went on. "I must see those transcripts."

"Get them declassified," said Clara.

"That will take three months of correspondence and explanations."

Clara did not answer for a minute and then she said, "It's impossible to get you those hearings. I could lose my job. But I certainly couldn't be blamed if a stranger picked up a key from my desk and helped himself to a pass. There are thieves all over this building nowadays."

"And when would that thief be most likely to strike?"

"At lunch tomorrow."

After a few more words Clara smiled, hung up the phone, and looked up to face a desperate young lawyer. "Clara, on that right to inspection in the disarmament treaty—"

"Stassen in Geneva, June 1958," said Clara. "I think it was the second day of the conference. Those were the first Soviet references."

The young lawyer looked so relieved that Clara, for a wild moment, thought he might kiss her. All those flirtatious young men wanted to do that, it seemed. She must be aging beautifully.

— 6 —

A beefy doorman was helping an elegant woman out of a limousine under the canopy of the St. Regis when a hippie with long flowing locks and a scar on his right cheek passed by. The hippie was spaced out on drugs, and the woman glared at him with loathing. "New York," she muttered to the doorman.

"Yes, ma'am," said the doorman.

The hippie turned down Fifth Avenue and headed for a passport photo shop in the basement of Rockefeller Center.

An hour later, Allen Lowell, the hippie, was talking to a girl on the second floor of a seedy establishment on 48th Street just off Broadway. The place was littered with gorilla heads, eighteenth century gowns, rifles, telephones, stage props of all descriptions. "I'm auditioning this afternoon," he said, "and I got this scar."

The girl said, "How did you get that?"

"Mugging," said Allen.

She nodded. "This stuff will take care of it." She handed him a jar of salve. "Flesh colored. They'll never see it from the seats."

"Covers it completely?"

The girl paused. "Well, not completely. People aren't blind, you know. But it won't look so fresh and red."

Allen thanked her and went out. Fifteen minutes later, in his room, he affixed the new passport photos and then tried out the salve. No problem, he thought when he looked in the mirror.

He called up Eastern air lines and booked a seat on Flight 500 to Nassau, departing Kennedy at eight P.M.

FAA BULLETIN
ALL AIRPORT SECURITY PERSONNEL
Man suspected of murder bears following description:
Age: late twenties
Race: Caucasian
Height: six feet approximate
Build: slim
Appearance: Neat, brown hair, short, gray eyes, fair complexioned, no identifying marks or scars. Artist's reconstruction of face appended.
Action: Detain if suspected. Search baggage. Contact Mr. George Williams, Justice Department, telephone 202-737-8209.
Mr. Williams adds special note that suspect may be traveling in disguise. Check suspected wigs.

Captain McGrady was a man under pressure. Reporters were driving him crazy with their constant questions; newspaper editorials were having a field day with his department. Apparently no one felt the need to report his statements that FBI men had been guarding Carson; the New York police hadn't even been informed. By three P.M. the day after the murder McGrady had had all he could take. He tracked down Williams by phone at the Plaza.

"Christ, you've given me a headache. I don't know what to release. And every newspaper clown in New York is spitting on me."

"No Jeff Bolton," said Williams. "No SDS. No Mike Gorgio. You'll blow it if you do."

"But I have to give them something."

"Refer all questions to Fred Jarvis at the FBI. Tell them it's an FBI matter—"

"But it's murder in New York!" McGrady shouted.

Williams waited until he had cooled. "It is not murder in New York," he said quietly. "It is murder up and down the coast, and in the Bahamas if we don't move in time. Interstate. FBI jurisdiction."

But McGrady was really worked up. "I don't give a shit if it's interworld," he said. "I have to give them something."

"All right," Williams said carefully. "If you promise not to say a word about the SDS and Mike Gorgio, I'll give you some concrete evidence."

McGrady sounded wary. "What?"

"The tape Bolton used with his voice and the whistle."

"YOU GOT IT?"

"It's been analyzed today at the FBI field office here. But it's no use, as I suspected. The filter masked the voice print. But it will make a nice little display at a press conference."

McGrady could just see that conference, the TV cameras, and then the astonished reaction as he produced the tape itself, the fantastic murder weapon. He'd have the glass ampule fragments too. Beautiful! He said, "Williams, I love you. Tell an old-timer something. Where the fuck did you get the tape?"

"Wastebasket on Lexington and 49th a half hour after the murder."

McGrady almost groaned. Who would have thought he'd dump incriminating evidence right next to the hotel? Williams would have thought, that's who. McGrady had not even had those baskets checked. He mounted a small counterattack. "You shouldn't have kept that a secret," he said.

"Well," said Williams, "in a way it was personal. The tape was in a box with my name on it."

As he hung up Williams could imagine the heavy face of McGrady wreathed in puzzlement. A good man, so far. Other police officers in a similar bind would have thrown the Billy Farran interrogation at the reporters and made himself a hero.

But things were moving too fast to worry about McGrady. He had phoned Mike Gorgio in Toronto, and found he had only just missed their man. Gorgio told him that the boys in Toronto were so furious at Bolton for implicating them in these murders he had put a watch on the Bon Soir tailor shop, where false ID papers were made. They had expected that Bolton might need new papers now, and they were right. Only Bolton had slipped in by conning the guard, got new papers, and fled. Mike had got the shop owner to talk, however. After much threatening he'd revealed he had made out papers for Bolton in the name of Joe Marconi, and told him Bolton used that identification to fly out of the country.

Joe Marconi! Why would Bolton use Marconi's name? Williams said: "You're being lied to, Mike. What's the name of the man who makes the papers?"

"Hell," said Mike, "he's our lifeline up here. I told you the Bon Soir, so find out yourself."

"Why did you tell me the Bon Soir then?"

"Because in case there's real trouble I want to show you we're cooperating all we can. Oh hell, I'll tell you, you'll find out sooner or later anyway. Robere Houard. H-O-U-A-R-D."

"I'll have the police up there contact him," said Williams. "How long have you known Bolton?"

"Known him! I've never even seen him. But he's a hero up here."

"How so?"

"He's been working for the deserters in the States for years—ever since his kid brother died. But he stays down there, doesn't even come to headquarters to see us when he's in Toronto. Mysterious, that guy."

Williams said, "What kind of work does he do?"

"Well, Bolton is one master thief, man. He is the greatest. He always delivered. We ask him to rifle the files from the Pentagon, he gets the files. We want him to install a bug in a Senator's office, he mails us the tapes. Whatever."

"What do you do with the information he sends you?"

"Feed it to the columnists and the congressmen who are trying to get us out of this hole. Not that it's done us much good with Hitler in the White House."

— 8 —

The Eastern air lines terminal at Kennedy Airport was crowded at eight P.M., as two security guards, Jim Aylesworth and Joe Leland, watched the line queue up for Flight 500 to Nassau.

"Did you catch that memo?" said Aylesworth. "A joke."

"More and more insane," said Leland. "We look

for a clean-cut square, but beware, he might be disguised with a wig. That takes in every guy from eighteen to ninety-three."

Nevertheless, they were watching keenly. They knew the hi-jacker "profile" by heart. It would have been hopeless if their man was one of the countless Negroes, Cubans, Puerto Ricans, Arabs, who passed through every day; at least he was white American. But what the hell to look for? They couldn't haul every clean-cut young guy out of line. Nor could they grab every hippie and tug at his hair.

Then they saw their man. Twenty-eight. Slim. Gray eyes when they got up close. Short hair. And carrying a bowling bag. A bowling bag aboard a plane? They pulled him out.

"What's the matter, men?"

"Open the bag," they said. The man opened the bag and there was the bowling ball.

"Shit," said Leland.

The man started laughing. "There's a fuse in it," he said.

They could have booked him for making a joke like that, but they had more important things to do. They scanned the line and saw a young man dressed in a neat blue blazer, an expensive tie, and well-creased slacks. He had a Prince Valiant haircut and an old scar on his face.

Aylesworth said, "What do you think of that beauty?"

Leland said, "Description states no visible scars. That one he's had for years."

Allen Lowell passed through the checking gate and up the ramp to the plane. He was not without his worries. He only had $100 left after paying for the ticket, and he knew he would have to get some money in Nassau. But that could be accomplished. Resort hotels were beautiful when the matrons went to the beach.

"Wild Bill" Donovan's OSS was not much of a factor in World War II. Hastily organized, working on an ad-lib basis, and utilizing such divergent characters as a famous wrestler named "Jumping Joe" Savoldi and an aristocratic academic named Allen Dulles, it nevertheless scored some outstanding successes, particularly in Rome and in Switzerland, where Dulles was in contact with disaffected Nazis.

After World War II, OSS died and the various military intelligence agencies took over for a while until President Harry Truman, recognizing the chaos, created the Central Intelligence Agency, to J. Edgar Hoover's intense displeasure. Hoover was concerned that CIA would infringe on his internal security empire, and over the years his FBI operated uneasily with the CIA.

In fact, CIA had much the worst of it in its early years. It was housed in ancient wooden barracks along the Mall, "temporary" barracks built in World War I. But gradually CIA grew, fueled by secret and unaccountable funds, and by 1973 it was a giant, housed in a great complex of buildings in Langley, Virginia, employing thousands here and abroad. But until now, except for one lapse during the Watergate affair, CIA had not, to the public's knowledge, ever interfered in internal affairs.

Nevertheless, in November 1973 there was still an internal security chief and his name was Talha Bahktiari. And this was interesting because the sign on his door read "Accounting and Budgetary Scheduling"—while the man whose office door three floors above read "Internal Security" was actually a stooge, a genial ex-newspaperman with no duties beyond courteously declining to pursue letters of inquiry.

On this day in early November, fall leaves brushed Bahktiari's first-floor window as he sat at his desk, staring onto the windswept lawn. Then he swiveled his chair around to a thin man whose rimless glasses were perched on a bony nose and whose name was Peter Hodkins. Hodkins was the personnel expert in the agency.

Talha Bahktiari said, "This Bolton is getting more and more dangerous."

"Who did he kill now?" asked Hodkins. "I haven't seen the papers."

"Us," said Bahktiari, bitterly. "He's traveling under the name Joe Marconi. Tying us into the murders all the way."

Hodkins was unconcerned. "So who knows about Marconi?"

"George Williams will know, that's who."

"And who is this Williams?"

Bahktiari said, "A man who hates us. And I'm not talking about the agency. I'm talking about *us*."

Hodkins was lighting a pipe. When he finished he said, "So what are you going to do about it? You won't find Bolton. He's going to be in deep cover with two murder raps on his head."

"I want someone to go to Toronto, see a man named Robere Houard at the address I will give him, and find the real name Bolton is using now. We know the Marconi name is a fake."

"There'll be three dozen police ahead of him."

"They won't use the measures our man will to get the truth," said Bahktiari.

Hodkins put down his pipe in an ashtray and folded his hands across his stomach while he gave the proposition some thought. "Johnson would be best for this," he said, "but he's in Lebanon."

Bahktiari stood up, looking irritated. "Johnson! What's wrong with you? You know the man we need. For God's sake, he *knows* Bolton!"

"I can't stand the bastard," said Hodkins, the profanity falling almost reluctantly from his lips. "He almost got us into trouble in San Francisco last year. He's gun-happy."

But Bahktiari only said, "In this case, that may be a plus."

"I'm advising against it," said Hodkins.

"I want to see that man this morning."

Hodkins left, and a half an hour later Bahktiari's secretary buzzed him to announce the visitor Bahktiari was expecting. Bahktiari was surprised to realize he was excited, but it was no surprise to him that he was nervous—this killer always affected him this way.

The man who came in the door was dressed in a suede jacket, heavy wool pants, and boots. He was tall, muscular, with square shoulders and hamlike fists. He sat down in the chair across from Bahktiari and looked straight into his eyes as Bahktiari detailed his mission: Bolton must be found before Williams got to him.

"Why me?"

"Because you have an in. You knew Bolton."

"And what do I do if I find the kid before Williams does?"

Bahktiari told him, and a few minutes later the man rose, his bulk dominating the room, and moved out. And Talha Bahktiari knew he had turned loose the one man who was sure to do the job. George Williams couldn't match him because Williams wouldn't use this man's methods—break fingers, cut tongues, blind eyes—anything to get results.

Lieutenant Colonel Carl Richardson had done all of those things at one time or another.

But the paunchy little internal security director didn't know his man *that* well. Idiots, Carl Richardson was thinking. Pointy heads that didn't know how to operate, what to do in a jam. Bahktiari had ordered him on a wild goose chase. Stupid! The real answer to Bolton was obvious. It might take Richardson weeks to track Bolton down. Williams, with the entire Justice Department behind him, might beat them to it no matter what Richardson did. Why take the chance? Why not kill Williams first? What was one more Justice Department stiff?

Not for the first time Lieutenant Colonel Carl Richardson decided to disobey orders.

— 10 —

George Williams got back to his hotel at seven o'clock. He had spent a frustrating day operating out of the New York FBI Office on East 65th Street. Houard in Toronto stuck to his Marconi story, even under a threat of being charged as accessory to the murders. NCIC in Washington fed both Bolton's and Marconi's name through their computers and came up with no one in the right age bracket except for a Negro in Providence, Rhode Island, who had stolen a car. Williams told them not even to bother following that up.

The rest of the day was another series of frustrating calls with the Pentagon Chief of Personnel, trying to track down other members of Richardson's platoon in Vietnam. None of them was listed; all of them were under CIA cover.

The Justice Department in Washington was in touch with the Toronto police who were cooperating eagerly enough. Despite the friendly attitude of the Canadian government, they didn't like American deserters; they thought they could get the name from Houard soon enough.

But Williams was afraid that Houard would not help. Bolton must have known Houard would be traced. What puzzled Williams most of all was the use of Marconi's name. Why had he picked that?

Had he somehow found out that Williams was on to that CIA platoon in Vietnam?

Perhaps Williams would know more when he read Marconi's testimony before Congress which was in the Congressional Library in Washington. But what would that reveal? Probably nothing but outdated information about Vietnam.

And meanwhile Bolton was on the loose, death was in the offing, and he was getting nowhere.

There was a knock on his door. Williams opened it to find Stephanie Spaulding, in a black chiffon pants suit with a gold pin at her throat, and a little sable wrap. She looked stunning and Williams wanted to throttle her. "I told you to stay home. To keep out of danger."

She came into the room, a faint scent trailing behind her. "But I wanted to surprise you." She kissed him on the cheek.

"Well, you succeeded. Two days after I warn you how serious this is you're blithely walking around the streets of New York."

"George, please. Can't you even pretend you're glad to see me?" Stephanie shrugged off her wrap and lay down on the bed, just like that. The chiffon pants suit was clinging, transparent, expensive-looking. "It's so boring to be holed up in Pound Ridge, George. I can't stand it. I'd rather be killed . . . tortured . . . anything."

Williams pulled up a chair alongside the bed and regarded her with amusement. Try as he would, he could never get angry at Stephanie. And when she felt kittenish, as now, it was impossible to reason with her. Still, he tried.

"What happened to the FBI Security assigned to you?"

She said, "They were brilliant, George. They still think I'm up in Connecticut. Besides, I couldn't bear them. They all smelled of hair oil, for God's sake."

Williams said, "Well, then, hire private guards a bit

more to your taste. You can afford them."

Stephanie sat up smiling. "I'm a bit destitute nowadays, George. My late husband's estate is all tied up while his relatives snatch at me. I've been borrowing, but you know how much fun that is." She was looking at George steadily, her green eyes luminous. "I must say, you are getting more handsome every year. Why don't you age?"

Williams said, "Maybe it's because I don't have to take care of you every day."

Stephanie sighed resignedly. "Believe it or not, I'm not here for a bravo seduction scene, George, no matter how it may look. But I just had to talk to you. You must have a *clue* by now."

"I have a lead—but I'm not getting anywhere," he stalled. He was wondering how much to tell her. Finally he said, "We do have something. Both Medwick and Carson had a run-in with CIA."

"So what?" said Stephanie.

"So did you ever have dealings with them?"

Stephanie smiled. "Really, George, you can't expect me to tell you everything. I'd have to turn in my Little Orphan Annie decoder pin." When Williams said nothing she laughed. "You ought to know I'm not the trenchcoat type. And as for picking up messages under statues after all the pigeons have been there, that's too messy."

"Still, CIA may be involved," said Williams.

She looked at him. "George, have you ever thought of the simplest explanation?"

"Which is?"

"There are some people who are still angry that Kennedy was assassinated. Millions of them. They think the country has gone downhill ever since he died."

"So he picks six names out of a hat and kills them in revenge?"

Stephanie was lost in thought. "That's what I don't understand. Even if he's some kind of a deranged Kennedy fanatic, why in the world would he pick me, when I'm a Kennedy fanatic myself to this day? People even kid me about it. But I say, 'What's to kid? What have we had since? LBJ . . . Watergate Nixon?' Kennedy made you think the country was worth working for. LBJ and Nixon make you blush when you see the flag."

"Maybe you met the letter writer in those days. He would have been about eighteen then, I think."

"My age," said Stephanie. "That makes it even more difficult. I didn't date many eighteen-year-old boys. How old were you when I met you, George?"

"Twenty-three."

"You fell in love with me that first night, didn't you?"

Williams said nothing. "You don't have to answer," she said. "I fell in love with you too."

"You showed it in a funny way," said Williams.

— 11 —

In 1963 George Williams had been living in Georgetown with two other young lawyers in a colonial red brick house with white shutters and a lantern with a live gas flame beside the front door. George Washington had not slept here, but Williams' two roommates more than made up for that with a variety of attractive Vassar and Radcliffe types who were thronging Washington in the Kennedy era.

Williams was regarded by his roommates as something of a square because more often than not he took to bed with a law book—until the night he landed the wildest girl in the city! It began one evening when the door burst open and an adorable eighteen-year-old with jet black hair came flying in, saying she was being followed. Williams' roommate, Ev Collins, was the only man in the house who had met Stephanie Spaulding, and Ev decidedly was not the one to charge out into a dark Georgetown night and tilt lances with one of Stephanie's inflamed lovers. Williams offered to take his place.

A yellow moon rode high over Georgetown's neat red blocks of Revolutionary War homes . . . but it was silent outside, too silent. Williams said to Stephanie, "Where is he?"

"Behind his car," she said. "I just can't get rid of him."

"Why is he following you?" Williams asked as they went down the street, but all Stephanie would say was, "He likes me."

The man's car was parked across the street, and Williams went over to find a pale-faced stocky man in his thirties, smoking a cigarette. Williams said, "I'm afraid you're bothering this girl."

The man laughed, a short barking sound.

Stephanie said, "Now Bill, you've really got to stop trailing me wherever I go. It's spooky."

"Yes," he said, surprisingly calm, "it spooks me too."

"Well . . . stop!" said Stephanie.

"I can't," he said.

Stephanie then did a surprising thing. She kissed him hard. His arms went around her, and they clung to each other. They were still locked together as Williams excused himself and walked back to the house.

But a few minutes later he heard a knocking on the door and when he opened it Stephanie was there. "You saved me," she said.

Williams couldn't help noticing she had the most beautiful green eyes he had ever seen. She came inside and curled up in a red velvet chair, looking very much at home. Ev Collins, who was in the kitchen making himself a cup of coffee, said to Stephanie, "What was *that* all about?"

"This man . . . he's married and just because I went to bed with him once it's like a . . . liaison! He thinks he's in love, or something. Stands outside my house at night staring up at my window. I don't know how to get rid of him."

Williams said, "That was a funny way to discourage him."

"It was the only way," said Stephanie. "God, he was making me feel . . . goosey."

Williams and Collins both laughed and later that night, after an expensive dinner at the Jockey Club which Williams couldn't afford (seeing Bobby Kennedy, his boss, come in with that pantherlike tread and shy smile accompanied by Justice Byron "Whizzer" White made it seem more worthwhile), Stephanie came home to bed with him. Her parents were in Switzerland, she said, so if it was all right with him she would like to stay the night.

Stephanie undressed in his room and he saw she had exquisite breasts, perfectly rounded and firm, and then she slipped off her panties and he saw she had an exquisite derrière, make that more than exquisite—call it extraordinary, one of those derrières that jut out provocatively—and this was all Williams could think of before a sweet face and half-lidded green eyes became his world, and Stephanie was kissing him on the face, and then browsing lower and lower, lips on his chest, on his stomach, and then on that part of him which ached most of all, and then not stopping there at all but moving with little nips down his thighs, while her soft hands played across his body touching sensitive spots, and when he was really throbbing, when he was about to burst, she suddenly looked up at him and said, "All right. Do me now."

Instead he rolled the virginal-looking young girl on her back and "did" her in the old-fashioned manner, rode her to kingdom come, she crying and pummeling him on the shoulders with small clenched fists, and both of them coming together, and she was saying, "Don't leave me! Don't leave me!" as he drifted off in serenity and calm, his lips in her dark hair.

He awoke to find her sitting on the side of the bed

smoking, her hand drifting along his thighs. "That was so wonderful!" she said. "I haven't done that in years."

"You haven't *slept* with anybody?" said Williams.

"Not in that normal way," said Stephanie. "You are really Mr. Straight, aren't you? You make me almost . . . embarrassed."

Williams reached his hand around her body, and cupped one of her breasts. "It's nice of you to take time off to teach me things, Stephanie."

Stephanie laughed and leaned down and kissed him. "You are kind of fun," she said. "I never met anyone like you before."

But the next morning he asked if he could see her again and she said no, because she just wasn't the Sunday School type.

— 12 —

"What did you mean by that?" Williams now asked.

Stephanie laughed. "I was afraid of you," she said. "You made me embarrassed, I guess, and I tried to hurt you. I only wound up hurting myself—as usual."

Williams smiled, and then said, "Stephanie, there's a killer who may be outside at this moment. Carson was killed practically under my eyes. So if you want a romantic chat about romantic yesterdays, wait until we find him and put him away."

"But you don't understand," said Stephanie. "That's just the point I'm trying to make. I remember those days as the most exhilarating of my life. You do too. Admit it."

"So?"

"And maybe the killer does too. It ties in there, George, believe me. Forget CIA. Who knows from CIA? I'll bet the others on that list had nothing to do with spying, either."

Every word she was saying was nudging at

Williams, for it could be the truth. He could be off on a dismally wrong tangent, wasting time and energy tracking down Green Berets and CIA agents. So Bolton had been in a Green Beret platoon. So he was using the name Joe Marconi, another man in the platoon. But his threat was addressed to six Kennedy people who had nothing to do with Vietnam.

— 13 —

The Navy man did not seem very military to Everett Mellon. He wore rimless glasses, and looked like a Professor of Romance Languages. But his uniform stripes counted to three; he was a commander all right.

"We'll need all the boats we can get for Tektite," he said, "Power stuff, mainly. Run our people back and forth between St. Thomas and St. John."

"I have only a few," said Everett. "Chris-crafts for small fishing parties; chair in the stern."

"Too small," said the commander. "We're thinking more of a motor yacht type, fifty feet, to use as a ferry and then to put our men aboard during the operation. We'll need it a minimum of three weeks."

Mellon and the commander were sitting on the patio of Mellon's home overlooking the beach at Nassau, the commander dressed in blinding whites, Mellon in Bermuda shorts. Mellon said, "Tell me something, Commander. You're in the Navy, right?"

"Yes."

"Why don't you use your own boats?"

With all the intrigue of the last few days, Mellon suspected everyone, including a commander who wants to charter a boat for the Navy. But he knew this particular commander personally, had known him since the previous Tektite project three years ago. The commander was smiling. "I don't blame you for asking. I feel silly myself. But the fact is, this is

not a Navy operation. It's Interior. We're just assisting—and with some reluctance."

"Why?"

"The Navy feels the Interior Department has no
business on these beneath-the-sea experiments. We're
doing our own work on the Sea Lab programs. And
now Interior comes busting in—and even wants our
help."

Mellon was beginning to understand.

"We feel that by chartering a boat we are lending
that assistance, but not gracing the enterprise with a
Navy vessel. So—"

"I have just the boat you want," said Mellon. "You
can have it for a thousand a week."

"No problem."

Mellon paused. "There might be one problem. If
you charter the boat from me I'll insist that I be the
captain."

The commander sat back, watching Mellon. Mellon knew what was going on in his mind. "I know
you're aware of the trouble I've been in," he said.
"But believe me, this is the solution. A killer who
wants to get at me in an isolated lagoon on St. John
surrounded by military and government guards is
going to have himself a problem. Right?"

"But still—"

"Please get back to your superiors and let me
know, Commander."

The commander picked up his gleaming white hat
with the salty gold braid and placed it on his head at
a slight angle. Mellon smiled, "Pretty snappy, Commander."

The commander was anxious to clear this up and
get back to Washington to his family. He said, "Con-
sider it a deal. But we can take no responsibility for
your safety." He paused. "We can, however, arrange
for four sailors to man your boat, and make certain
they're *tough* sailors. Might not even be sailors, if
you know what I mean."

Mellon knew what he meant. One problem solved.

A Bahamas government official had warned him that the flood of arrivals during the tourist season was a danger they could not cope with. Too many strangers on a tiny island—and the government could not jeopardize the vital tourist trade by screening every visitor.

Mellon had been to the island of St. John on the last Tektite operation, where aquanauts lived in a shelter beneath the sea for thirty days. No tourists in that lagoon. Only scientists and military people, everyone checked, everyone known. It would be an ideal hideout.

After the commander left, Mellon padded into the kitchen, and made himself a gin and tonic. Then he heard someone at the front door. One of his two Bahamian guards was trying to block off a teenage brunette in an orange bikini. "She won't go away, Mistah Mellon," said the guard. "Claims she's related to you."

Mellon looked into her blue eyes and thought if this is the killer I'll go quietly. "It's my niece," he said. "You can let her in."

A few minutes later the girl in the bikini was drinking a Coke on the patio with him and giggling, "You thought I'm the killer?"

"In disguise," said Mellon. "You're really a thirty-five year-old-man with a gun in your bra."

"Oh wow!" said the girl. She laughed again. "You're as cute as they told me. All the kids on the beach dared me to come up here . . . beard the lion in his den, so to speak."

"You're all sadists," said Mellon, not entirely in jest. "You want to be there when the old bullet comes through the throat and I'm choking—"

"See. That's what they all said. 'You *joke* about it.'"

"So what else is there to do? Somebody wants to kill me who doesn't know me and has nothing against me. So it must be a case of mistaken identity. I hope."

The girl was taking off her bikini. She had an extraordinary figure, absolutely perfect breasts, tiny waist, and bulging rear; he found the white lines of untanned skin at her breasts and hips erotic. The tan set off her only other article of adornment—a silver bracelet from which dangled a Kennedy half-dollar.

"How old are you?"

"Seventeen."

"And your mother and father are looking for you around the hotel right now?"

"Could be," said the girl, suddenly serious. "But come on. I haven't got all day."

Mellon stood up, feeling old and confused, but determined on one point. The girl was leaving. He had enough trouble. "I don't think we'll do any nude bathing today, Miss—what's your name?"

"Kathy."

"I think you're going home right now. *In* the bathing suit, not out."

"Oh wow," said the girl. "You're really old, aren't you?" She had come over to Mellon, and stood in front of him, looking into his face with a crazy sparkle in her eyes. She suddenly reached out, pulled his zipper down, and then a cool hand was touching a very warm subject. "I have to," she was saying, "they dared me."

It would be all over the beach tomorrow. Mellon pushed the girl's hand away, not without reluctance. Then he picked up the bikini, dropped to his knees, and grabbed her foot to put it back in her bikini, but this seventeen-year-old got an entirely different impression. She thrust her hips into his face and said, "Oh yes," and the Bahamian guards who were watching from behind the hedge with drawn guns started to laugh. "This man gon' to die happy!" one of them said.

Mellon got to his feet, blushing, and somehow the bikini did not seem so important any longer, and he and Kathy ended up in the bedroom all right, and before he could calculate how many years he could get for raping a minor the girl was giving him experiments major, and even at one point suddenly crouching on her knees and elbows and pleading with him to "kiss me back there," but Mellon did not oblige to the great regret of the merry Bahamian guards now taking turns at the window.

And later that evening, the teenage brunette reported to her cute new boy friend Jim Adams that she had succeeded, and to prove it, pulled out of her bag Mellon's underwear. Adams said he had never known a girl like her; the girls in Seattle were really square.

Later, after he had shown how much he appreciated her in bed, the girl mentioned something else. Mellon was going to St. John tomorrow. Something about an underwater project.

— 14 —

Late in New York now and Stephanie Spaulding was saying to Williams, "Enough already. Give up till tomorrow."

Williams put down the phone and regarded her. She was going to be a problem. "I haven't got *time* for you, Stephanie."

"But there's nothing you can do between now and tomorrow morning. It's after ten."

"And I suppose you have no place to sleep so you'll have to sleep here."

But Stephanie was already slipping her wrap around her shoulders. "Not until you've taken me to dinner," she said.

With Stephanie it had to be the 21. Williams did not turn her down for two reasons. One, he liked the 21's food when he could afford it. And two, they may as well go to a publicized place if he was to explain to Sarah later. And that would take some explaining, he thought. Sarah had a long memory.

Tall Chuck Anderson greeted them at the door of the 21, and winked at Williams. "You're in good company tonight, George," he said. "How are you, Mrs. Winthrop?"

Bob Kreindler came over to speak to Stephanie, and Chuck lowered his voice. "You don't want to be interrupted, I suppose."

Williams said, "There won't be any trouble here."

"You got a break on that case yet?"

"No."

"I've put some lines out myself. Mr. Carson was one of our regulars here. And a great guy. But it's strange. Strange. Nobody knows *anything!*"

"You've hit on our problem," said Williams. "But keep working."

Williams joined Stephanie in the big bar and they were seated, noticing the hubbub in the room stilling, and all eyes on them. And Williams did not like it, wondered if he was blown for all time as an investigator, was now a "name," a man whose picture had been on the front pages of all newspapers and now would be splashed beside society's Stephanie Spaulding and what would old Connors at Justice think of that! And a little while later as he was eating his dinner he glanced at his watch and saw it was midnight. November 8th. Two weeks to go.

An hour after that they were in a taxi heading for the Regency, where Stephanie had booked a room. Stephanie was in a marvelous mood. "That was great fun," she said. "My goodness, we're celebrities."

"I hope your next appearance in the newspapers won't be on the obituary pages," said Williams, not a tactful thing to say, but he was tired, tense, and concerned about his decision that Stephanie sleep at the Regency and not his hotel.

"Why can't I stay on another floor at the Plaza, for heaven's sake? Sarah can't be that suspicious."

"There are enough problems in this case without us

getting involved in any way," said Williams. They pulled up in front of the Regency. Williams went in first. "No one but no one for any reason goes to her room," he told the desk clerk.

"You don't have to worry about that," said the man. "We're aware of the danger."

But of course Williams should have known, should have been more careful, should never have let Stephanie sleep alone. For at 62nd and Park a car was waiting at the curb in the dark and the man at the wheel was Carl Richardson.

— 15 —

Darkness in Stephanie Spaulding's room. A sliver of moonlight across the foot of her bed. Stephanie was having a delicious dream; she and George Williams were young again and they were running across the grass of the Mall in Washington, and George slipped and when she went over to help him up he looked up at her and smiled that strange half-smile of his and said, "I love you," and the telephone rang, shattering the stillness, shattering her dream, and she could not wake up, did not want to, and she sat up suddenly, more frightened than she had ever been in her life. Still the phone rang. She picked it up.

A voice said, "I'm the man who sent you the letter. Meet me out front and I'll explain. And don't call the police!"

The phone dropped from her nervous hands. She picked it up and dialed the Plaza immediately. "George," she almost screamed. "He called. The killer!"

"Where was he calling from?"

"He said to meet him out front."

"Don't move and don't panic. We'll have fifteen FBI men there in a minute. Keep away from the door!"

* * *

In his room, Williams telephoned the Regency immediately and the clerk said he'd send security men right up to the room. "See who's out front," said Williams, although he knew it was a waste of time. Another stunt by that ingenious killer—but he had to make sure. He called the FBI and they dispatched three men immediately. Then he called Captain McGrady, woke him up at home, and McGrady put the Police Department in action.

Williams then thought for a minute, sitting up in bed. What was going on now? The last call like that the telephone had been booby-trapped. But to try the same call twice? And to know that Stephanie would call Williams; to even hint she should call the police?

Williams dressed fast, packing a snub-nosed .32. He had a feeling he would use it in the next hour. This time he was determined the killer would not get away.

He took the elevator to the deserted lobby, only a clerk at the desk, and slipped out the side door to 59th Street instead of the front, a move that took Carl Richardson, in his car at the corner, by surprise. Richardson was forced to make a U turn, which was stupid, and by the time he roared toward Williams the man had a gun out and a cab driver was reversing his motor to get out of there. Richardson placed his right arm across his left, steadied his Luger and fired, but instead of answering the shots Williams hailed the frightened cabbie and that was it. Richardson had a tail.

Race across Manhattan at two in the morning and twenty police cars would be alerted. Richardson wanted none of that. He screeched his car to a halt along Central Park, jumped out, and vaulted over the wall into the darkness of the park. But Williams kept right with him; Richardson cursed because he had underestimated his man, had thought surely that he would not pursue an armed man in the park, had not thought to stop and hit Williams when he was clearing the wall, a perfect target.

Richardson ran through the night. Far off he heard sirens coming closer. Oh, he had screwed up but good. This was the end. He could hear the man crashing along after him and he saw a boulder and dove for it and came up with the gun as steady as the rock, waiting. Williams did not appear. He was some son of a bitch.

Sirens in Manhattan . . . toward the Regency where Stephanie was now surrounded by guards pouring in from all directions . . . toward the Plaza, where the gunfire had been reported and a terrified cabbie was loudly telling about the man who had leaped out of his cab while it was still going and jumped over the wall into Central Park.

But Central Park is large, it is dark, and Richardson suddenly realized something: he had the advantage for the next few minutes. This was his kind of terrain.

Silence from the area where he had last heard Williams. The intelligent thing for the man to do was to withdraw to safety and wait for the police to come in from all directions and surround Richardson. But Williams would not do that. He was not the type. And, besides, he thought he had the killer in front of him.

Holy Jesus Christ! Richardson just realized something else. They would think *he* was the killer. Hadn't he made the call? Hadn't he fired at Williams? Suddenly he was desperate. He had minutes to live, minutes to make his escape. Soundlessly, he crouched and ran along the flank of the boulder out of Williams' sight. A minute later, gun pointing forward, he crept beyond the protection of the boulder and threw himself flat. No shots. A small rock was in front of him. He threw it thirty yards to the right. No shots. He got up and ran toward a tree and flattened against it. "Williams," he called. "Over here."

No shots.

He looked around wildly but the darkness covered everything. Williams could be anywhere. Then he saw him . . . behind a bush thirty feet away right in front of him. He aimed the Luger and fired once, twice. Nothing happened; the man didn't fall. And then he was running forward and hitting the ground, and a bullet varoomed over his head and that bastard had fooled him leaving his coat on a bush and he whirled and saw Williams for real this time and Williams fired and caught him in the shoulder, his gun falling away, and Williams was there beside him, picking him up and saying, "LET'S GO!"

And he found himself stumbling beside Williams, holding his shoulder, and Williams helping him over the wall and a police car right there and Williams telling the sergeant that Richardson was one of his men and the killer was still loose in the park.

— 16 —

Richardson was tough. In Williams' room in the Plaza a sleepy-eyed doctor came and dressed the wound. The bullet had penetrated muscle, not bone. Richardson never flinched as the doctor probed and stitched. Meanwhile Williams was on the phone to McGrady and later the FBI, who were reporting no success in finding the killer. He told them that the man who had been shot was a Justice Department assistant of his, and he was being treated right now.

Now, at three in the morning, the two of them sat across the room from each other, Williams with a gun in his lap. Richardson, he knew, was more dangerous with an arm in a sling than a platoon of normal killers.

Williams said, "You goofed *that* up."

The only answer was a grunt.

"Are you a man named Jeff Bolton?" asked Williams. "The man who sent me the note."

"Hell, no."

"Then why did you try to kill me?"

Richardson said, "I have to make a call."

"You don't want to make that call, do you? If your boys connect you with this stunt you're in trouble. I have a feeling you did it on your own."

"Why?"

"No cover. No lookout. No help. Why do *you* want to kill me, Carl Richardson?"

Now Richardson regarded him even more closely. "OK, so you know. So what?"

"So you were killed in a helicopter crash in Vietnam five years ago. Mighty strange to find you up and about."

"Shit," said Richardson. "Stop the kid stuff. You know that crash was just a cover."

Williams sat with the gun in his lap, talking quietly, but very, very watchful. "You made a real smart move tonight, Richardson. I don't think your bosses will be too pleased to find out. So I'll make a deal with you—"

"No deals." The voice was flat, angry.

"I can turn you over to the police, and make an announcement to the press that I've been attacked— and that's the end of your career. You're blown, for good."

"Or?"

"Or you can tell me everything you know about Bolton, and go free."

Now Richardson was looking really astonished. "Is that all?"

"We've had two murders on a list of six. I have to find Jeff Bolton before he kills again."

Richardson obviously was thinking fast. Williams knew he had to get out of this trap, if only to get another shot at him. "But you can't let me go," said Richardson. "I tried to kill you tonight. I could try again."

"I'll take that chance," said Williams.

"If I tell you everything I know to help you find

Bolton, you'll be dumb enough to let me walk out of this room."

"Right."

Richardson leaned his head back, and thought a while. Then he said, "OK, I'll tell you about Bolton. What made him join the Green Berets I'll never know."

— 17 —

February 11, 1964. Allen Lowell walked down the corridor to the office of his boss in USIA, Jim Carson. Carson, holding up a strip of 16 mm film to the light, put it down when he saw Allen.

"What's the trouble, Allen?"

"I want to thank you for the chance you gave me to work here. I really enjoyed the film editing bit."

"You're leaving?"

"Well, I'm draftable—but I don't want to wait. I'm joining the Green Berets."

Carson whistled. Then he said, "Now hold on, kid. That's rough stuff. If you're going to be drafted I can get you into the Army Pictorial Center in New York as a film editor, and you can enjoy the big city, and fight yourself a war."

"I want to fight a war my way."

Carson looked at the thin eighteen-year-old. "No offense, Allen, but you don't look like a Beret type to me."

"I'll take exercises. I'm still growing."

Carson gave up. "Whatever you think is best, but I don't understand. Why the Berets?"

"You have it on film," said Allen. "President Kennedy said to the Berets, 'Wear this as a mark of honor.'"

"I don't want to be harsh," said Carson, "but Kennedy is dead—and you may be joining him at Arlington if you go that Beret route."

"I wouldn't mind if it was for America."

Carson waited for the boy to smile. But no smile came. After a minute, Carson said awkwardly, "Well . . . uh . . . I admire that type of thinking, kid. I'm getting out myself now that Kennedy is gone."

"What are you going to do?"

"Try my luck in Hollywood. It's not *quite* the same as your decision, I know," he added quickly.

But all Allen said was, "I'll be leaving Friday. You'll fix up my pay and all those things?"

"No problem." He shook hands with the boy. "Good luck, Allen, and watch yourself over there. If I have any luck in Hollywood, call me when you get out of the service and I'll see if I can help you get back into the movie business."

Four years later Allen wrote Carson a letter saying he was in Hollywood, sick, and needed a job. Of course, Carson didn't answer.

— 18 —

EXCERPT FROM TRANSCRIPT OF TAPED CONVERSATION BETWEEN CARL RICHARDSON AND GEORGE WILLIAMS, MADE WITHOUT RESPONDENT'S CONSENT:

RICHARDSON: Right off, I have to tell you I didn't know his real name. None of us had real names on file. I got Carl Richardson as a tag when I entered the company.

WILLIAMS: Jeff Bolton was in CIA?

RICHARDSON: Not quite.

WILLIAMS: I don't follow. Either he was in or not.

RICHARDSON: Marconi, Greenwood, and me were a unit in 'Nam. We went wherever they needed us for whatever purpose, interrogation, intelligence, rough all the way. Nothing easy. As far as I'm concerned Marconi and the rest were heroes. And all the company men over there, hundreds of us, got all the absolutely dirty jobs. And then one of our men got hit—and we were in a hurry on a behind-the-lines job and I asked one of the infantry commanders if I could borrow a man from one of his platoons, just to fill in for a while.

WILLIAMS: What was his name?

RICHARDSON: Marconi went over to some grunt platoon and picked the first "warm body," I guess. Hell, I never did see the kid's real name. Didn't matter. We set him up with papers as Jeff Bolton.

WILLIAMS: Hold it. Hold it. The name of Bolton's previous commander. He'll remember Bolton's real name.

RICHARDSON: Dead. But really. Stepped on a pellet mine and tore his balls off. But I know what you're driving at. The unit. Now what the hell unit was it? (Pause on tape) The brigade that was near Chu Lai on September 12, 1967. Shit, that won't work.

WILLIAMS: It will if the brigade has a record of detachment of one soldier.

RICHARDSON: CIA would have destroyed Bolton's record.

WILLIAMS: We'll check anyway. Go on.

RICHARDSON: So the commander sent this Beret over to us, thin and wiry type, didn't look too much. But he was a hell of a soldier.

WILLIAMS: How so?

RICHARDSON: Smart. He made up in brains what he lacked in size. And guts. One time we were planting mines on a road that led to a VC chief's hut. The hut was empty but we knew he'd be back some day with some of his friends—Anyway, all of a sudden there's machine gun fire from three sides in front of us. We're caught. And Bolton takes a mine he was going to plant and does a funny thing. He sails it high in the air up the road toward the Charlies and it lands right in front of them. But it doesn't explode.

And that was the trick, Bolton's trick. He defused it first.

WILLIAMS: Why?

RICHARDSON: First off, the fucking Charlies are fascinated with that flying mine. They stop shooting and jump for cover, but that isn't all. When it lands they stare at it for five minutes expecting it to blow up and while they do we hightail it out of there. If it had just exploded some of them would have been hurt but the rest would have kept coming. Some kid, that Bolton. He hated me, though.

WILLIAMS: Why was that?

RICHARDSON: The kid was a real screwball, an . . . idealist, I guess you'd call it. Now all of us in the unit except him were . . . conservative.

WILLIAMS: Olympians?

(Silence on the tape)

WILLIAMS: I already know. So keep talking.

RICHARDSON: I don't know anything about Olympians. All I know is we were what you'd call hard liners, and Bolton was thinking he was doing some sort of good for humanity or some such shit fighting in 'Nam—and he didn't like what he saw or had to take part in once he joined us. I'll admit the rest of the men didn't like him. We kind of ganged up on him—made him do all the dirty work.

WILLIAMS: Such as.

RICHARDSON: Torture.

WILLIAMS: You made him torture people, the one man who didn't want to?

RICAHRDSON: It's a part of war. He joined the Berets on his own. Nobody asked him.

WILLIAMS: But you got him assigned to your CIA unit and then he saw there was a whole kind of another war going on.

RICHARDSON: That's it.

WILLIAMS: Did he make any protest?

RICHARDSON: Did he? Ran away three times. But you

couldn't get away from the 'company' in 'Nam.
No way. And when he hears he can get life in
Leavenworth for desertion he calms down and
stays with us.

WILLIAMS: Poor kid.

RICHARDSON: Hey, Williams. This is the guy trying to
kill you, remember?

WILLIAMS: Tell me how the Bolton business wound
up. How did he leave your unit, if he wasn't
really shot? Where did he go? What new cover
name did he use?

RICHARDSON: Well, it all started in the rain outside
Lon Sin with that prick Hu Ling. A double. We
had him nailed to the wall.

— 19 —

Rain tore at green mango leaves, rustled the underbrush and turned the ground into sloshing mud. Allen
Lowell lay in his tent outside Chu Lai and looked
over at Greenwood, that ass-kissing mental idiot, now
snoring peacefully, one arm flung back, and he
thought how simple it would be to slip a knife deep
into his heart or slit his throat—when the flap of the
tent opened and Marconi crept in, dripping wet,
saying, "What a fucking night. Hu Ling gone, and we
spend five hours chasing shadows."

"Where you been?" asked Allen.

"The honky wanted to see me. Says we're flying to
Lon Sin tomorrow."

"What's up there?"

Marconi stripped his wet fatigues, ending up in
long johns, and climbed into his sleeping bag. "He
says that's where Hu Ling will have to head. Nearest
village."

Allan lay on his back, looking up at the canvas
sagging from the weight of the rain. "You don't be-
long in this crowd, Joe."

Marconi rolled over his side. "That's a laugh coming from you."

"Let's you and I make a break for it tomorrow."

Marconi didn't answer for a minute, then he smiled. "Shit, man, Richardson says you're crazy and I'm beginning to believe he's right. You tried that act three times—but where you going to go in 'Nam? There's no way to fly. So relax, kid. I keep telling you. Sooner or later your number comes up and you're back in the States, all this little . . . untidyness forgotten."

Allen smiled. "Untidyness, yeah."

Marconi said, "So let's go to sleep, eh?"

Allen said, "You're forgetting one thing. We're not in the Berets any more. No regular leaves, rest period, return to the States after eighteen months. We're on special detail."

"War is hell," said Marconi, and went to sleep. Allen stared out the tent flap until dawn and then dozed. When he awakened, Richardson had a chopper ready for them and after breakfast they were off to kill again.

The chopper pilot pointed a finger down below. "The action's started," he said. They all looked out the right windows and saw firing on the ground. The grunts had some mortars in action and puffs of smoke among the trees indicated where they were hitting. "Hell," said Marconi from behind Allen, "they're too fucking far. They're nowhere near Lon Sin."

Richardson made his way back from behind the pilot's seat. He was dressed in full Beret regalia, ammo belt, grenades. He said to Marconi, "Scared?"

"Hell, no, sir."

"You want two more years over here without going home?"

"No, sir."

"Then be a good little boy and shut the fuck up."

But even Greenwood, even Greenwood the ass-kisser, remarked to Lowell, "I think he's flipping out. This

Hu Ling character has made him lose his brains."

In the village, consisting of huts flung helter-skelter with dirt paths between them, they could see movement below. Women and children walking, an ox pulling a cart, growing larger as the chopper started to settle outside the farthest hut, great clouds of dirt swirling up from the ground as the chopper's blades beat the earth into a fury. Then, Richardson first, they jumped down from the chopper, ran a few steps and fell flat and fired, setting up a covering fire, and no shots answered. A woman with a straw hat on her head ran into her hut. Richardson signaled and they ran forward, flung themselves down, and fired again. This time a wizened old man who had stepped around a hut to watch was hit and went down.

They lay there two full minutes before Richardson said over his shoulder, "I think it's clear."

Keeping to a crouch, they ran toward the village, passing huts with cowering people, and entered the village square. Richardson told them to start rounding up the civilians.

To the south, coming closer, they could hear the sound of gunfire and the crump of shells as they assembled a hapless group of women, babies, old men. Then when the firing was even closer, Richardson suddenly said to Greenwood, "Hold them here. We're going back." Allen saw Greenwood turn pale, afraid he was going to be left behind, but they rushed to the south of the village and took their position in the silent woods, the gunfire still hundreds of yards off, and suddenly twenty or more men in pajamas emerged from the brush with their backs to Richardson, their guns pointed at the forest, and Richardson stood up, training his machine gun on them, and shouted, "Drop your weapons."

The Charlies whirled, and not one of them fired. Lowell saw the agent Hu Ling immediately, a man so frightened his eyes were bulging.

The Charlies dropped their guns, and marched ahead of the Americans to the town square, and Allen and the others stood there, their weapons trained on the unarmed men, wondering what Richardson was going to do now. Regulations required them to turn them over to the GI's when they came through and get themselves a medal. But Allen knew Richardson. Richardson wasn't anxious to have any witnesses to what was about to happen next.

And then Allen's eyes were caught by a little baby in a woman's arms. His little hand was in the air and he was waving. Allen looked into the beseeching faces in front of him, the young VC Charlies, the old men, and the women with babies, and saw before him a tableau he would never forget, a side of war so ugly he wanted to cry. And just then Richardson was saying to him, "I'll shoot Ling and you waste the others," and out of the holster Richardson pulled the Luger he was so proud of and shot Ling first in the balls and then, when he bent over in agony, through the top of the head. "Shoot! Shoot!" Richardson was shouting at him, but Allen could not pull the trigger, was frozen, and told Richardson, "Get somebody else! I can't!" and Richardson said, "You shoot and be quick about it," before the regular troops could arrive and he said again, "Shoot or I make certain you stay in this unit forever." So Allen started firing, hitting people in the face and body and everyone was screaming and diving for the ground, which brought the American troops running into the village and one of them, a black, watched for a second with disgust and contempt in his eyes, and Richardson, furious, certain the incident would be reported and cause all kinds of fuck-ups, took them back to the chopper on the double.

And later, the chopper rising, Allen went for Richardson, throttled him and flung his head back against the cowling, choking him. Richardson turned purple and could not budge the steellike claws at his throat, and it took Marconi and Greenwood to finally pull Allen off, holding him on the floor of the chopper, kneeling on him, while he struggled to get free and cursed himself for not killing Richardson and then started to cry in frustration and hysteria.

The next day Richardson came in, smiling, to see him in the hospital. "You got your wish, boy. You're going home."

Allen looked at him without expression. "It will take three days to get all the papers through," said Richardson, cheerfully. "But it's an honorable discharge."

"I don't want to go home. I want to stay here and kill you," said Allen.

"I wouldn't recommend that," said Richardson. "Fact is, I'd recommend you keep your mouth very closed when you get back. You're in trouble."

"Why?"

"Jeff Bolton committed a massacre yesterday in full view of the troops. Now I have a plan to get that quashed. You're going to be killed—by me."

Allen just looked at him. Richardson said, "That's the cover story, in case someone kicks up a fuss. So just go on home like a good boy, take your old name back, and forget all of this ever happened."

But Allen did not go back so soon. That first night after Richardson left, he tried to commit suicide, swallowing a bottle of sleeping pills prescribed for the sergeant in the next bed, but they pumped out his stomach and saved him. The next day a psychiatrist with a blond mustache and bouffant hair started a series of sessions with him that lasted ten days.

After one of those sessions the psychiatrist was having a cup of coffee with a colleague. "How's the kid?" asked his colleague.

"Combat fatigue, stress, hatred of his commander, the usual."

"Nothing special."

"Just the delusions. He says he's been out on intelligence missions with the Berets, and tortured and massacred people. Normal compensation for a soldier of his type."

"What unit was he in?"

"A film editor with the Fifth Division. Never got near combat. It's all in the files."

The psychiatrist with the blond mustache looked up from his coffee and watched a nurse in green fatigues pass by. "Christ, I wish she'd give me a break," he said. But his colleague was still interested in the case. "If he has those delusions, maybe you should keep him over here until he's adjusted."

"We need every bed," said the psychiatrist. "So I'm sending him home. A few days with the family in the old home town and he'll be OK."

"Sure," said the other psychiatrist. "And if he isn't?"

— 20 —

"How did you know about the psychiatrist's conversation?" Williams now asked Richardson.

"Blond mustache was our man."

"So you turned an idealistic kid into a mental case."

"Have it your own way," said Richardson. He looked, sounded, quite at ease now. "I say he did what he had to do for his country. And if it was ugly, if he suffered in the process—hell, he wasn't the only one."

"Well, I'm still trying to get a line on him—where he came from, who his friends were. He must have given you some hints in all the time he was with you."

"Nothing to me. He hated me from Day One. Hated Greenwood too. The only one he got along with at all was Marconi—and that's because Marconi had a little Bolton in him too. I mean, he wasn't too happy with some of the stuff we did, either. But he never tried to desert, I'll say that for him."

199

"OK, this may be news to you. Bolton was in Toronto yesterday and got false papers in the name of Marconi."

"I heard," Richardson said angrily. "That son of a bitch. He's doing just what you want, dragging us into it to throw you off. Listen, Williams, here's news for you. We're looking for that freaked-out kid as hard as you."

"Why?" asked Williams.

"We don't tell *you* anything, Williams."

Williams leaned over and said sharply, "Don't play cute with me, Richardson, or this tape will be in CIA's hands tomorrow and you can start looking for a new career."

"A tape? You shit! You made a deal."

"The deal's on," said Williams. "But you're holding back information."

Richardson no longer seemed so confident. He was sweating. "You've got this whole thing on *tape?* And you want *me* to keep talking?"

"Or die," said Williams. He raised the gun and pointed it squarely at Richardson's eyes. And the odd thing was he meant it, he was not kidding. He would gladly have killed this sadist.

Richardson said, "Turn off the tape."

Williams reached below his chair and pressed a switch.

"Now, you lying son of a bitch, is it part of our deal that that tape is off?"

"Yes," said Williams.

"OK, let me give you some lessons. Number one, these murders of Bolton's have nothing to do with us. It's Kennedy. Bolton was a regular Kennedy nut when he joined us in 'Nam. Jesus, he even carried a picture of himself and Kennedy——"

"A picture of *him* with the President?"

"Yeah, but don't get excited. It was one time the kid managed to squeeze into a big reception at the White House, and he's so knocked over by the big man he jumps out and speaks to him—and somebody takes a picture."

"What did he say about Kennedy?" asked Williams.

"Oh, the usual left-wing crap. How Kennedy had ideals the young people understood. How he made them want to work for their country—and even to fight for it. Big goddamn inspiration bit. Jeez, I got tired of hearing it. I told him to stuff Kennedy up his ass one time."

"That's telling him," said Williams.

Richardson looked at him. "Man, I forgot I have another missionary in front of me."

"Did he tell you how he ended up in Washington working for the administration?"

"Did he? Ten times I heard about his aunt and how she had a stroke when he took off for Washington to work for those left wingers. The aunt knew what was what. But Bolton listens to the inaugural speech and has himself an orgasm, and gets all fired up and it's goodbye aunt and hello Washington, God Save the King."

"OK," said Williams. "Why are you looking for Bolton?"

"Because of *you,*" said Richardson. "You're dragging CIA into a mess we're not even involved in. And you hate us, man! We know that."

He leaned closer to Williams. "Let me tell you something, Williams. You're on the wrong track. Forget the Olympians! Hell, if Bolton wanted revenge or something for what happened to him in 'Nam, he'd be after *me,* not six Kennedy freaks."

"But he thinks you're dead—you were killed in Vietnam."

Richardson said nothing, and Williams looked at him sharply. "You mean he *knows* you're not dead. Have you seen him? *When?*"

"I don't know what he knows," said Richardson, after a pause, "but what I do know is he's going after six strangers on Kennedy's anniversary—and you're blaming CIA! He's not interested in CIA, Williams. *He wants you!*"

"OK," said Williams. "That's it."

Richardson said, "That is not it. I want the tape."

Williams was standing up. "Get lost, Richardson. My deal was that you would go free, and I'm keeping that deal. But think about that tape next time you feel like taking a shot at me. After you're blown, CIA will have you at a desk job in Uganda the next day."

Richardson walked angrily out of the room.

Williams started getting ready for bed. He knew now that he was definitely dealing with a sick boy in Jeff Bolton; those sadists in the Green Berets had seen to that. And it was a sick boy who carried with him a picture of himself and Kennedy. So he *was* a Kennedy fanatic; it tied in with the death threat itself on Kennedy's anniversary.

But where was the connection? Richardson had made a point. Williams was following up CIA leads—and the threat concerned six Kennedy people, not the Olympian goons. Why?

What a case! What a puzzle! Williams could not seem to get a handle on anything. He felt absolutely frustrated, absolutely helpless.

Tomorrow he would fly to Washington and go through the Marconi testimony, but with little hope. What could Marconi say that Richardson hadn't already told him? Nothing.

Wearily, Williams took a shower, slipped into his pajamas, and instead of going to bed sat down in an armchair and opened his briefcase once again. He knew he couldn't sleep anyway. So why waste time trying?

Files on all the victims were in the case. He took them out and laid them on the table beside him. What else? A copy of the death threat, a copy of the Medwick "suicide" note, a box with a copy of the

tape of Bolton's filtered voice. The NCIC check on
the Bolton name which had revealed nothing.

Williams read that computer print-out again. The
last paragraph read:

> SUSPECT JEFFREY BOLTON 1340
> MARLTON AVENUE, BALTIMORE,
> MARYLAND, HAS LEFT THAT AD-
> DRESS LEAVING NO FORWARDING
> ADDRESS. COMPUTER SEARCH
> BEING INSTITUTED THROUGH SO-
> CIAL SECURITY, INTERNAL RE-
> VENUE, AND DEFENSE DEPART-
> MENT IDENTIFYING NUMBERS.
> —0130799482

Williams studied that last number. These computer
types were in a gray world all of their own, with
numbers replacing blood, numbers replacing flesh,
numbers replacing everything.

It was two o'clock by his watch. Nevertheless he
placed a phone call to the FBI National Crime Information Center in Washington.

— 21 —

Late night in Washington. A few cabs nosed down
Pennsylvania Avenue, and there was still action in
Chanin's all-night coffee shop. Otherwise the street
across from the Justice Department building was
deserted.

But windows were lighted on high floors of the
FBI side of the building. And in one vast neon-
lighted area filled with bulky print-out and punch-
card machines, and bordered with tall gray cabinets
in which rolls of tapes revolved or rested, a young
man in shirtsleeves on night watch picked up the

ringing phone. What the hell was it now, he thought? Some police sergeant in Little Neck, Omaha, wanting a fingerprint check?

The young man's name was Fairfield. He said, "Who? Mr. Williams? What's this about—oh." He snapped awake. "Sorry, Mr. Williams, what can I do to help you?"

A girl in a white smock drifted through the room and went past his desk. Fairfield was listening to Williams explain about the NCIC print-out on Bolton. "Yes, sir," said Fairfield, "that was all we had on Bolton. I remember when they searched. A Negro in Providence was the only Bolton on file."

Williams said, "What does the number 0130799482 refer to?"

"Well, that's simple," Fairfield said quickly. "0130 is the code prefix which means no other information available."

"And the other numbers?"

"799 means a computer trace on all possible misspellings of the name has been conducted, and nothing was found."

"482?"

"False information."

"What?" Williams asked.

"False information, sir. Someone supplied information which was invalid."

"Jesus Christ!" said Williams.

Fairfield's face was burning, because he couldn't understand why Williams was angry. "What's the problem, sir?"

"FIND ME THAT GODDAMN FALSE INFORMATION!" said Williams so angrily the receiver crackled. "You computer types should be put in a cage in space—" but Fairfield was saying, "Yes, sir. Yes, sir. I'll try, sir," and took down Williams' number in New York just before he hung up.

His rubber-soled shoes made no noise as he walked over to the computer-typewriter on the 501 set. But his heart was making a regular commotion. Why did it have to be him on night watch when Williams called? It wasn't fair. And what had he done? He had given Williams the information he wanted.

He sat in front of the typewriter and punched in the following numbers: 0130799482.

Then he consulted a black looseleaf folder next to the typewriter and typed in: 717598/475.

Then he sat there and the computer-typewriter sprang to life. FALSE INFORMATION AUTOMATICALLY ERASED ON THIRTIETH DAY FROM RECEIPT.

The girl in the white smock was beside him. "Want some coffee, Bill?"

He turned to her, "Hell, yes. I got a hairy bastard all over me—" He looked around at the typewriter to see what it was clacking out now: DATE DATE DATE.

Fairfield typed in the current date, and the typewriter almost immediately started jumping:

FALSE INFORMATION TO BE CANCELLED:

TWX NCIC WASHINGTON TO SYRACUSE OFFICE FBI: SUBJECT JEFFREY BOLTON ADDRESS 1340 MARLTON AVENUE BALTIMORE MARYLAND SUSPECTED OF EXPROPRIATING TWO STICKS OF EXPLOSIVE FROM US STEEL PLANT IN LARGO FALLS NY CHECK REQUESTED ON NAME

TWX SYRACUSE OFFICE FBI TO NCIC WASHINGTON: AGE IN TWENTIES SIX FOOT SLIM GRAY EYES NO DISTINGUISHING MARKS OBSERVED WEARS HAIR FAIRLY SHORT DESCRIBED AS QUOTE ALL AMERICAN TYPE UNQUOTE THAT IS, NO HIPPIE

But by that time Fairfield was saying, "Oh Christ! Oh Christ!" The assassin was coming to life in the clicking typewriter, and Fairfield looked up at the girl in the white smock who was staring as transfixed as he was at the print-out, and said, "Williams will have our *ass!*"

Excerpt from Allen Lowell's diary . . . entry dated
November 9, 1973:

I should hate Richardson and Marconi, but I don't.
They are stupid robots in an organization that con-
trols them. It would be a waste of mental energy to
hate two such hollow-heads.

Tektite III was the most ambitious oceanographic
project since the ill-fated Sea Lab III mission.

To this day no one has ever explained what went
wrong during Sea Lab III, a daring experiment conducted in 1968 in which Navy aquanauts would live
and work out of a habitat three hundred feet beneath
the sea in rugged ocean off San Clemente island, California. One of the Navy commanders in charge on
the mother ship later testified at a congressional hearing that he believed it was sabotage.

At one point, he testified, he had happened to pass
by a pressure chamber aboard ship in which
the aquanauts were undergoing training and found that
the oxygen valve had been closed. Within minutes all
five men inside would have been dead. Who turned
the valve off?

Later in the training period, preparing for a re-
hearsal run, the rescue chamber with the aquanauts
inside was hoisted fifty feet above deck, when suddenly the chamber broke loose from its moorings and
plummeted toward the deck. Five feet above that
deck, a steel prong broke the velocity of the fall, al-

though not sufficiently to save the chamber from being destroyed and the aquanauts injured.

And then, on the first day of the experiment, with VIPs aboard the mother ship and television crews and correspondents covering the momentous event, tragedy struck. Three aquanauts had been lowered in the so-called rescue chamber to the floor of the sea, three hundred feet below in the icy depths of the Pacific, where the water was so cold you shivered even inside electrically insulated rubber suits. The chamber descended smoothly to the ocean bottom and the three men had begun swimming to the habitat fifty feet away. But suddenly the two men behind saw the leader clutch at his throat. Frantically they grabbed him, hauled him to the rescue chamber and signaled for him to be pulled up, but the leader was already dead. Investigation showed that the carbon dioxide scrubber had been removed from his diving equipment. Who had removed it?

Strange. And now in this more modest experiment, Tektite III, where aquanauts would live only fifty feet below the surface of a clear lagoon, security men were still nervous. And the presence of Everett Mellon was the last straw.

John Ludlow pulled alongside Mellon's boat in an LCT and jumped onto the gangway. Mellon, in white slacks and sports shirt, leaned over the side and watched Ludlow come up the ladder. "We're scrubbing your charter, Mr. Mellon," said Ludlow.

Around them on this beautiful blue lagoon were ships of all types, even an old LST converted to cargo hauling. The Navy had chartered a whole platoon of small power boats which darted back and forth between the LST and Mellon's boat to the encampment in the forest a few yards back from the beach.

To their left on the other side of St. John was the well-known area owned by the Rockefellers, a tourist attraction. But this end was closed off by barbed wire and guards, and it was strictly Navy right now. No one got through without a pass.

Mellon did not answer Ludlow's remark, but led him into the saloon of the ship, outfitted in leather and steel chairs with a bar on the port side, and a large galley through a door at the rear. "What's the uproar, Mr. Ludlow?" he said at last.

Ludlow was Navy Intelligence, in plainclothes, which on St. John consisted of green shorts and jumper and old sneakers. "I put in a request to the Navy Department," said Ludlow. "I told them we had enough trouble without worrying about a civilian murder case."

"So?"

"So we'll fly you off by chopper, and book you on an inter-island flight to Nassau."

Mellon was behind the bar. "Want a Coke?"

"Thanks. I'm glad you're taking it right. For myself I'd be glad to have you. And we appreciate the boat."

Mellon poured two tall glasses, watching the Coke bubble and froth, then brought them over to Ludlow who was sitting rather erectly on one of the leather chairs. "Relax, Mr. Ludlow," he said with a smile. "I don't think the killer is on board."

"Who knows?" said Ludlow. "Anybody who can kill through a telephone isn't human!"

"You have a point. But then wouldn't I be safer in this lagoon with marines and Navy Intelligence men all over the place than in my home in Nassau? If I die, Mr. Ludlow, the death will be on your head."

Ludlow was studying him. "No offense, Mr. Mellon. But are you *joking* about this? I don't see what's funny to be on that list myself. I've got eight years training in intelligence and self-defense and karate and pistol marksmanship—and I'd still be jumping every time a door opened in the dark."

Mellon sipped his Coke. "Everyone wants me to fall over in shock because of this thing. You say I'm joking. On the contrary, I'm taking it perfectly seriously. I could be on the beach at Nassau with pretty girls, and here I am watching an oceanographic project in a deserted lagoon. It doesn't beat sex, Mr. Ludlow."

Ludlow almost bit his lip. He knew of course about Mellon's escapade with the teenage girl. The guards' report had been treasured reading throughout Intelligence circles on Nassau. But he said nothing. Mellon said, "I will admit I compromised a bit," he said. "I did bring some . . . company. Come out here, Kathy."

And the teenage brunette he had first seen in the orange bikini emerged from the galley. Ludlow was on his feet, angry. "She doesn't have a pass. You stowed her away!"

"Do you blame me?" asked Mellon, indicating the girl who, although now in a purple hot-pants outfit, still seemed to be bursting every stitch. "But don't draw wrong conclusions, Mr. Ludlow. It's entirely innocent."

Ludlow said nothing. Mellon went on. "In fact, I have her parents aboard with me. They're ashore right now."

"Which ones would they be?" said Ludlow. He was trying to keep his eyes off that girl. The Intelligence report. The details! And this middle-aged moron had done that with her! Mellon was saying, "Her father turned out to be Jackson Simmons, one of the Navy oceanographers. He and his wife both have passes, as he is a participant, and he was glad to stay on my boat."

"Well," Ludlow said, "all of them can stay, all right. But not you."

"You mean you haven't heard—"

"Heard what?"

"The Admiral of Oceanography sent word to me today. Here's the cable."

Ludlow, confused, read the cable:

URGENT YOU REMAIN WITH SHIP UNTIL COMPLE-

TION OF OCEANOGRAPHIC EXPERIMENT IN THREE
WEEKS. ACTING AT JUSTICE DEPARTMENT RE-
QUEST.

Ludlow tried to apologize. "Somebody always
doesn't get the word. I'm sorry, Mr. Mellon."

"That's all right. To tell you the truth the cable
came as a shock to me too. I expect George Williams
at the Justice Department put the word in."

Ludlow was all business. "In that case, we take
rigid security precautions. I'll have two boats, starboard and port, lying off your ship on a twenty-four-
hour watch. No one gets aboard. At night we flood-
light the sides. I'll put five armed marines aboard and
if you want to go ashore, or to another ship, you take
two of them with you. All right?"

"Listen, I'll cooperate all the way. I'm aware of the
danger."

But Ludlow, walking down the gangway, and step-
ping into the LCT, was not so sure. There was something about Mellon's attitude. He was not frightened
enough by far.

Ludlow was no Justice Department brain but he
thought he would be quizzing Mellon pretty good if
he were in charge of this case.

— 24 —

George Williams had called Fred Jarvis from New
York the night before with the news of the missing
NCIC information, and this morning he flew into
Washington and arrived at Jarvis' office just before
noon. Jarvis said he had contacted the US Steel plant
in Largo Falls and gotten all the information. Bolton
was a free-lance film editor working for a motion picture company right next door in Baltimore. The name
of the company was Leonard Coleman Productions.

Williams tried to absorb this information. A free-lance film editor? That's what Bolton was?

Jarvis went on, "The reason the information was cancelled was that the security chief at the plant was trying to save the job of the boy who let Bolton steal the explosives. He admitted he put out a fake report that the explosives had been found."

But Williams was not listening. He said to Jarvis, "We have a killer in his late twenties who was once at a Kennedy reception and was photographed. Question: How did he get to a reception? Pretty big stuff for a young fellow.

"We have a killer who was a Green Beret and was taken over by the Olympians and trained in murder and electronics and all the dirty tricks he needs.

"And now we have a killer who is a free-lance film editor. Apparently, a real one who's actually had film jobs before with Coleman, according to what you tell me."

He stopped, and Jarvis said, "A Kennedy follower, a Green Beret sadist, and a film editor. Are we talking about one man?"

"I hope so," said Williams. He picked up the phone on Jarvis's desk and asked his secretary to place a call to Coleman Productions in Baltimore, even though Jarvis was saying, "We called him. He's away until tomorrow." When the phone was answered, Williams told Mr. Coleman's secretary that he would be in tomorrow at noon for an appointment, and to make sure Mr. Coleman realized the urgency.

"What shall I tell him it's about?" the secretary asked.

"Jeff Bolton."

"Oh *him!* He was nice."

"Nice?"

"I liked him. I felt sorry for him."

Williams asked why. She said, "He was always so . . . nervous. And yet he was a good boy too. Mr. Coleman will tell you."

Williams thanked her and hung up. Coleman

would not be back until tomorrow. He said to Jarvis, "I'm going over to the Library of Congress."

Jarvis was staring at him. "The Library of Congress!"

"I'm going to read what Marconi had to say at those hearings. He knew Bolton."

Jarvis was upset. "Jesus Christ, George. You have a hot lead right now in Baltimore, and you're going to start digging back ten years into the past."

"That's the way I work," said Williams.

The way he said it made Jarvis drop the subject. Instead he said, "Well, we got one victim taken care of, anyway."

"Who?"

"Mellon. He's in St. John in the middle of a whole bloody flotilla surrounded by an army of marine guards."

"St. John!" Williams said angrily. "That's the worst place he could be. Who knows from the uniforms?"

Jarvis looked worried. "Connors pushed it through. He thought it was a good idea."

"Can we get him out?"

"Maybe. But Mellon wants to stay. He feels safer there."

Williams said, "Well, then, put in a radiotelephone hook-up to that boat, and have the guard report in every hour on the hour to you. Anything at all unusual . . . report. Understand?"

"Will do, George. Sorry."

Williams stood up and Jarvis said, "George . . . I'm worried about you. You're getting edgy as hell."

"I can't break this case," said Williams. "The deeper I get into it, the farther away he flies. I almost feel as if I'm being *lured* into false trails."

"You could use a vacation, George—"

"It's not on his schedule," said Williams.

— 25 —

George Williams arrived in Clara Abbott's office in the Library of Congress at twelve thirty P.M. and found a key and a book of passes on her desk. Also a note which said "James Patton." A secretary across the room looked up. "Can I help you?"

"I had an appointment with Miss Abbott."

"She's gone to lunch," the girl said. "Be back at two probably."

"Thank you. Tell her that Mr. Williams called and will be back."

Outside he took marble steps into the lobby, and in the main reading room he filled out his pass.

The elevator brought him to the basement. He showed his pass to a guard at the door. The pass was signed "James Patton." The guard let him through, and clanged a door after him.

He was in among a century's congressional hearings. Shelves rose to the ceiling crammed with big bound books. He found the date he was looking for: the House Military Affairs Committee Hearings, October 10, 1967.

He skimmed rapidly, because he knew all the facts now. What he was looking for was any mention of Bolton. What he found made his hands tremble, and his heart begin to pound. If it were only true! If only Marconi hadn't been lying.

— 26 —

Excerpt from House of Representatives Military Affairs Committee hearing October 10, 1967:

Present. The Honorable Congressmen Kasswell, Burton, Flagler, Rogers.

FLAGER: You were there when Bolton was buried?

MARCONI: Well, sure, we grew up together.

FLAGER: You grew up together and you ended up in the same platoon. That's unusual in the Army that I remember.

MARCONI: Well, what happened, sir, was Major Richardson told me to pick up any old grunt for our operation, and I found my buddy Bolton in one of the grunt outfits so I picked him.

FLAGER: What did Richardson have to say to that?

MARCONI: We never told him, sir. In fact, till now, I never told anybody.

FLAGER: Why not?

MARCONI: Well, Richardson wouldn't have liked it. In this kind of an operation you couldn't take any chances. The officers didn't want any buddy-buddy types under them.

FLAGER: Are you saying you were on some kind of . . . classified operation?

MARCONI: Yes, sir. Although you already know what it was about. We were picking up a double agent that had escaped.

FLAGER: All right, now about Bolton. Counsel, do you have the Bolton file?

COUNSEL: Yes, sir.

FLAGER: All right, where did you and Bolton grow up together? Chicago? That's what he gives as his address.

MARCONI: No, sir. Steubenville, Ohio. He went to Chicago after his mother and father were killed in a traffic accident. He went with his stepbrother, Tommy Schovajsa . . .

Tommy Schovajsa! It had to be the same one! Williams closed his eyes. He couldn't go on reading. Jeff Bolton was Tommy Schovajsa's stepbrother? If it were true, he knew at least why one man was on the death list. Himself, George Williams.

March 1969, Williams' boss, Harley Connors, had called him into his office.

"Look, I know you're up to your throat over there in civil rights but we have a problem here and you can help us."

"I've got too much to do in my own office——"

But Connors was waving his big beefy hand at him. "We got twenty thousand deserters up there in Canada. OK. And we've been waiting for the Army to do something about it——it's their baby. OK. But they're doing nothing."

"So?"

"So we have to stop it, for Christ's sake. We have to at least make an attempt."

"So make an attempt." Williams was sure he could get out of any Connors nonsense by speaking to his own boss. Connors said, "So we made an attempt. We got the FBI off their ass in St. Paul and in two minutes they had bagged the civilian who was routing all of the deserters through, getting them over the border, for a price of course."

"I heard about that. Good work."

"Good work, your ass," said Connors, not known for his delicacy of speech. "Those crewcut friends of ours across the way acted with their usual expert efficiency. The two of them escaped."

"Two?"

"The guy had a helper. The main man was Fred Caldwell. A draft dodger named Tom Schovajsa was helping him. Schovajsa was just a kid, nineteen, jumped his draft board out of Chicago and got tied up with this deserters net."

Williams looked at him with amusement. "Sherlock Holmes is dead, Bill. What am I supposed to do——go

to St. Paul and study a footprint in the snow and
track them down?"

Connors said, "You just wrote your job description."

Tommy Schovajsa was frightened. All night he and
Caldwell had slept in a barn, although Tommy hadn't
slept at all, just lay there. What had he gotten into?
Maybe he shouldn't have listened to Allen

God, he was worried about Allen. The brother he
adored in high school had come back a sick man,
wary, suspicious, introverted. His aunt had put up with
him for three days, then told him he would have to
leave the house. Tommy had joined his brother in a
crummy rooming house on Chicago's south side.

"What happened in Vietnam?" Tommy asked Allen again and again. But Allen would say nothing,
only repeat to his brother: "I made a mistake going
in. And you're not going to make the same mistake."

Then Tommy's draft number came up, and Allen
took the letter and the envelope and tore it up right
in front of Tommy's eyes! He said, "You're never
going into that sick war!"

Tommy was worried, but Allen told him to sit
tight, and a few days later he had some news. He told
Tommy to meet him in a bar. "I've been doing some
work down here through SDS for the deserters up in
Toronto, that's how strong I feel about 'Nam," he
said when they were seated at a table. "I wrote to the
head of the group up there, somebody named Mike
Gorgio, and he had an idea."

"What was it—shoot LBJ?"

"Gorgio says he's heard about my work for the
SDS and anybody so hot against the war is his kind
of man. He wants to use me some more. So he says if
I'll help him and his boys on some special deals, he'll
take double care of you."

"And what does that mean?" asked Tommy.

"Well, you won't even have to leave the country,

go to Sweden or Canada or anywhere. Gorgio has an operation in Minnesota with a man named Fred Caldwell. Caldwell runs the deserter network over the border."

Tommy was worried. "Allen, that only gets me in deeper. I'll be helping other people break the law."

"But you'll be safe," said Allen. "Because you'll be loose. Those kids in Toronto are living from day to day, wondering when the Canadian government is going to change its mind and ship them all home to face the music. And everyone up there is under surveillance . . . the FBI knows every name. With Caldwell you'll be the invisible man, able to swing either north or south if anything happens, and even able to get home on the sly."

After a while two girls from a nearby table came over and joined them and they talked but nothing happened and that night they were lying in their beds in the rooming house and Allen said, "You're out of style, Tommy."

"What do you mean?"

"I came home, four years in the Berets there in Vietnam, and what did I find . . . the people my age laugh at me. They say the Berets are sadistic goons fighting a stupid war against some peasants. Three years I was fighting for an ideal. I thought. And all those three years my own friends and classmates and buddies back home were thinking I was some kind of idiot. And they were right."

Two days later they were up to see Fred Caldwell, a shifty-eyed young man about twenty-five.

"Take care of Tommy," Allen said. "He's my only brother. Anything happens to him I'll kill you no matter where you go and hide."

"Nothing like a friendly introduction, I always say," said Caldwell. "All I'll tell you is he's as safe as I am—and I've never had any trouble yet. You a friend of Mike Gorgio?"

"I've never met him—but we've done some business by mail and through the grapevine."

"One hot ticket, that Gorgio," said Fred. "He came up there a year ago and really took over. For once, things are organized."

"He's got me doing about ten things," said Allen, "and I think it's great. I only wish I'd had enough sense to go up to Canada instead of 'Nam."

But later that night, in a beer parlor in St. Paul, Tommy said to Allen, "I don't want to be a draft dodger. I want to join the Army. I want to serve my time."

But Allen was grabbing his shoulders, white-faced. "Don't ever let me hear you say that again. Ever!"

And then he subsided a bit. "This isn't World War II, buddy, this is a whole new sickness."

The next day Allen went back to Chicago to look for work, and a day after that Tommy met a pretty girl named Peggy Barton. Peggy was an activist on the University of Minnesota campus, and into grass and sex. Tommy had never met a girl like her, but Peggy liked him right away. And when she heard he was into the deserters' network, she couldn't believe it. "You?" she said.

"Me," Tommy answered. "What's so strange?"

"You don't look the type. If I didn't know different, I'd bet you would *want* to join up yourself, let alone help others dodge the draft."

Tommy smiled. "You'd be right," he said. "But my brother just got back from the Berets, and it turned him into a sick man."

Peggy, a petite auburn-haired girl who wore a GI field jacket with the word "Killers" ostentatiously scrawled across its back, had a strange reaction. She said, "But he shouldn't control your life. If that's your bag, join the Army."

"I'm afraid it would make Allen sicker," said Tommy, simply.

"You in love with him or something?"

"He's a great guy. He's been more than a brother all my life. Sure, we love each other. Why not?"

Peggy was smiling. "I've never met an old-fashioned boy," she said. "You're cute."

She introduced Tommy to grass and to uninhibited sex, and then to love, and one night riding bikes along a cold Minnesota road she said, "I want you to go home, Tommy."

Tommy said, "Why?"

"I love you and I'm afraid for you," she said. "You could go to jail! And it's ridiculous when you really want to serve."

And that night an FBI informer telephoned the St. Paul FBI field office and Fred Caldwell and Tommy Schovajsa were picked up and held without bail. What was odd was the informer called from long-distance.

Allen heard about the arrest in Chicago and was in a bind. He had no money, had been unable to hold onto any kind of a job ever since getting back. He was moody, unable to concentrate, constantly making errors, and even the most patriotic employers, wanting to help an ex-Green Beret, had given up on him.

And now he was in panic. His brother was in jail—because of him! And he didn't have a damn cent, didn't have one friend with influence, had no way to stop his young brother from being sent to prison for years for something he didn't want to do.

An hour later he was on the road, hitchhiking to St. Paul, and a truck driver driving the type of trailer that had killed his mother and father picked him up and took him all the way to Des Moines where he stopped on a deserted lot on the outskirts of the city and made a pass at Allen, and Allen took him out with a chop beneath the ear.

And still later it was snowing on lonely roads

across Minnesota and there wasn't much traffic, and what there was was slowed by the snow, and Allen was freezing alongside the road, eyelids covered with frost, and finally a car pulled up with four women and the ex-Green Beret found himself in the back seat with two sweet-looking nuns in black habits who were very nice, very Irish, who took him all the way to St. Paul, ten miles out of their way, and offered to pray for him.

He was in a snowbound city, and somewhere in this city his brother was in jail. In St. Paul, federal prisoners are kept in a building behind the federal court. Allen went to the jail and asked about visiting hours and was told that a hearing was set for tomorrow. Allen identified himself as Tommy's brother, and asked whether Tommy had a lawyer. "The judge will appoint one," said the man behind the desk. "Don't worry about that. His rights will be fully protected."

And in fact they were being protected more fully than the man behind the desk realized because that night fifty students from Minnesota U. raided the building, and in the melee someone stole the cell keys and freed Tommy and Fred Caldwell, and the next day three of the student leaders of the riot were held for aiding a jailbreak, but their fathers got them out within hours, although they were expelled from school.

The man who got the keys and opened the cells during the melee was Allen Lowell. The students had no idea the prisoners were going to be actually released, which was one of the reasons the three student leaders were given suspended sentences.

Two days later George Williams arrived in St. Paul and checked in at the FBI office. The inspector, John Moley, was a thirty-five year old collegiate-looking type with the approved conservative suit and dark tie but an air that suggested he would be more comfortable in a blazer and loafers. He was also, Williams soon noted, totally incompetent.

"Did the police cooperate?" Williams asked.

"They threw up roadblocks, and put men in the train station and at the airport with descriptions. But—"

"How long can they keep the roadblocks?" said Williams.

"That's the problem. It's snowing and freezing out there, and the normal traffic keeps piling up, and the police chief only had the blockage on for twelve hours."

"Well, hell," said Williams. "They're gone. They aren't going to sit around St. Paul and wait for you to bag them again."

"So what do we do?"

Williams looked at him. "We find where they're gone. And that's easy."

"It is? How do we do it?"

"We call in the informants."

That afternoon they came in, one by one, scared college kids who were earning extra bread informing on their classmates—and justifying it by telling themselves they were really *for* the war, anyway. Williams interviewed them all, and when the last one had left he went into John Moley's office and sat down heavily on a green sofa beneath the inevitable portrait of J. Edgar. He had a sheaf of notes in his hand and shuffled through them for a moment before saying, "Well, it's unanimous. Everyone says they went to Toronto. To get out of US jurisdiction."

"So we call the border people."

"So we know they went the other way," said Williams. "We're gambling that they're intelligent. Toronto is too obvious."

Moley was watching him, fascinated. Williams said, "You can't check every car between here and Chicago, right?"

"Right. It's just not a big enough deal to put roadblocks all the way down. The police chiefs couldn't care less about two deserters up in Minnesota."

"But the State Police could look for a specific car—a car driven by three young men."

Moley was excited. "That's right! Somebody helped them, one guy—according to the informers. So all three would probably go together."

"So you telephone the State Police and tell them to stop every car with three young men in it. Do it on the Toronto roads too, if you want."

Moley was looking at him. "Christ, you make it all seem so simple. What am I earning my pay for?"

But Williams was saying something that brought him up short. "Personally, I hope you don't find them."

Moley didn't know how to handle this statement from a top Justice Department official so he kept his mouth shut.

Rolling along a two-lane asphalt road between snow-locked forests and then plains, they were exposed as could be. No traffic to hide them. Nothing. Allen was worried. He drove as fast as he dared, eyes glued to the rear-view mirror.

Fred said, "Take it easy, Allen, before you kill us all. They have to think we went to Toronto. Half their informers are my people, and I know they spread the word."

Tommy said nothing, huddled in the back seat, still looking confused. Now he spoke up, "I was going to tell the judge at the hearing that I want to serve in the Army, and maybe he'd give me a break."

"Sure," said Caldwell, "and what about the thirty boys we got over the border in the last month?"

"But nobody knows his name," said Allen. "You're known—but Tommy isn't."

"Thanks a lot."

"I got you out, didn't I? You could still be rotting in that cell."

That night they found a path leading to a deserted hunting cabin, and broke in and made a huge roaring fire and toasted some frankfurters they had bought at a general store in one of the small towns they had passed through.

The next day they stopped at a drugstore and Caldwell called one of his people in St. Paul, and was told that a top-flight Justice Department type named George Williams had come up to handle the investigation.

That seemed to worry Allen, for he said, "We can't stay on the road now," and he turned the car around and headed back for the cabin. "We can hole out there. They can't investigate every tumbledown shack in three states." And he almost got there, too, when, passing a billboard, they saw too late a state trooper on a motorcycle and like lightning he went to the radio on his bike and Allen knew they were lost, lost, and he turned off at the first dirt road and drove as far as he could go and then abandoned the car.

They were all three in the snowy woods when they heard the dogs. The fucking trooper must have called in his friends and picked up the car tracks in the snow. How could he miss?

And then they got a break. The trooper was a hero. He was coming up the road right after them, not waiting for the others, for the dogs. The roar of his motor filled the forest and then the big bike was skidding in the snow as it approached their car, and Allen was on the trooper like a cat, arm around his throat, grabbing his revolver, and then clubbing him over the head with its butt.

The trooper lay, arms outflung in the snow, and Allen said, "Fred, you and I will make a break for it on this bike. And while we do, you get lost, Tommy."

He was hoping they could cause enough confusion to allow Tommy time, but he really thought he was going to die and he didn't want Tommy riding into gunfire, and apparently Caldwell was having the same thought. "No way," he said. "I'll stay behind and you can be a hero."

But Allen had the gun on Caldwell. "It's got to be

two," he said, "if Tommy is to have a chance."

A minute later he was gunning the trooper's cycle down the road, holding the revolver in his right hand on the handle bar, with Caldwell clutching him around the waist. The snow on the hump-backed dirt road caused them to skid but Allen hung on and as they burst out of the forest they saw the dogs and state troopers with looks of amazement on their faces. One of them fumbled for his gun but it was too late—they were already down the road and away before the patrol car could make a U turn.

In the forest Tommy crashed through underbrush not knowing where he was going, icy limbs slashing his face, and the sound of dogs in the distance. And then the blizzard struck and it was a beauty and he was so tired he could barely see and he suddenly came staggering out on the road where they had started, almost on top of the trooper Allen had decked. The man was sitting up now and he cried out to the three men who had come to his assistance, and two of the men whirled and fired as Tommy cried out, "NO!" and the first slug tore into his brain and he was catapulted back against an oak tree, and then crumpled like a broken puppet, blood dripping on the snow.

— 28 —

George Williams returned the transcript of the congressional hearing to the shelf. He had solved the mystery in at least one case. His own. He knew why Tommy Schovajsa's stepbrother wanted to kill him.

And as Williams had exploded that moment he heard the boy was killed, had shouted at those bonehead troopers who had fired without cause, had known in his heart that he alone had killed the boy because without him those geniuses up there would never have caught him—for all these reasons

Williams had an odd feeling. He no longer blamed the man who intended to kill him. He did not blame him at all.

He left the library, went to the FBI office, and in five minutes the name of Tommy Schovajsa's stepbrother was clattering out of a teletypewriter. Allen Lowell.

— 29 —

AP . . . Washington . . . November 10 . . . An informed FBI source said today that the murders of James Carson and Thomas Medwick were committed by a man named Allen Lowell, a former Green Beret, whose last address was Chicago.

Pictures of the suspect were released to the press late today by the FBI. His description has already been circulated.

The FBI spokesman stated that he could not say at this time how the suspect's identity was discovered, but hinted that a large part of the manpower of the FBI had been laboring on this case since the murder of Representative Thomas Medwick.

George Williams, the Justice Department official who broke the first news of the "Kennedy" list last week, was out of town and could not be reached for comment.

FBI sources say that it is now just a matter of days before the suspect is apprehended.

— 30 —

The man who came to Laura Morgan's door was not the sort of FBI man she expected. His hair was rather

long, his suit was unpressed. Nevertheless, he showed
the thin old woman his FBI identification and she let
him into the living room of her two-story frame
house on the north side of Chicago.

The FBI man said, "You're Laura Morgan, Allen
Lowell's aunt?"

"Yes, sir," said the woman, sitting primly on the
edge of her sofa. "I always said that boy was no
good."

She noticed the FBI man look up quickly from the
pad on which he was taking notes. "Was he in any
trouble in the past? There's nothing on the police
blotter."

"No. Just with me. Never would listen to me, always running off at the mouth about what he was
going to do as soon as he could get away from me.
You see, my sister was his mother, and when she and
her husband were killed in an accident I had to take
the two kids over——"

"We know the background, Miss Morgan."

"Oh . . . well . . . anyway, I made him finish high
school and then he went off to Washington like a
shot. Never sent me a dime, that boy, after all I did
for him."

"Did he have a job to go to?"

"Nothing. We were watching that Kennedy get
sworn in as President—President, him!—I remember
so clear, Allen and Tommy were sitting right there on
the floor in front of the TV set, and Allen was listening to every word like he was in church. Tommy was
different. He didn't care one way or the other, but
Allen, I don't know, something was *wrong* with that
boy. I mean, it isn't right for him to get so excited
about something some politician says a thousand
miles away."

"Did he go to join the Peace Corps or something
like that? We haven't traced where he went in Washington yet."

"No," said Miss Morgan. "That was for college

226

types, wasn't it? This was just an average kid, no college, no money behind him, no contacts. I kept saying to him, what do you expect to *find* in Washington? You're nothing, Allen."

"And what did he say?"

"Oh some smart-aleck reply. Like . . . 'if I was just average, I wouldn't want to go.' Thought a lot of himself in those days, that boy."

— 31 —

Everywhere he went, headlines screamed his name. ALLEN LOWELL HUNTED. ALLEN LOWELL KILLER.

Nothing about it worried him. Nor the fact that by now George Williams might be telegraphing Jim Adams' name all over the world, no doubt congratulating himself on making poor Robere spit blood.

Allen had learned one thing in the Olympians: the necessity of staying ahead to survive. He now carried the ID papers of Sergeant Harold Daub he had stolen from Robere's office—an identity which would last him through the death of Mellon. And by then he would have new papers, already being made up in Washington.

By tomorrow, Mellon would be dead. Spaulding would be easy—he had heard she was ducking away from her guards at least twice a day. In three days he could get to her. Then that fag Warneky—allow a week for that. That would mean a week and a half to get ready for Williams, and for that he already had the location chosen, and the very special weapon for killing this most dangerous of antagonists.

Allen shouldered a heavy tray of glasses and kicked open the swinging door to the restaurant of the Paradise Hotel in Nassau where he had been working as a bus boy. He placed the tray on a table near a prosperous-looking businessman who was just signing his check. Allen's eyes took in the room number: 641.

So far he had stolen more than $2,000 by simply checking room numbers, sighting the people off for the beach, and entering their rooms through a master key he had stolen. The beautiful thing was there had been no publicity. The last thing the hotel wanted was to announce that tourists were being robbed. All Allen had noticed was a sallow-faced plainclothesman hanging around. But he wasn't worried. One more good strike and he was through. He figured twenty-five hundred would be ample.

The robbery took place one hour later. No problem. Then Allen went to the little room he rented in town, and examined the 35 mm camera he had bought yesterday. He took a razor and carefully started working on its insides.

— 32 —

An enthusiastic Conners was on the phone. "You identified him starting from nothing, George! I told them over here you would."

But Williams set him straight quickly. "I feel I'm worse off than before."

"Why?"

"The motive. He has a motive to kill *me*. It's obvious—I helped kill his own brother. But what about the five others on the list who *never heard of* Tommy Schovajsa!"

"You have a point there," said Connors. "But I have a theory. When you can't figure out a motive, when you're all screwed up, and you think you're going crazy—jump for the jugular. FIND THE GUY, THEN CHOKE THE MOTIVE OUT OF HIM."

Williams was smiling on his end of the phone. "I couldn't express it as eloquently as you, but that's exactly what I'm trying. I'm seeing the last two men who spoke to him, Leonard Coleman in Baltimore and Robere Houard up in Toronto. I'll check Gorgio up there too, although Gorgio never did see him in person. Still he worked with him and might know something about his tactics, hideouts, disguises . . . something. Somewhere out of those three we might find the clue we need because Harley—" he stopped.

"Yes?"

"I think Lowell has every murder planned, scheduled, and on track. And that includes changes of ID cards, disguises, cut-offs, the works. In fact, if you want to know the truth, I say we're *never* going to find him."

Connors sounded shocked. "We're not! Then what the hell are we doing? You might as well stay home and get yourself shot in comfort."

"I've been playing hunches all the way through, and every hunch has worked out, and still I can't stop him. And I won't until—"

"Until what?"

"Where does the Kennedy angle come in? If the motive is to avenge the death of his brother, why kill *me* to observe Kennedy's anniversary? That's what haunts this case. That's what makes him unfindable. We can't trap him because we don't know the lure. I hope to God you're checking Spaulding and the others. This publicity might flip Lowell out. He might go for the nearest victim fast."

"Fred Jarvis has a constant check on all the guards, twenty-four-hour basis, just like you ordered."

"OK," said Williams. A few minutes later he was talking on the telephone to Robere Houard in Toronto, but once again with no luck. "You must understand," said Robere, "Jeff Bolton was like a son to me. Years ago one of my own sons, Paul, was mixed up with drugs. He was selling them to deserters, and using them himself. Then the police cornered him with some others at a drug party and Jeff managed to get him away. Everyone else was arrested and convicted; my son was free to change his ways."

The man stopped talking for a moment. Then he went on, "Today my son is a lawyer in Quebec, respected, happily married, and it is all because of that American boy. I will not help you."

"You must help us," said Williams. "He's not the same boy you knew. He's insane."

"But I just saw him, M'sieu. He was sane as ever. Of course he has always been . . . nervous since his brother died. But he is reasonable."

Williams said, "I'll be up to see you."

Silence, then Houard said wearily, "Do not bother, M'sieu. I will tell you, as I told the police, I made him papers in the name of Joe Marconi."

"Don't go away," said Williams.

— 33 —

Off St. John, the scuba diver clung to the stern of the motorboat near a support ship and then flopped over backward into the green depths of the Caribbean lagoon. Mellon was watching with binoculars from his own boat, and it was surprising how deep you could follow the diver in the clear water.

Underneath, the diver, who was one of the aquanauts in training, approached the habitat placed on the floor of the lagoon. A silvery fish hung motionless near him, then an eel flashed by—a harmless eel, not a Moray—and then, arms propelling slowly, the aquanaut was at the steel door, pushing some levers, and swimming into the entrance lock. He waited while compressed air emptied the water from the lock, then opened the inner door and found the other two aquanauts sitting at a table in their undershorts

playing poker. One of them looked up at the ceiling and said, "Tell me what he's got, Les!"

The other aquanaut laughed. The television eye above them was being monitored on board the support ship, and the answer came fast, "Two kings, two threes, and a five."

"Damn you!" shouted the aquanaut whose hand had been exposed.

"Gentlemen, watch your language. We have a lady on board up here."

"Hey, Bob, turn on the screen," said one of the aquanauts. The newcomer went over to the TV, and soon the screen was filled with some kind of chick in a bikini! A seventeen-year-old sweetheart, Mellon's friend Kathy.

Whistles from the aquanauts. "Send her down!" "When do we get introduced?"

The voice from above was reproving. "Gentlemen, this is Kathy Simmons, the daughter of Mr. and Mrs. Jackson Simmons, whom you've met. So mind your manners—MY DEAR!"

Kathy, smiling, had pulled down the top of her bikini for a flash, exposing her breasts. Then, slowly she replaced the bikini and turned to the unseen man above. "Sorry, Mr. Haddon," she said. "It slipped."

"Oh Christ," said one of the aquanauts. "After that they expect us to spend thirty days down here!"

On board the ship above, Kathy was facing an angry scientist. "I'm going to tell your father about that."

And, in truth, she was furious at herself. Jim Adams would kill her if he knew she had called attention to herself when he told her to be especially discreet. But those aquanauts were so darling and looked so forlorn, like fish in an aquarium.

She was a nut, an absolute nut. She was always doing absolutely nutty things. Like promising Jim Adams to keep track of Everett Mellon.

She said to Mr. Haddon, "Please don't tell my father. The boys down there looked so lonely . . ."

"Miss Simmons! You're only a baby."

And let me get *your* trousers off, thought Kathy to herself. But she started to cry instead, and finally old Haddon told her he would say nothing to her parents. But he also said, "I can't allow you to stay on the support ship any more, Kathy."

And that made Kathy cry for real. Because the support ship was where Jim Adams was going to meet her, and now she had messed up the whole thing.

In the small boat riding back across the lagoon to Mellon's yacht she looked around and saw that marines were all over Mellon's boat and two boats were lying thirty feet to either side. Jim would never be able to reach her. She'd never see him again.

She climbed up the gangway, said "Hi" to Mellon who she thought was a really nice guy. She had never told Jim that she really enjoyed that session with him in bed. Jim wouldn't have liked that at all. He was the jealous type.

In her little stateroom she changed into slacks and a halter and for the hundredth time wondered, what did Jim Adams have against Mellon? Every time he mentioned Mellon's name he got a quiet unnatural look on his face. And Mellon was really a sweetheart. He wouldn't hurt a fly.

That last night in Nassau she had tried to argue this point with Jim, as they lay on the beach. But he had said, "If he's so nice, why does someone want to kill him?"

"But Mr. Mellon doesn't even believe that threatening note that was in the papers. He says it's a case of mistaken identity."

Her boyfriend said nothing. He was lying on his back on an Indian blanket they had brought to the beach, looking up at the stars.

"Why are you trailing him, Jim? It's not right. It's

scary. I don't want to get involved in anything wrong."

Jim raised himself to one elbow, and looked at her. "I could be fired for this," he said. "But I'll tell you because I love you, and I don't want you frightened. FBI."

"You're an FBI man—with hair like that?"

"Undercover." He laughed. "Nowadays there are more FBI men with long hair than short."

"And Mr. Mellon's done something . . . bad?"

"He's done something bad, all right. I'm not going to tell you what or you might spill it to him. But I'll give you a hint. When his yacht goes to St. John you'll see some strangers aboard, and at least two of them will be FBI men. Figure *that* out."

Later on, they had made love on the beach, and afterward Jim had given her the bracelet. He told her it was a good luck charm, and she promised to wear it always.

Now, dressed in her slacks, Kathy was thinking Jim was wrong about Mr. Mellon. They had been in this lagoon three days and all she had seen were men in uniform. Some cute marines. So Jim was lying to her after all.

Out on deck she saw two men coming up the gangway, looking very out of place in business suits. Mellon showed them into the salon, and ten minutes later he bumped into Kathy on deck and said, "What do you know? FBI men. We've got everybody but the Air Force on board."

Mellon couldn't understand why his remark brought such a smile to Kathy's face.

— 34 —

Coleman Productions was housed in a modest brick building with white facing in the beautiful hill coun-

try near Towson, Maryland. Williams was led to the cluttered corner office of the president, a ruddy, freckle-faced man with tufted gray hair and a hearty manner.

"Yes, hell, don't mention that chemite film," said Coleman. "Nothing but trouble, beginning with Bolton—uh, Lowell, if that's his real name. We haven't even been paid for it yet."

"Why not?"

"Bolton got the client so mad up there he hardly would cooperate with us. Then, of course, I've had the usual trouble with the writer—but that's no worry of yours. You want to know all I know about Bolton, right? You don't mind if I keep calling him that?"

"Was the chemite film his first one with you?"

"No, we hired him for a few other jobs beginning about a year ago. You want some coffee?"

"Fine."

They sat there without talking until a secretary brought in the ritual cups of coffee in cardboard containers, and Williams sipped his, waiting. Coleman said, "That boy came looking for free-lance work about a year ago. He was desperate. Number one, he couldn't hold a steady job any more. He told me straight out he'd been in and out of mental hospitals since he left Vietnam. Number two, he had just had a disappointment that really hurt him."

"What was that?"

"He had applied for and gotten a job up in New York on a TV special on the anniversary of Kennedy's death, and at the last minute they fired him. Didn't like his attitude, he told me."

"What was the name of that company in New York?" Williams asked.

Coleman smiled. "Never miss a beat, do you, Mr. Williams? Well, old King Cole is ready for you. Here's the resumé he gave me, and the name is on the bottom of it." He shoved a mimeographed resumé across to Williams. Williams read the name at the bottom:

International Television Packaging
30 Rockefeller Plaza
New York, N.Y.
Duration of employment: August to October, 1972

Coleman said, "His home address on there is NG. We checked it out when he stole the chemite. Just a rooming house." But Williams was looking at the top of the page and reading:

USIA
Washington, D.C.
Duration of employment June 1963 to May 1964

So Lowell had worked for USIA! Carson had worked for USIA. A connection! He folded the resumé and put it in his pocket, then said to Coleman. "Lowell is killing some people who worked for the government at the same time he did. Any clue as to why, from your knowledge of him?"

"Sure I have a clue," said Coleman.

"What is it?"

"I saw the film he carried around on the President's funeral."

"A movie? You mean a photograph of himself and Kennedy at a White House reception?"

"No," said Coleman. "It was motion picture footage taken at the funeral. He used it as a sample reel to get jobs."

"OK. So how is a film on Kennedy's funeral a clue?"

"I have the *shot list*. He took the film with him when he left, but he didn't take that. I dug it out of the file today. I don't mind telling you I was a *bit* surprised."

Coleman had lighted a pipe, and now leaned back, puffing, watching Williams' face. He was the type of man who loved to tell stories in his own way, and that was in his own sweet time. Williams said, "What was on the film?"

"We-e-e-l-l," said Coleman, and Williams waited for another puff of blue smoke to drift to the ceiling. "Lowell told me he was only an apprentice editor over at USIA when the funeral came around. But for that event the agency sent every man they had out on the street to cover it from all angles. Lowell went along with a crew and ended up doing filler interviews with the people in the crowd. Those interviews didn't make it into the *Years of Lightning* film—but Lowell was proud of them anyway. He kept the reel as a sample. When he's applying for a job he screens the film to show what he can do. Usual thing in this business."

The Kennedy funeral! Lowell *interviewing* people! Coleman read off the shot list the names of four people Allen Lowell had interviewed at Kennedy's funeral, November 1963:

> Everett Mellon
> Thomas Medwick
> Robert Warneky
> Stephanie Spaulding

— 35 —

Williams called Connors. "Change of plans. I'm stopping off in New York tomorrow on the way to Toronto. A company called International Television Packaging. Lowell worked there last year."

"You found something in Baltimore?"

"I don't know. But Lowell carried a little film of the Kennedy funeral. Used it as a sample reel to help him get jobs. The film shows him interviewing four people at the Kennedy funeral—and those four are on the list of victims."

"Jesus!"

Williams said, "Tie that together with the fact he was working on a Kennedy anniversary TV special in New York before coming to Baltimore last year, and he told the Baltimore producer he had been fired from the New York outfit."

Connors was silent on the other end of the phone, then he said, "*You* tie it in. I can't."

"I can't—but I must. If Houard and Gorgio give me nothing new in Toronto, that's all we have to go on. That film tie-in. And it doesn't make sense."

Williams stayed in a Baltimore motel that night, went to dinner alone, then up to his room, and he was thinking of nothing but that interview film. As he had been doing ever since this nightmare began, he cast his mind back to 1963 . . . those days when Kennedy was still alive before that dark November, and the town was swelling with bright eager people, Mellon, Medwick, Spaulding, Warneky among thousands.

And now, ten years later, he wanted to kill them.

Williams knew why *he* was on the list. And—who knows—Lowell might have some grievance against Carson from USIA days. These were concrete grudges that a mentally disturbed boy might decide to kill for.

But four people that Lowell had interviewed at the funeral? Four people at random in the crowd, and they're marked for death ten years later. Why?

— 36 —

On a dock in St. Thomas, Allen Lowell waited for a small boat that would take a camera crew to the lagoon in St. John. It was Dive Day minus one.

Allen wore a tan windbreaker and blue jeans, and carried the small Nikon 35 camera slung from his shoulder in a case. He had been hired as a grip by the camera crew when their own man had mysteriously disappeared the day before. The disappearance had been engineered by Allen, who told the man he was a diving fanatic and just had to see the experiment. In exchange for a crisp $100 bill and the promise of another tomorrow, the grip gave Allen his badge. No one would question Allen once it was on, least of all the young marine guard on the dock.

Allen stood in the sun on that dock in St. Thomas and watched sea gulls making precision dives at the blue water, striking sharply, coming up with fish every time, a flash of silver in their beak, and they were off. They never missed.

A boat circled into the dock, a line was thrown over, and Allen carried battery boxes and camera equipment for the crew into the boat. A few minutes later they were speeding across the water to St. John, the island rising green and lush to its ridge of hills, first the Rockefeller park, and then after twenty minutes they rounded a peninsula and saw a Navy operation underway, boats at anchor, huts on shore, and a helicopter landing slowly and gracefully on a dock.

Approaching the lagoon, the white froth at their bow, Allen saw the two ships he was looking for: Mellon's—and the LST support ship.

On Mellon's ship, an FBI man was making his scheduled call on the radiotelephone to Williams' switchboard operator in Washington. "Nothing unusual. Nothing to report. Will call back in an hour."

And on the water Allen was looking at the two boats guarding Mellon's—and seeing marines aboard, and thinking it would be impossible to break through that cordon. He had been wise to arrange his rendezvous with Kathy on the LST instead.

Their small boat came to a rest against a dock, bobbing and scraping. Allen said to the coxswain, "Where are you going now?"

"Don't know. We just stand by to wait instructions."

"You want to make twenty dollars for a little trip?"

The first cameraman looked down at Allen from the dock and said angrily, "Hey, Adams, you're hired to help!"

Allen said to the coxswain quickly, "Meet me in half an hour."

"Where do you want to go?"

"I've got a chick on the support ship."

"All right," said the coxswain. "I'll be here."

Allen jumped hurriedly onto the dock and did more than his share of the heavy work helping the crew set up.

The helicopter which Allen had seen landing had been a stroke of wisdom on the part of an Interior Department coordinator. The Navy had been grousing ever since Interior had launched this operation: to soothe them some genius had come up with the idea of inviting a Navy admiral to participate in the diving ceremony which would launch the thirty-day experiment.

In fact, the first aquanaut to descend to the habitat would remove a large golden key from its hatch and swim up to the surface and hand the startled admiral the symbolic key to the experiment while the television cameras ground. Beautiful.

Admiral Jason Bingham was chatting with Captain Mazur in the wardroom of the LST. The admiral said, "I got a call from the Justice Department before I came down here. They're worried about that man Mellon being here."

"It was the Admiral of Oceanography that insisted on it, sir. We were ready to send him packing."

"Well, hell, I don't like it. This experiment is costing the government a fortune, and all we need is to get some civilian murdered in the middle of it. After the last fiasco, we could really kiss Tektite goodbye."

"It's not too late," the captain said. "We could lift him off in the chopper."

"And I could get my head handed to me in the Pentagon—if I order him off—and he gets murdered in his home tonight. No. The mistake has been made. But we're going to make certain nothing happens to that man while I'm here at least."

The captain explained the security precautions that had been taken on Mellon's boat, and the admiral was satisfied. "Nobody gets past marines," he said. Then he heard a boat come alongside.

On LSTs the wardroom is right next to the gangway watch. And the admiral heard the conversation clearly. He was to remember it well in the future. A man was asking the gangway watch, "I'm here to see Kathy Simmons."

"Who?"

"A girl about seventeen years old—"

"Yes, sir. I remember *her,* sir."

The unidentified voice said, "Well, I made arrangements to meet her here at this time."

"Well, she ain't here, sir. Mr. Haddon, the chief oceanographer, sent her back to Mr. Mellon's boat over there. She ain't allowed on this here boat no more."

In the wardroom the captain was smiling at the admiral, wondering if he should tell him of the impromptu television show the Simmons girl had put on for the aquanauts below. But he thought better of it. An admiral couldn't afford to laugh at a scene like that.

The voice was asking the gangway watch, "Not that it matters. But what did Kathy do?"

"She done exposed her tits," said the gangway watch, and the admiral started to laugh. Relieved, the captain laughed too.

Outside, Allen Lowell was not laughing as he went down to his boat. This was going to be tricky.

The FBI man was talking to Kathy on the bow of

Mellon's yacht when a small boat approached the guard boat on the port side. The FBI man saw a young man at the wheel, and then the girl beside him was shouting and waving. "Jim! Over here!"

"Who's that?" asked the FBI man.

"My boy friend. He told me he'd be working with a camera crew." She turned to the FBI man, "Oh, sir, can't he come aboard? Just for a minute? I haven't seen him in days."

Mellon was coming out on deck, but the FBI man was already saying, "No chance." He picked up a hailer that lay beside him for communication with the guard boats, and said, his voice magnified metallically: "Tell him to get lost. No visitors!"

He saw the man in the small boat hand what looked to be a camera in a case to one of the guards, and then roar off in his boat toward the dock. The guard yelled through a megaphone, "He left a present for the girl."

The FBI man said through the hailer, "OK, bring it over."

The boat pulled alongside. "Can you catch it?"

"Sure."

He threw it up and Kathy caught it. Mellon and the FBI man were beside her. They took the case from her, opened it, and saw the Nikon camera. "I forgot to bring it with me," Kathy said, although she had never seen the camera before. But Jim had briefed her what to say if there were any questions. The FBI man was turning it over in his hands. "Can't see anything wrong with this," he said to Mellon, "Specially as the man isn't aboard."

"I'm going to use it to photograph the diving ceremony tomorrow," said Kathy. "It's all right, I promise."

But the FBI man wanted to be doubly sure. He opened the back of the camera and saw a film neatly in place, rolled onto the take-up reel. Then he replaced the back cover, held the camera to his eye, squinted through the lens, and pressed the button. It clicked, and the film counter knob advanced. He handed the camera to Kathy. "Just wanted to be sure it was a camera." he said, although he never really had doubts. A teenybopper like Kathy was bound to have young men running errands for her.

Allen Lowell worked all that day in the sun, lugging heavy boxes and equipment, sand in his boots, sweat on his face. But he was used to working with film crews. Then the men took the small boat back to St. Thomas, and that night in a native bar along the water Allen handed another $100 bill to the real grip and told him he could go back to work tomorrow. It had been a thrill, he said.

Then he went to his hotel, and from his suitcase removed an Army sergeant's uniform. That night Sergeant Harold Daub, 1st Cavalry, flew Pan-American to Miami, and changed for an Eastern flight to Washington. Tektite III was behind Allen Lowell.

Stephanie Spaulding was ahead.

— 37 —

Ten forty-five A.M. St. John. The camera lay in its case on the dresser in Kathy's room. But things had already gone wrong. The way Jim had explained it, she was to take a picture of the diving ceremony, and then pretend she had flubbed it, advance the roll, and ask Mr. Mellon to take another.

But the FBI man had already advanced the roll and now she didn't know what to do. Did she still take a picture, then hand it to Mr. Mellon, or did the marine's shot count and should she give Mr. Mellon the camera right away?

Whatever, she had better hurry. The ceremony was to begin at eleven A.M.; the aquanauts were on their boat, getting suited up; and the admiral and all the VIPs were assembled on the dock.

Kathy thought she'd give the aquanauts one last break. She squeezed into a blue bikini and stationed herself on the bow where she could wave at them before they dived. Give them something to remember all those long days underwater.

As she walked down the corridor past the radio room, one of the FBI men saw her and whistled.

In Baltimore George Williams had spent the morning on the phone before taking a noon flight to New York. He talked to Stephanie Spaulding and Bob Warneky, and Stephanie remembered the interview at the funeral right away. Warneky had to think a minute. "I was interviewed a lot of times as a coach, you know. But I can't honestly remember whether someone stuck a microphone that day in my face or not . . . Wait now . . . oh, you mean that . . . sure, some kid came up to me in the middle of the street after the funeral procession had gone by. I was just staring after it, crying like a baby. He asked me if I worked for Kennedy and I told him I couldn't talk now. That was the interview! Hell, that must be him. That kid!"

"That's him," said Williams. Then he hung up and tried to get through to the telephone contact man on Mellon's boat in St. John. After a lot of static and disconnects, he made it. "You keeping a close check on Mellon?" said Williams.

The FBI man said, "I'm telling you no one's been near this boat." He paused. "Well, one young guy yesterday."

"What?"

"There's a girl on the boat. Daughter of one of the scientists. A young fellow tried to visit her yesterday but we shooed him away."

"Get that girl and keep her away from Mellon!'

"He never got to her! Just left her camera with the guard boat."

"A *camera!*"

243

"Well, yes . . ."

"Where is it now?"

"What?"

"Where is the camera now?"

"I . . . I don't know."

"Throw it overboard this minute!"

"It's a real camera. We tested it. We took a picture with it."

"FIND IT AND THROW IT OVERBOARD THIS MINUTE!"

Admiral Bingham was enjoying himself. Someone on his staff had got word to him that he would be receiving a gold key from the habitat below, and that pleased him. His staff men, captains and commanders, were immaculate in whites and gold braid as they stood beside him on the deck. To the right was the cabin cruiser from which the aquanauts would dive. The pleasure craft was a jarring note in what should have been a military operation, but the Interior Department didn't have much of a Navy. The admiral smiled as one of the aquanauts already in his diving gear gave him a salute.

Farther out on the lagoon was the LST with the electronic cables leading down to the habitat, and now coming alongside was old Kurt Manning, television's science expert. A camera crew on the stern of the boat aimed its cameras at the admiral. Manning said, "Care to comment before the dive begins?"

Without waiting for a reply, Manning leaped onto the dock, to the annoyance of the other television crews in their own boats. The admiral had refused to speak to them before the dive in case something went wrong—he didn't want to be photographed heralding a technological break-through with a diver dead below as had happened at Sea Lab III—but Manning apparently had an in.

From the deck of Mellon's yacht, about thirty yards away, it was a colorful glorious scene. The weather was brilliant, a clear blue sky with sun sparkling on the waters of the lagoon. The aquanauts were enjoying a last cigarette before going without for thirty days. One of them looked up and saw Kathy in her blue bikini. "Nature girl is back."

"She really knows how to hurt a fella," another responded and then heard his name being called from the dock. A pretty young woman stepped out of the crowd and threw him a photograph in waterproof plastic. She blew him a kiss.

The aquanaut waved the picture of his wife and smiled at her. Compared to the girl in the bikini, she suddenly looked very old.

On board, Kathy remembered with a start. The camera! She had been so absorbed in the spectacle and those poor aquanauts, she had almost forgotten Jim's instructions.

She removed it from its case and held it to her eye. She had decided that since the marine snapped the first picture Mr. Mellon was supposed to take the next. But where was Mellon? Jim must have assumed he would be right here on the bow with her.

She looked around anxiously and saw him standing on the wheelhouse with one of the marine guards. She hurried up the ladder just as a frantic FBI man came racing out of the door below. He didn't see her.

"Mr. Mellon," she was saying, "would you take a picture of me with the aquanauts in the background? My parents would love it."

Mellon took the camera. "Sure. Tell me when you're ready."

"Let me just get up on the railing."

"MELLON!" The voice boomed from the deck. The FBI man had spotted them.

"Just a damn minute," said Mellon, focusing the camera. "OK, I think I've got it."

"THROW THAT CAMERA OVERBOARD! IT'S A BOMB!"

Mellon lowered the camera and started to laugh at the panicky face beneath him. "Are you kidding?

Your FBI friend took a picture yesterday, and he didn't blow up! You guys are getting jumpy——"

But the FBI man was clambering up the ladder desperately. "Hurry," said Kathy, "before he takes my camera away and I'll never have a picture."

"He rigged it for the second exposure!" the FBI man yelled, as he vaulted over the edge of the wheelhouse. Mellon brought the camera to his eye, but before he could push the button, the FBI man tackled him and he went sprawling across the wheelhouse roof. The camera arched through the air and people aboard ship watched in a frozen tableau as the camera landed on the deck railing below, depressing the button. There was a giant WHOOMPH! and an explosion tore apart the deck and the adjacent cabins and cracked the hull and a marine was blown overboard, his arm in shreds.

BOOK V

11-22-73

— 1 —

Cold in New York, wind whipping the passengers as
they deplaned at the Eastern air lines shuttle terminal
and made their way across the tarmac to the swinging
doors and warmth. Williams went outside and hailed
a taxi.

On the way into Manhattan, the cabbie said, "You
know about them murders? The one in the Ambassador Hotel . . . Carton or Carson or something? And
now that bomb in Nassau."

The cabbie, a man with heavy black eyebrows and
a nose that looked as if it had been broken more than
once, glanced into the rear-view mirror. Williams
said, "I read about it."

"Well, my kid solved it last night. We're watching
the news on TV and he comes up with the answer.
It's Oswald."

"Lee Oswald?"

"That's right. The real Lee Oswald. You know he
had a double. My kid made me read one of them
books about the conspiracy, and there was this evidence that one Oswald is in one town buying something at the same time the other Oswald is in another
town at a rifle range or something. Anyway, my kid
says, one of them Oswalds is still loose."

Williams had worked with the Warren Commission
on the case, helping to investigate every conspiracy
theory. The CIA connection had worried everyone:
Oswald had gone to Russia to live; everyone in Washington knew that meant he was at least *approached*
by CIA. But in the end all evidence pointed to the
fact Oswald had acted alone, and Williams believed
it. He said to the cabbie, "Well, whoever it is, we
ought to know by November twenty-second."

"Why?"

"The note mentioned the anniversary."

The cabbie said, "But that's only two weeks away. You mean he's going to kill four more people in two weeks, with the whole government after him?"

"I think he's going to try," said Williams.

Rockefeller Center soaring above midtown, growing older but still majestic, braceleted with modern glass towers that seemed whimsical fancies that would some day blow away.

The cab turned off Fifth, but Williams was oblivious to his surroundings. Now more than ever he knew he had to find some way to lure Lowell into going after himself, at once! Sheer luck and timing had saved Mellon's life yesterday. If he had called the FBI five minutes later, Mellon would be dead now.

Once again the newspapers were in an uproar. The attack on Mellon had drawn angry denunciations of the "flabby" FBI which could not protect known victims with the help of hundreds of marines.

Well, Williams had news for them. A killer like Lowell, who planned everything ahead, always did something unexpected and executed his killings with such precision and daring, could not be stopped, short of actually jailing the victims, which neither Spaulding nor Warneky would accept, although it had been seriously suggested by someone at FBI. By now it was clear that routine custody—guarded hotel room, safe house—would be useless against Lowell's methods.

The cabbie let him off in front of "30 Rock" and Williams took the elevator to International Television Packaging on the eighth floor.

Its suite of offices was furnished with quiet elegance: regency antiques and original oil paintings throughout, including the reception room. Williams was shown into the office of the vice-president in charge of production, a tall thin graying man with a pleasant smile named Tom Jackson. "I've been told to give you one hundred percent cooperation, Mr. Williams. And, speaking for myself, I'm happy to do so. This is the most dreadful affair."

"How long has your company been in business, Mr. Jackson?"

"Two years and a half, I think, give or take a month. Why?"

"I wondered why you would need free-lance help."

Jackson smiled. "Yes, well, this was a special project, Mr. Williams. We advertised extensively for anyone with original footage never before shown on President Kennedy for an anniversary special last year. Bolton was one of the people who answered the ad. He had some interviews taken at the President's funeral. Quite affecting, actually."

"Did you see the film?"

"Yes. And I believe it was my idea to send him out to reinterview those four people nine years later. Bring the story up to date."

"And did he do that?"

"Yes, sir. Bob Torley was the producer of the film. I'll let him tell you what happened."

In a few minutes a man in a gray cashmere sweater, gray slacks, and Gucci loafers came in and shook Williams' hand. "Some kook, that Bolton, eh?"

Williams said, "How did Bolton react to the four reinterviews?"

"React? It just about finished him—and he was in sad shape to begin with. I mean, the first time I saw him I could see he was too nervous to work. I think Mr. Jackson here was just doing him a favor to hire him because he was a Vietnam vet and all that."

Jackson said, "Well, I *did* think we could use his film."

Torley said, "Not after what the kid found. You see, we wanted him to do some checking into the people before he barged in for interviews. So when he comes back, looking ill, I ask him what's the mat-

ter. He said he found out that his four Kennedy idol-
izers of 1963 were now a whore, a crook, an alco-
holic beach bum, and a fag."

Williams' mind was working. The first three he
could identify, so that left Warneky as the fag. Warneky? A football coach? "Did he identify which· was
which?" he asked.

"No. What was the point? He said he didn't want
to use them in a Kennedy memorial—not the way
they'd desecrated, that was his word—everything
Kennedy stood for. He said he wouldn't allow us to
use his film from the funeral after what he'd learned,
and I said OK, we'd do without. And that was it."

"And that afternoon," Jackson said, "he walked
out—and we never saw him again. Disappeared.
Didn't even pick up his last check."

Williams said, "He told a producer in Baltimore
that you fired him because of his attitude."

"Attitude! He had a perfect attitude. He loved
Kennedy and was working his head off for the show.
We had him editing some sequences, and doing research on the Kennedy years, and he was happy as a
clam."

"So as far as you know he soured on the project
after he found out what had become of the four people on his film."

Jackson spread his arms out. "What else could it
be? He just walked out of the door that day and
never came back. Period. Now I won't say his leaving
was a blow to us—he was just free-lance, after all—
but he was so hot about not using those four people
some of it must have rubbed off. Anyway, we decided
to drop them entirely, including, of course, Bolton's
original interviews at the funeral."

Williams asked if he could see the special.

"You want to see the special Bolton was working
on last year?"

"Yes."

"I'd be happy to cooperate, Mr. Williams, but actually there's nothing to see. It was never finished.

You can see this year's version, though."

"Why wasn't last year's special finished?"

"Bolton's? Well, the network news departments hate independent documentary producers, Mr. Williams. They want to produce all their own news shows . . . it's a well-known fact in the television business. So at the last minute they got word to us that the prime time wasn't available and the sponsor pulled out. We were stuck with half a year's work. But this year we have a strong sponsor, and we're getting our new special on. Definitely."

Williams knew what Jackson was saying was true. He had once been involved in an anti-trust case against the networks which cited the monopoly of prime time, and the rejection of independent shows by the news departments in particular. He said, "You don't have Lowell's film?"

Jackson shook his head.

"Then I'd like to see the new show."

"Of course," said Jackson. "Let me check with the editor." He buzzed his secretary and told her he wanted to speak to Herb Sanchez. When Sanchez came on the phone, Jackson said, "I have someone here who wants to see our new Kennedy special. Is the rough cut ready? . . . What can you show him? . . . I see. Just a minute." He said to Williams, "They haven't patched the rough cut together yet, but he can show you some sequences on different reels."

"When will the rough cut be ready?"

Jackson asked Sanchez over the phone. "Can't say yet. They're waiting for some stock footage that hasn't come in yet."

"I'll be back," said Williams.

Jackson looked at Williams. "I still don't see what our special this year has to do with Jeff Bolton. He wasn't in on this one at all."

But instead of enlightening him, Williams said, "When is your show going on the air, Mr. Jackson?"

"November twenty-second, eight o'clock."

Williams thanked him and Torley and left the office. But on the way out he stopped at the desk of the receptionist, a brunette of sizable proportions, who favored him with a smile. "Mr. Jackson says that you were on duty the day Jeff Bolton left. Do you remember?"

"Oh sure. He was a nice boy. Nervous as a tick, though."

The phone rang and Williams had to wait while she plugged the call through the switchboard. Then she looked up at him and said, "All I know is Mr. Brockway came in to see Mr. Jackson. And five minutes later Jeff came back from lunch, looking shook. Ever since he started looking up those people he had interviewed he was looking sick, poor kid."

"So?"

"So I don't know what happened. He went inside to see Mr. Jackson and ten minutes later he was out here looking like death. But death. I said, 'What's the matter?' And he said, 'Nothing. Nothing.' And he went out and I never saw him again."

"Who's Mr. Brockway?"

"One of our financial backers from out of town. He comes in from time to time on business so he keeps an office here. Mr. Jackson is always very nice to him."

"So a man named Brockway was in Jackson's office when Bolton went in to see him?"

"That's right."

"And ten minutes later Bolton walked out and never came back?"

'Right again," said the receptionist. "And he looked green! Said he was never coming back."

Williams thanked her and left.

— 2 —

A driving snowstorm lashed Toronto, and Williams' plane circled for what seemed hours before diving into the gray swirling maelstrom. It broke clear at five hundred feet for a skidding landing on an icy runway.

Williams asked directions from the girl at the counter where he had rented the Peugeot. She gave him a map and circled the two addresses he had mentioned. Then she added a warning. "They clear the streets very quickly here, but still it will be bad for an hour. If you're not familiar with our roads you might want to wait."

"I'll take the chance," said Williams, and a few minutes later he was regretting it. The snow was still falling, and the tires crunched halfheartedly into the slippery white slush beneath; to make matters worse, his breath began fogging the windows, while the window wipers laboriously creaked to clear his view.

The plane's delay had already caused him to fall behind schedule and in a crisis where every minute counted this could be fatal. Somewhere in Toronto there must be a clue. Houard *must* be forced to tell the real names on the ID cards he had prepared for Lowell. And Mike Gorgio and his friends *must* know more than they had revealed about someone who had worked with them for years.

What he had learned in Baltimore and New York had brought him a long way toward solving the greatest riddle of all: Lowell's motive. All Williams' instincts told him he was right.

From New York Williams had called Mike Gorgio who said he would put him up overnight; he'd just move out one of the transients. But first, Williams wanted to see Robere Houard.

The snow was tapering off as he parked before the Bon Soir tailor shop. Inside he waited until a stout woman in a blue smock took care of a customer, and then he identified himself. "Ah," the woman said, "we expect you. I am Marie Houard." She hung a sign which read CLOSED on the front door and took Williams into the back.

A giant Negro was at the presses. She led

Williams up the stairs to a bedroom where Robere was sitting up in bed, looking wan and peaked. "Now, Robere," Mrs. Houard said, "no more foolishness. Tell this man what papers you made for Jeff."

Robere said, "Marie is of the opinion that I should not protect Jeff so far as to help him murder people. So, I am sick. But I believe she is right."

He gave Williams a sheet of paper from the table beside his bed. "I am sorry, I spilled tea on it this morning."

Williams read the name and address:

> Jim Adams
> 135 Oak Street
> Seattle, Wash.

Robere said, "He has a passport, a Gulf Oil credit card which he will not use, and a membership in a Seattle sailing club."

Williams said, "How do I know you're not still lying to protect your friend?"

"He is not lying," said Mrs. Houard angrily. It was obvious to Williams who had been the moving force in Robere's change of mind. She said, "I tell you myself. On his way out that morning I said, 'Au revoir, Jeff.' And he smiled and said, 'The name is Jim now, Marie.' "

Williams believed her. He asked them if he could use their phone, and called Connors in Washington collect with the information. Connors said, "Right on!" He said he'd get it on the wires at once.

— 3 —

The blizzard had stopped abruptly and the streets were being cleared as Williams left the Bon Soir. Driving cautiously, he made his way through the late afternoon to the northern outskirts of Toronto. By the time he reached the semi-attached brownstone where Mike Gorgio lived, it was almost five o'clock and dark; Williams had been expected at noon.

He pressed the bell and a young man with tousled blond hair came to the door. Williams introduced himself and said he was there to see Mike Gorgio.

"Come in. But he's not here."

Williams stomped his shoes on a mat, and saw three other young men sitting around inside, reading.

"I'm Frank Powers," said the boy. "Mike thought you'd been grounded by the storm so he went out half an hour ago. He's kept a room for you just in case, though."

"Good of him," said Williams. He could feel the apprehension sweeping out at him from the three young men. He was Justice. They were deserters.

One of the boys rustled up a cup of steaming black coffee. Williams sat down on a creaky couch with battered cushions. He said, "Any of your fellows ever run into Allen Lowell?"

A tall dark-haired boy across the room burst out: "That creep who's been murdering people? I suppose you're going to tie us in with that freaky bit, too?"

"But we never even saw the guy," Powers said. "None of us. I asked all over Toronto myself. In fact, I was the one who found out he had been up to see Houard last year."

"Did you see him then?"

"Hell, no. He slipped in and out of town."

Williams said, "But how do you know? He might not have used his real name."

"We use real names," Powers said angrily. "We're proud of what we did, no matter what they say about us in America."

Williams said, "Allen Lowell was about six feet tall, slim—and had short hair. Any of you ever see someone like that? All-American type?"

"Well, now," said Powers, "most of these guys are fresh out of the Army so a lot of them have short hair, depending on the command they were in—

257

Yeah, now hold it. There *was* one oddball like that who came in here about a year ago and asked for Mike. The guy acted weird . . . like he was nervous, or something. Couldn't sit still. I told him Mike would be back around dinner time and said he could sleep in your room upstairs. But when Mike got back the guy was gone. He never did see Mike."

Williams was not too impressed. He said, "There could have been a hundred reasons he decided to push on."

"Yes, but when I took him upstairs he sure looked like he was going to stay. He plunked himself down on that bed and looked all worn out. Hell, I thought he was sick."

Williams felt his stomach tighten. Lowell disappeared suddenly from International Television. . . . Someone who fits his description suddenly disappeared from this house. . . . Still, deserters were always coming and going. Williams finished his coffee. "Where's that room?" he asked.

Powers took him upstairs to a little cubicle with a single bunk and sagging springs. Powers was saying, "Mike's room is right next door. We call it the presidential suite. The bathroom's down the hall. Make yourself at home. We're always nice to FBI spooks."

"I'm not FBI, I'm Justice," said Williams.

"You're all spooks to us," said Powers, and he left.

Williams went down to the bathroom to wash up, and on the way back passed Mike's room and looked inside. One thing he saw immediately was that Mike was a football nut. He had action pictures of NFL games all over the walls. Well, that was one thing he had in common with Allen Lowell, Williams thought. Williams had obtained a copy of the Steubenville High yearbook and discovered that in his sophomore year Lowell was the star end of the team, catching ten touchdown passes.

Seeing no one in the hall, Williams entered the room. In addition to the NFL photos, there was a picture on the bureau of a quarterback giving a hand-off. The athletes in this picture were younger; high school or college age. Evidently Gorgio, like Lowell, had had his moments on the gridiron, too. Williams studied the picture for a long time.

He walked over to a desk in the corner and the strangest thing happened. A buzzer went off.

The boys came charging up from downstairs. "What the hell is that?" Powers asked. But Williams was down next to the wall, examining an electric eye. The buzzer was still buzzing. "Gorgio must want privacy," he said to the faces at the door. "Who knows how to stop the alarm?"

"We didn't even know he had one! I never heard it before."

Williams traced a wire along the baseboard behind the desk to where it terminated in a switch plate, obviously newly installed. Paint and plaster chippings were still on the floor. He threw the switch and the buzzing stopped.

Why a buzzer to protect a desk? To the boys he said, "OK, emergency over."

But they were reluctant to leave. "Listen, mister, if he had an alarm rigged, there's something he didn't want you to see."

"Like what?" said Williams. The papers on the desk and in the drawers yielded nothing—letters and bills, absolutely nothing of an incriminating nature, not even a record of the Bolton robbery they had contracted for.

The boys were looking at each other. "What's to hide?" said Powers. "Maybe the names of the deserters in case the Canadian police changed their mind and crack down."

"Still," said another, "an electric eye?"

They went downstairs just as Mike Gorgio came in. He was stocky, curly-haired, engaging. He stood there rubbing his hands and saying, "Jesus, I will never get used to this cold—" He saw Williams and stopped. "Hey, you're George Williams, right?"

"Right."

"Well, make yourself at home. Hey Larry," he said to one of the others, "go up to my room and dig out a bottle of Scotch I've been hiding. It's in a suitcase under the bed."

"I can't get through the electric eye," Larry said.

Gorgio laughed. "Christ, I forgot. Listen, it's only a foot high, so just kind of lift your leg over it."

He plunked himself down in a chair. "I can see that thing's going to be more a nuisance than it's worth."

"When did you put it in?" asked Williams. "The boys here didn't even know about it."

"Well," said Mike, "when I heard a Justice Department type was going to be sleeping right next door I got me the fixings. I put it in last night. Used to be an electrician before I became a war criminal, you know."

Williams smiled. "Well, I tripped it off, so you were right."

Mike said, "Sure, hell, that don't surprise me. You're on a murder case so you got to look everywhere. Did you find the gun under the pillow?"

Williams smiled, "Actually I was more interested in your football pictures."

"Sure, I'll bet," said Mike. "Anyway, Mr. Williams, I'll let you in on a secret. That little gadget wasn't intended for you. It was intended for me! I've been ripped off three times since I came to this crummy city. Now I got me a .38 under a pillow and an electric alarm, and somebody's gonna find himself full of holes if he tries to sneak in on old Mike again."

"You keep money up there?"

"You Justice Department types," said Gorgio with amusement. "Don't you know the rip-off rule? You got the guy you got the money. You lead him to it—by his nose. Shit, I lost every penny . . . every penny I had saved in five years when two fucking spades caught me asleep. On top of that, they smashed two of my ribs." He started to laugh. "Jesus, that's cool. I set the trap for .spades—and a Justice Department mad dog walks into it. Well, by God, I know one thing. It works!"

Larry came down with the Scotch and Mike poured drinks for everyone. He said, "When are you going to see Houard?"

"I saw him," said Williams. "He gave me Bolton's new name."

Mike looked at him, impressed. "You are something, Mr. Williams. I didn't think old Robere would ever rat on Bolton. He gave me a sob story about how Bolton had saved his kid's life."

They finished their drinks and Williams asked Mike if they could talk in private. The others were willing enough to leave Mike with the disturbing guest from the Justice Department.

Williams waited till they were gone and put his drink down on the coffee table. "What time is Carl Richardson walking through that door Mike?"

— 4 —

Gorgio's eyes were blank. "*What* Carl Richardson? I don't know anybody by that name."

"I think you do, Mike. I think you were with him in Vietnam. That's because I know something Allen Lowell didn't know for three years. Mike Gorgio's real name is Joe Marconi."

Silence in the room, then Gorgio said, "I think my little old electric eye has given you ideas—"

"You made a slight mistake, Mike—but you made it twice. You keep a football picture on your bureau which is mighty interesting to me because I just saw the same picture in your high school yearbook."

"You what?"

"So I know who you really are. And I know the Olympians infiltrated you into the deserters group in Toronto years ago so you could use them without their knowing it, and to recruit others. And the carrot they dangled—someone already working for the SDS in the States because he hated the war and all it stood for—was none other than your old high school and Green Beret buddy, Allen Lowell—"

"I never heard of an Allen Lowell!" said Gorgio.

"A guy with his Olympian training was just what you needed. It made your job that much easier. So you wrote to him under your new name and made some kind of deal. Was it his brother, Mike? Were you involved in that? Because one thing always bothered me. The person who informed on Caldwell and Tommy Schovajsa did so long-distance from Toronto!"

Gorgio said nothing, and Williams went on. After his brother was killed, Lowell was hooked, Williams said. He'd do anything for the deserters—and that meant for the Olympians. "But you knew if he came up to Toronto to talk to Mike Gorgio your whole undercover deal would be blown, so you always wrote to him under the name Mike Gorgio, kept him distant, and arranged to be out of Toronto whenever he came to town."

Nothing but silence and uncomprehending eyes, and Williams said, "So for years you had Allen Lowell down there in the States doing all kinds of dirty work for the deserters, he *thinks*. He's electronically bugging offices, stealing files, listening in on telephones, all the time sending you incriminating information which you funnel ninety-nine percent to the Olympians to use for blackmail and pressure against liberal politicians and newspapermen, and one percent to the deserters. Beautiful, Mike. I congratulate you."

Mike looked at him as if he were raving. He said quietly, "Williams, you're off on a wrong horse. My name isn't Joe Marconi. That football picture upstairs wasn't in the Steubenville yearbook—" he stopped.

"Steubenville? How did you know I meant the Steubenville yearbook?"

"YOU'RE A PRICK, WILLIAMS!"

"Maybe," Williams said calmly, "but I'm not dumb, Mike. Even now you still don't know that when Lowell turned up here a year ago it was because he had bumped into Carl Richardson. Richardson was supposed to have been killed in Vietnam, but now after all those years, here he is, alive—and still watching him. Was it possible the Olympians had been watching him all these years, too? Lowell was suspicious and he came to Toronto to check you— and naturally you were out. But this time he went right to your house, right into your room. You were smart enough to hide out, but you forgot one thing. He saw that *picture*, Mike."

Gorgio's eyes flickered, and Williams knew he was right. And if he was right about that, then he knew at last one possible answer to the riddle of the six on Allen Lowell's list. If only the location were right . . . and Richardson could confirm it.

Mike was leaning over, very close to Williams, and whispering, "You die, Williams. That gun wasn't under the pillow." He took it from his belt. "Why don't we just finish our drinks. Richardson should be here any minute. That electric eye buzzes in the apartment we got for him. I'll let him do the honors."

"It's a great suggestion," said Williams, "but not at this time. I'll have to be moving on." He opened the closet and put on his coat. Mike was at first dumbfounded but then followed him. He said, "You're going nowhere!"

Williams smiled, opened the door, and went out. He knew Gorgio wouldn't dare risk shooting and bringing the Toronto police force down on his neck. Richardson would have to do the dirty work, not an Olympian in place as a deserter.

The Peugeot was about a hundred feet up the street. Williams was still on the sidewalk when he looked over his shoulder and saw Gorgio standing in the open door, debating whether to take a chance, while the distance between them widened. Then Gorgio made the wrong decision. He aimed the gun and fired. The sound of the shot reverberated in the quiet street, but Williams quickly ducked and was now running behind the parked cars. He unlocked the door of the Peugeot, turned on the motor, as Gorgio ran down the sidewalk toward him. His tires were slipping in the snow, spinning uselessly, he couldn't get purchase. Gorgio brought the gun up, running while aiming, and slipped and went head-long on the icy pavement, the gun skidding free. As Williams crunched slowly out of the parking space, a cruising car almost hit him and when he looked over at the driver angrily he saw it was Carl Richardson.

Marconi was up, going for his gun, and Richardson took in the situation at a glance—doors opening, people at the windows—and gunned his motor and took off down the street. Williams followed him, skidding wildly around the corner, determined this time Richardson would not get away.

— 5 —

Ahead the red taillights of Carl Richardson glowed. Where was he going? South, toward Hamilton? No. The car pulled off the main road and turned left and they were heading north toward the mountains on roads packed with ice.

Williams was unarmed, although Richardson wouldn't know that; still, it was suicide to race after him into the lonely hills where all Richardson had to do was stop and kill him at short range. But the lives of three people might hang on whether he could somehow stop Richardson, brave the gun, and find out what he knew.

Suddenly Richardson's taillights disappeared. Williams roared around a snowy curve but they were no longer ahead. And then he realized Richardson had turned off his lights, a dangerous gamble on a dark road at night even though no other car had passed in half an hour. Richardson must be preparing some sort of stunt.

They were moving into the mountainous territory now, climbing roads hugging the side of steep hills. The full moon betrayed Richardson, when the clouds parted Williams was able to see the car ahead, a shadow flitting up the road.

Richardson was doing exactly what Williams feared. He was leading him high into the mountains where he could pull over, set his ambush, and kill him when he roared up.

Suddenly Williams did something unexpected. He pressed the accelerator to the floor, taking a terrible chance around curves on the lip of cliffs, but getting closer and closer, and then he stamped his hand on the horn as hard as he could, holding it there for five minutes, and then pulling over to the side of the road and parking.

Richardson heard the horn and thought, what the fuck! He's signalling me. But what did the signal mean? He needs help? Help! Richardson was sure of only one thing: he was going to kill Williams now that he had him out in the open. And no cutesy Central Park stuff would throw him off again.

But he slowed. That horn. It had to mean something. Maybe Williams was warning him? Maybe his car had a radio, as his did not, and he'd heard the police put up a roadblock somewhere ahead? –

Richardson pulled into a spot where the road widened for some tractors parked on a road-construction site, threw the car in reverse, angled it between two tractors, then managed to squeeze a turn on the road and started downhill very, very slowly. He had his Luger on his lap.

And then he realized what he was doing. That bloody Williams had turned the tables on him again! Put *him* on the defensive! The dimensions of his situation were suddenly bright to him. If Williams was out of his car and waiting on the cliff above, and if he, too, had a gun—

Son of a bitch! He looked around wildly and realized the road was too narrow to make another U turn—and then not thirty feet away he saw the Peugeot parked across the road, blocking it completely. He was trapped!

And then he saw it. The horn in Williams' car was blaring but there was no one at the wheel. He must be crouching on the floor, or had a pin in it or something. But why the horn?

This was when Williams underestimated the experience and skill of the ex-Green Beret. For while Richardson didn't know exactly what was happening, he did know *something* was happening and that horn was meant to distract him. He grabbed two grenades packed in cotton batting from his glove compartment, ducked out the car on the side away from the hill above, and lobbed a grenade at Williams' car.

A blinding explosion inside the Peugeot, glass shattering, and then Richardson felt a shock and tumbled backward. A goddamn piece of steel from Williams' ripped-apart car had whirled thirty feet through the air and slammed into his chest! He lay on the ground, cursing his stupidity, still clutching the other grenade, as Williams came scrambling down the hillside.

He leaned over the bleeding man, and easily disarmed him. "I'll take this before you blow yourself up again, Richardson." Then he stepped over him and opened the door to Richardson's car.

The man on the ground groaned, and Williams saw the fright in his eyes. The CIA man said weakly, "You going to leave me here?"

"Why not?" said Williams. "You would have left me here . . . in pieces."

"Jesus, Williams, I don't want to die." Blood was staining his shirt, the stain spreading. He had to *think*. He would die if Williams didn't take him to a hospital fast. He said, "Take me with you, Williams."

"No."

Richardson was showing panic. He grabbed at

Williams' ankle. "Take me back and . . . I'll tell you something you want to know."

"Make your pitch, Richardson, and make it good."

Richardson said weakly, "Williams . . . I'll tell you . . . *why Lowell wants to kill you six guys!*"

The Justice Department man looked down at Richardson, the "butcher" whose eyes were brimming with fear. He said, "I already know what triggered him off. Lowell bumped into you a year ago at 30 Rockefeller Plaza, and he recognized you . . . *Mr. Brockway.*"

The shock was apparent on Richardson's face. "You're not so . . . smart . . . you . . ." Richardson was coughing red blood now . . . "bastard. You didn't fool any of our people at International Television yesterday."

But before he could finish, Williams was gone. When a truck pulled up to the wrecked car ten minutes later, Carl Richardson was dead.

— 6 —

George Williams flew into Washington and reported directly to Harley Connors' office. Connors jumped up when he saw him. "Christ, what happened up there? The Canadians are screaming for your hide."

"Richardson came after me, and he had an accident instead," Williams said. "I didn't kill him."

Connors sat down and smiled. "Everybody dies but you."

"My luck may not hold much longer," said Williams. "And I can't wait any longer. I've got to meet Lowell fast."

"And how do you plan to arrange that?"

Instead of answering, Williams scribbled something on a note pad. Connors was irritated. "Come on, George. Let's have it. What have you found?"

Williams handed him the note he had written and Connors saw it was addressed to Allen Lowell. The note read: "I saw your TV special, and you're right."

"That's it?"

"I want you to release that as a statement in my name," Williams said.

"What TV special? The one he was working on a year ago in New York?"

"Try out that statement and see what happens," said Williams.

"Now wait a goddamn minute," said Connors angrily. "Fill me in here. What the hell is in that special?"

Williams said, "I don't know. I haven't seen it."

But later, Williams had coffee with his friend, John Newhouse, and Newhouse quickly perceived something. "You're not yourself, George. You're supposed to be cool, remember?"

"Everything's out of control," said Williams, "I can't win either way. If he doesn't go for that press release, we've had it. He'll kill us all in his own sweet time, whenever he's ready. We won't be able to lift a finger to stop him."

"And if he comes after you?"

"I'll never know the answer. A dead man can't learn much. I can't save the others, so either way I lose."

"George, as your friend—"

Williams stopped him. "I'm not running away, John. I have to meet Lowell. I have to hear from him why he started out to kill six strangers instead of Marconi and Richardson."

"But your message to Lowell about the TV special?" said Newhouse. "I got the impression you're on to something there. It's as if it's a code of sorts between the two of you to show you know his motive."

"I'm entitled to guess," said Williams. "If I'm wrong, he won't go for it."

"And if you're right, you're dead."

— 7 —

Excerpt from Allen Lowell diary . . . entry dated
November 20, 1973:

. . . Today the newspapers are filled with
Williams' statement, "I have seen your TV
special, and you're right."

Once in World War II Churchill said in
Parliament in reference to General Rom-
mel, "We face a cunning and flexible adver-
sary and, may I say across the havoc of
war, a great general."

I have this same feeling toward Williams.
What I have spent a year preparing, step by
step, he has pierced in weeks . . . even my
motive.

But what kind of a man is Williams?
What kind of a man would track down
deserters and have them killed . . . and
then say to me ten years later, "I have seen
your TV special, and you're right?"

He is cunning and flexible and dangerous, and he is one of *them,* and he must
die. Now! That press statement was his
death warrant.

. . . I will make the videotapes today at
Capitol Film Recording . . .

Weapons Checklist

1) Kidnapping   Rifle
                   .38 pistol, on hand
2) Death, and   Chemite (2) . . . . SDS
   Building 3   Two detonators (2) . . . . SDS
                   Thirty feet, slow-burning fuse
                        (2) . . . . SDS

Thirty feet, fast-burning
primacord .... SDS
Adamsite gas, signal mortar, gas
mask from CIA Building 3.

— 8 —

At four o'clock Williams was back in Connors' office at Justice. "All right," he said, "call off the guards. I've been watching them all day."

"Damn it, Williams, no. No matter what you say. You're the best man I've got."

Williams came around Connor's desk and looked down at him. "Don't you understand? It's now or never."

"Who says he's going to come at you now?"

"I'm counting on that statement."

Connors threw up his hands. "That statement! What the hell has that got to do with anything?"

Williams looked at him a moment, then said, "If you don't call off those men, my resignation is in—"

Connors stood up angrily. "Don't push me, Williams—"

"Call off those men . . . or I'll shoot them. I mean it. I'll say I mistook them for the killer's men."

Connors dropped back into his chair. Finally recovering his poise he said, "There is no one . . . *no one* . . . who makes me explode like you." He paused. "You and I are on different sides of the political fence, George. But goddamnit I'm here to do a job for the country—and you're the best man in the whole department and I'm going to swallow my pride again, eat crap again, and say yes, have it your way, do whatever you want. But if you're bleeding to death on a lonely road tomorrow night I won't shed a tear. Get me?"

Williams said, "Take the men off, Harley." And he was gone.

9

The National Archives building sits beside the Justice Department on Constitution Avenue. On its pediment is graven the famous saying, "What is past, is prologue." Inside are civil servants, most of them old librarian types who care for the documents and microfilm libraries, and provide research for scholars on such subjects as General Custer's court martial, Lincoln's papers, Jefferson trivia.

There is a guard at the door but he does little more than make certain no unauthorized documents are carried out. Another guard sits in the basement in front of a cage which contains, among other memorabilia, the sealed documents and X-rays on the Kennedy assassination, and the evidence in the case, including Oswald's effects, and his Mannlicher-Carcano rifle.

Allen Lowell drifted into the building just before the rush-hour exit, showed the guard at the door an FBI card that Robere had made for him three years ago, then took the stairs to the basement. The guard down there was a fragile old man, seated on a high stool behind a desk, a pistol slung at his hip. Allen showed him the card and said he wanted to check something in the secret portion of the Warren report.

"No chance, young fellow," said the guard. "We have to have special permission for that area."

"Well, here's the special permission," said Allen. And he produced a snub-nosed .38. The old man panicked. "Now just don't get excited," said the guard excitedly. "Take it easy."

"Open the door and shut up," said Allen. The guard looked over his shoulder in hopes the other security man somehow might have been alerted, but Allen had timed it perfectly. It was rush hour and the guard at the front door would be too busy checking passes to notice what went on in the basement. The guard hesitated, then picked a key from a ring and opened the wire gate. Allen hated to do it but he had to. He clubbed him over the ear with the butt of the pistol as lightly as he could. The old man slid to the floor. Allen took his ring of keys and passed through a large area of files and documents until he came to some cardboard cartons. And there were Oswald's belongings, and atop them all, in a plastic sheath, the rifle.

The rest was easy. Allen took the rifle and, locking the door behind him, he placed the rifle to one side of the stairs. He rushed upstairs and flashed his FBI card at the guard at the door. "What the hell's going on?" he said breathlessly. "Your man down there is unconscious. Someone must have decked him."

"You kidding?"

"Come on. There must be someone still down there!"

The guard brushed through the crowd, taking the stairs two at a time with Allen following behind. At the bottom, Allen hit him with the pistol butt. Then Allen picked up the rifle, wrapped it in an old newspaper he had found inside with a headline that said, "World Leaders Will Attend," and carrying it under his arm melted into the employees pouring through the unguarded door.

Later, in his room, he examined Lee Oswald's rifle. Looking into its muzzle, he felt sick knowing the result of this cheap rifle's action, the squeezing of a two-penny trigger, the detonation of a pinch of powder, the tiny bullet whirling through the rifling and then, guided by an idiot's eye, the classic coward's shot in the back of the head.

But the evil rifle in his hands would serve one good purpose in its lifetime.

10

Five fifteen P.M. Williams was alone in his house. He had sent Sarah off to her relatives in Virginia. She had protested but had gone anyway, knowing George had to do it his own way.

Sitting in the car as he kissed her, she felt tears threatening, and Sarah was not the type who cried easily. She said, "I'm frightened, George. You're being . . . stubborn about this."

"I can't expose you to—"

"I don't mean that. I mean the guards. For heaven's sake, at least—"

But Williams shook his head. "What good would guards do, Sarah? We had them on Carson. We had men all over Mellon. Lowell always thinks of a way."

"So that makes it more . . . awful."

"I'm prepared. And, besides, I want to meet Allen Lowell. That's exactly why I gambled on that statement."

Sarah turned on the ignition, then said to him, "How do you meet a man who wants to kill you?"

"By not letting him kill you," said Williams, and managed a smile as his wife backed down the driveway, still angry and worried, turning the car in a flurry of gravel and racing off.

He went back inside and Fred Jarvis called to tell him that Oswald's rifle had been stolen, and that nothing about it was to be released to the press, nothing.

Unless I am killed by it, thought Williams as he hung up. But in truth he was dismayed. He had wanted a chance to talk to Lowell, but Sarah's intuition had been right.

Instead of an insight into Lowell's motivations, more likely he was to be treated to a far-off

CRACK! and a bullet in the brain.

The Archives building was in an uproar. FBI men had been dispatched next door two minutes after the theft had been discovered. The old guard in the basement was being treated with cold compresses. "I been expecting this a long time," he said, sitting up on the floor.

"What happened?" an FBI man asked. The guard told him, and the FBI man knew immediately it was Allen Lowell. He went to the phone and called Fred Jarvis, his task force head on Lowell's case.

But when he came back the old guard was grinning. "Yeah, like I said I been expecting it quite some time. These Kennedy fanatics trying to make a case for conspiracy in the assassination, they've tried every way to get in here outside of this." He touched the back of his head gingerly. "So I set up a little display, just in case."

"A display? You mean he took a phony?"

"Sure. The real stuff is in the safe. What that boy got was the rifle they used to compare shooting times with the real rifle. He ain't got a thing."

Allen Lowell cradled the rifle to his cheek, sighted through the scope, and then put the rifle down.

At one A.M. he went to sleep in a cheap rooming house on the northwest side of downtown Washington, almost at the same time as Williams, some miles away. But Allen set the alarm for four o'clock.

Night in McLean, Virginia. Allen Lowell traveled very slowly toward Williams' house. He was carrying a rifle and a small Pan American flight bag. He had inspected this house three times since returning to Washington. The first two times he could see it was unguarded, but on the third visit he spotted two men in the shadows and Allen had disappeared quickly before he could be seen.

But he couldn't believe Williams would allow guards. He knew his man by now, and Williams was too clever, too intelligent to allow guards to frighten Lowell away. Williams knew Lowell always could come back months later when the guards were gone and the publicity was over and it would be so easy to kill.

Williams sat in the pitch dark by his first-floor bedroom window, looking out at the back lawn. He had not been to bed yet. The absence of an expected telephone call from Lowell had worried him, set him thinking again, set him remembering the rigged telephone and the camera bomb and the knowledge that Lowell was a cunning killer who never did what was expected.

Maybe he was wrong, maybe he was overestimating the man, but he had made the little sign in the back yard anyway. As he sat in the dark, he could barely make out the swimming pool—how that pool must confirm Lowell's hatred of him—and now he took a small pair of binoculars and searched the shadows. He scanned the hedges, stopping at a small light which he had affixed on the far lawn, the only spot of light in the total darkness.

He continued along the hedges with the binoculars, then froze. A shadow was coming through, holding a rifle. He could not make out the man's face, but he knew it was Allen Lowell. Keeping in the shadows, the man ran quickly toward the house. Then he stopped. He had seen the light, and the small sign it illuminated. Williams had made it with black crayon after Jarvis had called the second time.

Backed against the hedges, Lowell read the sign:

WRONG
RIFLE

Involuntarily Allen looked down at the rifle in his hands, then up at the darkened house, and he was in a rage. Williams had outguessed him. He was awake, no doubt covering him with a gun from one of those windows. Like lightning Allen put the rifle to his shoulder and fired into Williams' bedroom window, which he had located on a previous surveillance.

He heard a cry of pain and turned, rushing through the hedges and running the hundred yards to his car. He had no illusions. It would be a miracle if he had hit Williams on a blind shot with Williams watching him, no doubt through binoculars. He'd have to ditch the car in a minute or so and go the rest of the way on foot. Williams would be on the phone and every police car in the country would be on the roads.

Williams' cry of pain had been half simulated, half real. Glass from the shattered window had sliced into the back of his neck as he ducked away. He held a handkerchief to the cut while he called the special police number he had set up. The sergeant on the phone said the extra cars and men standing by would block all roads.

Williams applied two band-aids to the cut, and remembered what Connors had told him, "Everyone dies but you." But Williams had the feeling his luck was running out.

— 11 —

McLean, Virginia, is an area of "gentleman" farms. On his three previous trips Allen Lowell had prepared well. He knew his route.

He abandoned his car by the side of the road, pointing away from the direction he was headed, then traveled on foot through the back areas of farms until he came to the lavish property of one J. Ginsberg. Some hundred yards from the main house was a small wooden two-story building which was unoccupied at the moment. Ginsberg apparently rented it out, but no one was renting it now. Two nights ago Allen had used it for a comfortable night's sleep. And tonight he was prepared to do the same, the rifle on the bed beside him, a .38 under his pillow. Yes, he was more than prepared. But nature has a way of interfering.

Police cars combed the road and soon found the abandoned car. A check with headquarters showed it had been stolen off the street a few hours ago; the owner didn't even know it was missing.

Minutes later the police were at Williams' house. He seemed unsurprised by the abandoned car. "He's on foot," he said, "and it's a long way to Washington. Cover all the bridges, and assign men with binoculars to scan the water."

"Will do, sir," said the young sergeant who was excited to be in on this fantastic case. But Williams was saying, "And search all the houses."

"It's not even six," said the sergeant. "You want us to wake up everybody in McLean?"

"All the houses near the road to Washington," said Williams.

And then, suddenly, the phone was ringing. Williams picked it up, and a voice said: "You win. Arlington Cemetery, six o'clock tomorrow night." And the phone clicked.

Arlington Cemetery. So that *was* the reason for the Oswald gun. But why had Lowell come after him tonight then? He turned to the sergeant. "That was Allen Lowell. He's either in an outdoor phone booth or a house, and he can't be too far away. Get moving."

The police disappeared, all but two who would not leave no matter what Williams said, and Williams didn't say much. He knew Lowell wouldn't come back here.

But would he be in Arlington tomorrow in full view of hundreds of police and guards? Could it be that Lowell simply wanted to *die* at Arlington?

Williams knew Lowell too well for that.

It came up rain that night . . . slanting, torrential rain that battered the small house where Allen Lowell lay thinking. He knew he was playing a chess game with a master, but it was a game that Williams couldn't win if Lowell kept his wits. For it was his move, and Arlington was a master decoy.

It could have been any place where there were bound to be large crowds of guards and people. But Arlington was the best place for one reason. If something should go wrong—if he should somehow slip up—he would die at Arlington, die among the white crosses up the great hill, among the men who had fought (killed for what reason?), where the two Kennedys now lay (killed for what reason?), where the beauty of a gentle hill overlooking the white Capitol could not hide the despair so close to the surface.

— 12 —

November 25, 1963. Allen Lowell could not be everywhere. He did not want to be where he *was*, with a two-man USIA camera and sound crew, deployed along the funeral route.

Allen still did not believe the news of Oswald's act, could not believe it, would not let himself believe it. But a few moments ago he had been up in the great rotunda of the Capitol, and there beneath paintings of the "Landing of Columbus" and the "Embarkation of the Pilgrims" and other historic scenes was a coffin draped in red and white stripes and stars on a field of blue, and that was all that remained of the President he had idolized for a thousand days.

It had been less than a week ago that he had seen the young President in the flesh, and even had his picture taken with him. It was at a White House reception for the Supreme Court justices, the only reception in the year to which all kinds of government people could get invited, even clerks and secretaries, simply because there were so few Supreme Court justices and their wives. And Allen had asked Carson, and Carson had asked the USIA boss, and somehow they had wangled him a pass.

He had taken his place with perhaps a hundred strangers in the East Room downstairs while on the floor above Jack Kennedy and members of his family met with the justices. Then the Marine band in its scarlet tunics struck a martial chord. Ruffles and flourishes and then "Hail to the Chief!" and Allen had looked up and the President and his lovely brown-eyed wife, both looking radiant, had come down the stairway, little knowing it was their last time.

> *Hail to the Chief who in triumph advances!*
> *Honor'd and bless'd be the evergreen pine*
> *Long may the tree, in his banner that glances*
> *Flourish, the shelter and grace of our line!*

Allen found himself in line, and the President was coming toward him, shaking hands, a tanned, freckled, vibrant young man with quick intelligent eyes, and then—he didn't know why he did it—he stepped out of line, impulsively, and reached in front of other people as a Secret Service man said, "Hey!" and Kennedy whirled, saw the young boy's outstretched hand, and smiled. He shook Allen's hand firmly, a camera going off blindingly, and asked him his name and where he worked and when Allen told the President, "USIA," Mr. Kennedy said, "You're doing good work over there," as if Allen *was* USIA and not just a fringe employee, and then hands were pulling Allen

279

back and the President swept by, not without another good-humored glance at the impetuous young man— and that was the last he ever would see of the President. Until now.

Nine pallbearers from the Army, Navy, Marines, Air Force, and Coast Guard were carrying the coffin slowly down the steps, between two lines of sailors and marines with arms presented and Bobby Kennedy and the black-veiled widow waiting solemnly below and the band was playing the Navy hymn, the most sorrowful tune Allen had ever heard, a tune he could never hear again without a sudden sharp pain in the heart.

And now the drums, the coffin placed on a caisson and three pairs of matched gray horses, the right row saddled but riderless, and behind it the great black horse, Blackjack, carrying empty boots reversed in the stirrups, and that horse rearing as if in protest.

"For Christ's sake, Lowell! Pull yourself together."

Jim Noli, the cameraman, was gesturing to him angrily. They were off to their next position at the Lincoln Memorial, and so Allen missed the proceedings at St. Matthew's Cathedral, and found himself instead in a line of people four feet deep around the Lincoln Memorial, interviewing four young people in tears.

— 13 —

MEDIUM SHOT of crowd at Lincoln Memorial awaiting the funeral procession. CLOSE UP a young nervous-looking Allen Lowell with a microphone. CAMERA PANS WITH him as he turns to crowd and TRUCKS BACK TO MEDIUM SHOT, Lowell and a boy in sports shirt and slacks. The boy is crying.

LOWELL: Your name?
BOY: Ev . . . Everett Mellon. I'm a page at the Senate.

LOWELL: What are your plans now?

BOY: To stay in government and show the insane idiots in this world that we can't be thrown off by one jerk with a gun. We won't! Oh Christ!

LOWELL: What's the matter?

BOY: They're coming!

CUT TO:

Caisson and procession as seen from crowd along the street. Sound of drums.

CLOSE UP a middle-aged man. He is crying CAMERA PULLS BACK to reveal Lowell walking up to him.

LOWELL: Pardon me, sir . . .

MAN: Yes?

LOWELL: What's your name?

MAN: I'm . . . I'm sorry. I can't talk right now.

LOWELL: Just your name.

MAN: Bob Warneky. I knew the President. I worked for him. (Turns away to hide tears, then turns back) I loved that man. I'll never forget him. Never.

TWO-SHOT . . . Lowell and a young man with glasses.

MAN: I'm Thomas Medwick. I worked for Senator Fulbright.

LOWELL: Are you going to continue to work here now that this has happened?

MAN: President Kennedy stood for everything I believe in in this country. We have to go on. We can't let the right-wingers use this freak accident to take over the country.

CLOSE UP . . . an eighteen-year old girl in the crowd. The girl is crying. Lowell steps up to her.

LOWELL: What is your name, miss?

GIRL: Stephanie Spaulding.

LOWELL: Do you work for the government?
GIRL: I did.
(She starts to cry again)
LOWELL: Where did you work?
GIRL: The . . . the State Department. And now God I
don't know . . . but I'm going back to work. I have
to do something! (Sobbing) *I can't let them get
away with this just when everything was getting
started—*

Four people in the crowd, chosen at random, and
all four his brothers and sisters. Allen Lowell had felt
then that he shared a blood bond with these four;
that all of them, immersed in this tragedy, would be
united forever. They were of a generation; they
would prevail.

Those filmed interviews had been the only motion
picture footage in which Allen Lowell had ever appeared on camera. How often had he viewed them in
the intervening years while showing the film to motion picture companies as a sample of his on-camera
work, how often had he seen those four Kennedy
people crying out in hurt, how often had he heard
them promise to remember, pledging themselves to go
on with the fight.

— 14 —

A sudden battering at the door. Grabbing his pistol
Allen let himself downstairs. The door cracked as
some force was smashed against it. What was going
on? The storm? The thunder?

He peered out a side window and saw a frightening
sight. A Great Dane, frothing at the mouth in hysteria, gathering itself again and again to leap at the
door. Allen knew right away what was happening;
Marconi had had a dog like it in Steubenville, a dog
that lost its mind in terror at thunder storms.

Such a dog could not be controlled until the storm stopped, he knew, even if he let it inside the house. He feared that the owner of the big house might hear the noise and come investigate. It seemed unlikely— the main house was three hundred feet away, and the fury of the storm obscured all barking—but still. . . .

CRASH! The dog hurled itself at the door—and this time it gave! The lock sprang open and a leaping, yelping Great Dane was inside the dark room, smashing Allen in the chest knocking him over and then going for his throat by instinct. Allen wrestled free and made it to the stairs as lightning flashed and the dog ran crazily in circles in the dark below. Safely in his room upstairs, Allen looked out of his window and saw lights go on in the big house and knew he couldn't afford to stay here any longer. But how to get by that dog without killing it?

He took the rifle in his left hand, the pistol in his right, and crept down the staircase. Then suddenly the dog ran out the front door, barking. Was there someone outside?

Frightened for the first time, thrown by the unexpected, Allen ran from the house. The thunder and lightning had stopped, the rain cleared, as he headed south through the farm. Eventually he came to a fence and climbed over it into a corn field.

All that day he traveled south and then west through fields, taking cover whenever police helicopters came over. At four P.M. he was lying on his back in a forest. Two hours to go.

The storm had thrown off the police, too, delayed their search too long, and as dawn came Williams knew he had failed. Lowell would be gone by now.

But where would he go? Would he really be foolhardy enough to keep that appointment in Arlington tonight? Advertise it to Williams so a hundred police troopers could surround the whole area?

No, it was a blind. Williams had considered the idea and discarded it. And then Williams had the answer. Maybe Lowell knew him better than he thought. Maybe Lowell would gamble that Williams would meet him alone, would not alert the police.

Because that was exactly what Williams intended to do. But he would arrive at Arlington by a route Allen Lowell would not expect. He would first check the roof of the Custis-Lee mansion, which overlooked the cemetery and where he fully expected to find a young man with a rifle.

— 15 —

Excerpts from Communication Between Officer Clay Monahan in Police Helicopter 78, and Controller Sergeant Jay Pierson

PILOT: Not a damn thing's moving down there. I can see your patrols sweeping the woods.

CONTROLLER: Affirm. Take a look over the Chain Bridge area.

PILOT: Affirm. Yeah, I know that river by heart. Some kids in canoes, the usual. They don't seem to be going anywhere. I'll get over there (Pause) Arlington 8, this is 78.

CONTROLLER: Come in, 78.

PILOT: There's an overturned canoe in that stretch above the falls and a kid holding onto a rock. Oh Jesus.

CONTROLLER: What happened, 78?

PILOT: The kid lost his grip and—yes, yes, he's got it! He got himself another rock. I'm going down there to investigate.

CONTROLLER: Affirm. Report action, 78.

George Williams turned up at the Justice Department and said to Connors, "I give up."

"I told you," said Connors, "this is too big to play the one-man hero gig. Too many people are involved. Too many people still carry some sort of a dream about Kennedy. I admit it, even though I think they're crazy."

"Well," Williams said, "it's apparent I can't shake everybody so I've got a proposition for you. Lowell told me he would meet me at the Kennedy grave at six o'clock tonight—"

Connors leaned back in his chair. "So that's the reason for the rifle! Well, I'm glad."

"Why?"

"The people over at the White House thought the rifle was meant for their man."

"He doesn't care about him," said Williams. "It's me he wants."

Williams spread both hands palm outwards in front of his chest. "All right then, you call the shots. But make them sensible."

"Put as many men as you want around the place, but keep them hidden. And here's the route I'm going to take. First I'm going to the Lee mansion where I think he's going to be, then if he isn't there I'll go on to the cemetery and wait . . . but alone. I don't want tourists there, or troopers standing around me."

"What the hell do you have—a death wish?"

"Just curiosity, Bill. Curiosity. I want to hear from his own lips why he wants to kill five innocent people."

"Six," said Connors.

"Five," said Williams. "I'm not innocent." He looked at Connors. "And one more thing. Don't kill Lowell! Tell your men!"

After Williams left, Connors got on the phone with the FBI, and then the police department. He told them he was taking personal charge of this operation tonight. He wanted men around the Lee mansion, out of sight, and men throughout the cemetery ringing the grave, but out of sight. And no one was to fire until he, Connors, gave the word. They wanted to capture Lowell alive, if possible.

Afterward he had time for a cup of coffee with Fred Jarvis who had come over from the FBI. "I've been through a lot of situations," said Connors, "but I never saw anybody with two murder counts on his head go after a third man out in the open with a hundred troopers with guns. What kind of a man is this Lowell? How crazy is he?"

"That's what Williams wants to find out, I guess," said Jarvis. "But a bullet goes faster than words. And why does Williams want to do everything he can to give Lowell the chance to kill him?"

"That's another thing that's been bugging me. Hell, he wanted to be alone out there with no cops around!"

But Jarvis was musing, "I'll tell you. One on one between Williams and Lowell, I'll go with Williams any day."

"There's always that one little mistake," said Connors.

— 17 —

Talha Bahktiari, Director of Internal Security at CIA, glanced over at Joe Marconi, sitting bolt upright in his office. Bahktiari had chewed him out but good for that Richardson foul-up. Bad enough that Richardson was killed, but then Lowell had to get away! With what he knew, and with what Williams might find if the two of them ever got together!

Right away Bahktiari got on the horn, and the look on Marconi's face when he heard the names of some of the networks, newspapers, and wire services contacted all across the country reflected his amazement at the scope of the intelligence network. As phone call followed phone call, Bahktiari began to regain his sense of control. The one missing gap was being closed—and that gap was not knowing what *evidence* Lowell had. Talk they could take care of . . . Lowell was an assassin, no one would believe a wild story from him about a secret group in the highest echelons of government. Hadn't Watergate exposed everything? What was left to expose?

Well, Bahktiari knew that Lowell had been on dozens of sensitive assignments. And he knew he had forwarded every tape of every intercepted phone call, every photograph of every document to the "deserters" —which meant that Marconi had quickly relayed them to Bahktiari and the Olympians through their courier set-up. And those documents had been more explosive than anything those blundering Watergaters had found. Lowell was a pro and, unknown to himself, he had been manipulated by even greater pros—the Olympians. Revealing those documents could be damaging, even fatal.

Bahktiari placed one final phone call. "That's right. The networks are all taken care of. . . . We're covering the locals, too, so relax . . ."

When he hung up, Marconi said, "What the hell's that about? TV coverage?"

"Among other things," said Bahktiari. "I must say your boyhood buddy has given us more trouble than anyone in years."

"And now?"

Bahktiari stood up. "Now . . . *we* have his evidence."

"How the hell did you—"

"Come to the Com room," said Bahktiari, "and I'll show you."

Marconi gratefully followed him out of the office. It meant he was going to be allowed to live.

Bahktiari's Olympian office was not at CIA headquarters in McLean. Instead, it was on the sixth floor of the Ring Building facing Connecticut Avenue, an entire floor which functioned under the front: Harrison and Harrison. Insurance Underwriters—and had real insurance underwriters, trained at the Olympians' expense, located in offices near the elevators.

Beyond that, no visitors ever ventured because of an obstacle: a wall. Only when a key was inserted in a lock in one of the "underwriter's" offices did the wall slide back. There was very little bustle of office personnel; the few people who worked here were all alumni of CIA. The two top men were ex-CIA types who devoted full time to the enterprise. Bahktiari, who was No. 3 in the Olympian set-up, was the only one still working at CIA.

He led Marconi into the Com room, which Marconi had never seen before. It had Telex machines along one side, closed-circuit TV monitors ringing the top of the room on tilted shelves, looking downward, a map of the United States with bulbs at key cities, a simple desk and a few chairs. Marconi guessed that a TV camera was aimed at the desk, because when Bahktiari sat down behind it he straightened his tie.

Marconi looked around at all the TV sets. Nothing but scrambled blurs. Then he noticed each set was marked with the name of a city.

Bahktiari turned to a command console, set on an extended arm next to his chair. It was filled with buttons and knobs. Bahktiari pressed one of the buttons and said to Marconi, "Watch the set on the righthand wall, third from the end." It was labeled "Detroit."

Marconi said, "What the hell," as the picture of a man at a desk came into clear focus. But the man was talking gibberish!

Bahktiari was now pushing more buttons and TV sets were springing to life with other men speaking unintelligible syllables. The room was a cacaphony of unfamiliar sound. Marconi wanted to hold his ears!

"What's going on!" he shouted across the din.

Mindlessly, the talking faces mouthed nonsense, crazy syllables tumbling out from sincere faces. From all around the US, faceless men reported in on call. My God, thought Marconi, if all regions are reporting on those TV monitors, this Lowell business must have the "Company" really on its toes.

Buttons pressed and the TV screens went black. And in the semi-darkness Marconi, for some reason, suddenly felt frightened. My God, what was he into? This was even more powerful than he had dreamed. He said, "What the hell language were those guys speaking?"

"English, of course. What did they teach you in the 'Company'?"

"But the picture was clear."

"So we scrambled the sound on each tape! No problem. Luckily for you we intercepted Lowell's stuff in time. You want to see it on screen?"

"Sure."

Bahktiari spoke to a projectionist through an intercom. "Roll the Lowell stuff." To Marconi he said, "Got the first print just an hour ago."

A screen dropped over one wall, it was lighted brilliantly, and there before the camera appeared a nervous young man, Lowell, with a table full of documents and a sound-tape machine beside him.

Lowell was saying, "I am Allen Lowell, the man you know as an assassin. Tonight I will show you documents I photographed in secret, and play you tapes of intercepted telephone calls made by me at the direction of an organization you have never heard of . . . the most dangerous revolutionary group ever to form in this government. They call themselves the Olympians . . ."

— 18 —

TRANSCRIPT OF BROADCAST FROM ARLINGTON POLICE HEADQUARTERS ALL CARS . . . PROCEED TO VICINITY ARLINGTON CEMETERY AND PUT YOURSELVES AT DISPOSAL OF MR. CONNORS FROM JUSTICE DEPARTMENT AND MR. JARVIS FROM FBI HEADQUARTERS.

Conversation Between Officer Clay Monahan in Police Helicopter 78 and Controller Sergeant Jay Pierson

MONAHAN: OK, we fished him out of the water. He's all right. Any instructions?

CONTROLLER: Affirm. Take him to shore and let him off. Then go to the Arlington Cemetery immediately. A man in a gray business suit will be Williams. Any other man that approaches him will be the killer. Williams says he saw killer last night and he is dressed in tan shirt and levis.

MONAHAN: Affirm. You gave me that before.

CONTROLLER: Affirm. I'm telling you again, you dumb Irishman.

MONAHAN: Over and out.

— 19 —

In the police helicopter, not much more than a bubble on skis, Monahan turned to Allen Lowell who was holding a pistol on him. His co-pilot was handcuffed and gagged. Monahan said, "OK?"

"You should have laughed when he made that joke," said Lowell.

"You try laughing with a gun pointing at you," said the officer. "Hey, what the hell are you doing?"

Allen was undressing the officer on the floor who tried to swing at him with his handcuffed wrists. The pilot turned his head to look and the helicopter dipped crazily. Allen was crouched with the gun pointing straight at Monahan's head. "I've killed a lot of people," he said.

Monahan turned and steadied the chopper. He was wondering what he could do. Signal somehow? Drop something out—a note, anything? But he had to be careful. He knew a real killer when he saw one. Lowell was the goods.

Then he heard a sigh, and looked and saw his co-pilot now limp. The kid had taken him out with the gun or a karate chop. Lowell said, "Face forward!"

Ten minutes later he was joined by a man in uniform, only this time his co-pilot was Allen Lowell. He was saying, "How often do you report in?"

"No regular schedule."

The butt of a gun smashed his cheekbone. It started to bleed. "Every quarter of an hour," said Monahan, "but it don't have to be to the minute."

Swinging lazily over the Potomac, the Lincoln Memorial ahead to the left, cars on the Rock Creek Parkway, and farther ahead the Washington monument, a white sword pointing at the sky, and gray government buildings marching up Pennsylvania and Constitution Avenues to the Capitol, and pretty grass, really pretty green grass on the Mall, and now swinging south and away to a jet landing at National Airport, and a hillside just ahead with people ducking as the chopper swept in, trying to keep out of sight. Hundreds, thought Allen. There must be hundreds of police there. But where was Williams?

And none of the policemen on the ground saw anything unusual in a police chopper with two policemen on board. To their right another chopper circled the area. Monahan checked in on the radio:

"On station. What are new orders?"

"Affirm. Observe area around mansion and graves. Do you see Williams?"

"Negative. Where is he?"

"He's supposed to be at the Lee mansion right about now."

The chopper swung down over the roof of the mansion. Williams was not there. Now the other chopper broke in on the channel:

"I see Williams. He's walking toward the cemetery."

"Maintain close watch on area around him."

"Affirm. But there's a cop every ten feet."

Monahan's chopper pulled into a circling pattern behind the other, and that's when Lowell realized he was being tricked. The other chopper radioed, "Hey,

Seventy Eight, what are you doing?"

"Executing my pattern."

"On *my* altitude?"

Monahan flushed and went up five hundred feet, and hoped to God that maniac wouldn't shoot. "Tell him you forgot, you're so interested," whispered Lowell.

"I got so interested in the action, I forgot," radioed Monahan.

"Affirm. Just keep off my tail."

And below them on the ground, in this most beautiful of cemeteries, Williams made his way to the Kennedy graves, and stopped there seemingly alone, a quiet man absorbed in the epitaph which ended "and this glow will truly light the world."

He stood in the open, the center of all hidden eyes, and waited. In spite of himself he was elated—he knew Lowell had triumphed again. Williams had long since figured out Lowell's plan because, of course, there could be no other plan. It had to be from the air. It had to be from one of those choppers, unless a third one came into view.

But aboard the chopper Allen Lowell was having a problem. Tears were blinding his eyes and Monahan was watching him, waiting his chance. Allen had to stop and he did, wiping away the tears with the back of his hand. Monahan was sure now the boy was mentally unbalanced. He knew it was wrong, but he actually felt compassion for his captor. "What's wrong?" he asked.

Allen said nothing, but he glanced down at the tableau . . . the man he hated standing there beside a grave with a flickering flame . . . and he realized he was crying because after this, dead or alive, he would have no more hate in his heart . . . he had done all he could . . . all anybody ever could in this stupid, insane, maniacal nation.

Monahan's chopper suddenly altered course and dipped toward Williams. A rope ladder dropped, and a voice on a hailer was heard by the police hidden in the vicinity. "We got orders to take you to the White House, Mr. Williams."

Consternation among the police. Connors was staked out with Jarvis but the announcement caught him by surprise. The White House? It could be! He turned to a cop with a walkie-talkie behind them. "Contact that chopper and find out who gave him those orders!"

But by the time he turned back Williams had already grasped the rope ladder and was climbing hand over hand into the chopper cabin, and the police nearby were waiting for Connors' signal, and the cop with the walkie-talkie was saying, "He ain't on my frequency, sir," and the chopper with Williams aboard lifted gracefully off in the direction of the White House, the other chopper speeding after it, and a hundred troopers on the ground looking at Connors with disgust.

And on board the helicopter Williams said, "Hello, Allen."

— 20 —

Allen Lowell clicked a pair of handcuffs on Williams and then sat down on the floor across from him. The pilot was saying nervously, "Where to? Where to?"

"Langley. CIA."

"What?"

"I want you to put her down on the ground behind CIA's headquarters. What's so difficult about that?"

The pilot said, "Well, hell, that's guarded over there. They won't let us come in without some fireworks."

"Get going," said Allen. "And tell that other chopper if he doesn't get off our tail, Williams will get it."

The pilot started talking into the radio. Then, swinging the chopper in a wide arc above the crowds below, he flew toward Langley.

Allen Lowell was unzipping his Pan American bag and taking out two sticks of an explosive.

"Chemite," said Williams. "Stolen from Reynolds Chemical."

Allen looked at him. "You found out about that too?"

"Sure," said Williams. "What are you going to do at Langley? You'll need more than two sticks to take that place out."

"They'll do for what I want," said Allen.

Lowell plunged detonators in each of the two sticks, then removed a little gray box from the bag and connected the wires from the detonators to terminals on the box. He replaced the box and the explosive back into the bag.

Williams said, "I think I know what makes you tick, Allen, and if I'm right I'm on your side."

"Oh sure," said Allen. "And that's why you killed my brother."

"Some trigger-happy cop did that."

"But you set Tommy up. You showed them how to find him. Why, Williams? What's a Kennedy man doing shooting young kids?"

Williams said, "I didn't want it to happen. But your brother was breaking a law, and I was in the Justice Department."

Allen said nothing, but a small smile played across his face. "You have the gall to talk about law—in *your* Justice Department?"

"You're right, Allen, and that's why I say I'm on your side. I think you may even have hit on the right idea to *want* to kill."

And now Allen looked at him, really puzzled. But a shout interrupted them. "Langley right ahead," the pilot called back. "There are choppers all over the place. They're not going to let us through."

Allen stood up and looked over the pilot's shoulder. Outside it was dark, but the red and green lights of choppers ahead were plainly visible.

Just then one of the choppers swerved and came in at them at an angle, and a machine gun started spitting fire. Bullets tore through the chopper and the pilot shouted into the radio, "Christ! They're *shooting!*

Stop them!" and Lowell was punching his shoulder,
"Down! Land it."

The pilot shoved the wheel forward and the chopper dropped at a dangerous angle toward the CIA
complex, and guards on the ground started firing as
they neared the high fence, and one of the bullets
tore through the pilot's head just as they reached the
fence and the chopper crashed at an angle, great ro-
tor blades tearing ground, the chopper flipping, and
inside chaos as Williams was thrown against the ceiling and then forward, and Lowell was not out, he
was conscious and hammering a window with his
gun, and then dragging Williams free and prodding
him across the lawn toward a dark building. Bullets
ripped past them and Lowell suddenly dropped to
one knee and fired at someone in front of the building, then he got up and pushed Williams on the run
to the door and was opening it when a bullet found
Williams, spun him around, and sent him crashing to
the ground. He lay there, his left shoulder numb, and
Lowell reached out and dragged him inside. Then he
slammed the door shut and locked it. "Can you
walk?" he asked Williams.

Williams stood up. He had cracked his head
against a stone step, falling down, and he was woozy.
"I'm OK. It's just my shoulder."

"This is the building I want," said Allen. "We're
going to the roof."

They ran up darkened stairs to the top floor, then
up a narrow staircase to another door which opened
to the roof. The shooting below had stopped and all
was quiet except for the drone of choppers with searchlight beams criss-crossing the ground. Williams sank
against a balustrade. Blood was seeping through his
coat. "We'll last about two minutes here," he said.

Lowell was smiling. "They'll think twice about
shooting into this place. It's Building Three."

"What's that?"

"Richardson called it the Dirty Tricks warehouse.
It's filled with explosives and chemicals. One shell

from one of those choppers blows half of CIA apart."

Williams said, "You could do it yourself with the chemite."

"I intend to," said Lowell.

Word must have reached the choppers because now they were circling but not shooting. On the ground, guards in bulletproof vests and helmets fanned out around the darkened building. One of them had a bullhorn. His amplified voice came up to them through the night. "Surrender, Lowell. Open the door to the stairway and then raise your arms."

Williams looked at Lowell. "What are you going to do?"

"First get the guards out of the building," said Allen. "Tell the people below I have two sticks of dynamite and I'm going to blow up the building."

Williams stood up and leaned over the balustrade. Below he could see flashlights stabbing up at him, illuminating his face. He shouted, "Get back! Lowell has dynamite and is going to blow up the building! Tell your men inside to get out."

The lights below wavered as the guards took that in. But none of them moved. A few even pressed forward as if to rush the building. Williams said to Allen, "They're not buying it. Nobody's moving."

Allen was remembering a sandy desert in upper New York State; the explosives man throwing him a stick of chemite, and he throwing it on to the Reynolds man standing below them on the hill, the stick tumbling into his frightened hands. And the tests they had run, the fire, the shooting, the cleaver cutting into the chemite—and his surprise when it didn't go off. He would get a bonus out of that experience here.

He opened his Pan American bag, unhooked the wires and detonators attached to the chemite, and fastened two long fuses to the two sticks. He handed the sticks to Williams and unclicked his handcuffs. "Hold these up so they can see them. Then light the fuses and throw the fuses over the side. Don't throw the chemite or I'll kill you."

Williams said, "You *are* going to blow the building?"

"It's part of the plan," said Allen. "For your information, you were always scheduled to die here—where your buddies operate. Building Three."

"You'll have to light the fuses then. I only have one good arm."

"OK," said Lowell. He lighted both fuses, then handed the chemite to Williams. Williams stood up again and saw the guards were now very close to the building. He held up the two sticks and shouted: "Here come the fuses!" He threw the two long lengths of fuses, sparking and flaming at the ends, across the balustrade where they dangled high off the ground. The guards fell back in confusion, and then the man with the bullhorn was calling to his guards inside the building, "You men inside. Come out of that building on the double!" and they heard footsteps clattering down the stairs.

Williams handed the two sticks of chemite to Lowell, and Lowell clicked on the cuffs again. Williams said. "It worked. They're running. Now what happens?"

Lowell said, "It won't blow, Williams. We roasted that stuff in New York in a bonfire, and it didn't go. It only blows with an electric detonator. But they don't know that down there."

"Pretty clever. You got the guards out of the building too," said Williams. "Not that it will do you any good. You'll never escape, Allen."

Alongside the building the flame on the slow burning fuses crept up the wall, crackling. Williams knew that one of the guards was on the radio to the choppers with the information, wondering what to do.

Lowell looked at Williams. "One thing I don't understand. Why is everyone shooting at *you?* I thought you'd make a good hostage."

Williams shifted against the wall to free his aching left shoulder. "Richardson and Marconi tried to kill me in Canada last week. A set-up. Marconi knew I was going to be up there and got word to Richardson."

"But you're Justice Department," Allen said. "You're their man!"

Williams said, "Apparently the Olympians don't think so."

"What happened?"

"Richardson is dead. Marconi is still running his fake operation."

"That bastard," said Allen. "He made an idiot of me for three years. He even set up my brother with Caldwell, knowing he'd be arrested and I'd work all the harder for what I thought were the deserters. He set Tommy up for *you*, Williams."

Only one chopper still hovered above them. Williams knew that the other had flown out for sharpshooters to pick off Lowell. But they would have to hurry. He said, "Then why didn't you kill Marconi? Why six strangers?"

Allen said, "As if you didn't know, Williams. I had it all arranged. I was going to kill the girl, then Warneky, and you I was saving for last. Then you forced my hand with that telegram, you threw off my timetable. So you found out about International Television BUT YOU WON'T STOP ME!"

A chopper came in low, its searchlight sweeping across the roof and then pinpointing them sitting against the wall. Lowell put up his left arm, steadied his pistol across it and shot the light out. "You are some kind of shooter," said Williams.

The flame of the fuses now crackled across the walls toward the chemite in Lowell's hands. Lowell scrambled over. "Time's up, Williams. Richardson talked to me for years in 'Nam about the goodies inside this warehouse."

"The building's surrounded, choppers and troopers coming in from all over, and you think you're going to walk out of here alive. Allen, wake up, it's over."

But Allen was ripping the fuses off the chemite, and replacing the detonators and wiring, and now with the choppers coming in lower he got Williams to his feet and shoved him toward the stairway. As they went downstairs, the sound of the choppers' engines came in louder; by now their floodlights would show them the roof was empty and they might chance a landing.

Off a hallway on the first floor, Lowell opened a door labeled RIOT SUPPRESSION CHEMICALS, shoved Williams in and locked the door. Williams saw brown aluminum containers with black labels which meant nothing to him: XF 111, TF 23, OTT 101.

Lowell was back inside without the chemite, looking redfaced and breathless, a gas mask snapped to his belt. He went over to the shelf which contained grenades labeled OTT 101, and put ten of them in an empty container. "What's OTT 101?" asked Williams.

"In 'Nam we called it 'vomit gas.' It takes a crowd out but good."

"And the chemite is in the explosives room with a timer, ready to blow? And in the confusion of the gas and the building blowing up you're going to slip away?"

"That's it."

"Crazy, Allen. You're not going to begin to make it. You're going to die, and you're dying for nothing. You haven't succeeded, no matter what you think."

Lowell crouched next to Williams on the concrete floor. "Listen, I know the odds. But last night before I started after you I sent copies of a videotape I made to the head of every network news department in New York. The whole story is there . . . tapes, documents . . . The Olympians will be dead when my video tapes go on the air, Williams. I'll stop them, all of them."

"By killing six innocent people?"

Allen said, "Innocent? Those four traitors I interviewed! They *deserve* to be killed. *It's people like them who made the Olympians possible.* It was the only way—"

Williams looked into Lowell's intense eyes. A mind twisted and destroyed by the Olympians—or was it thinking clearly? Perhaps he *had* hit on the only way to expose and destroy the Olympians. Killing six Kennedy people on Kennedy's anniversary would shock the country. Even the Olympians couldn't stop that publicity. . . .

"I could have kissed you when you called that press conference after Carson got it," Allen was saying. "Listen, Williams, after tonight the networks have *got* to use my tapes—even the White House can't stop that news story. No matter what happens to me, it's going to work! It's going to be worth it!"

"But it won't work, Allen. THE NETWORKS WON'T USE YOUR TAPES."

Allen's face went white.

"Remember that Kennedy TV special you were working on last year? You know why I sent you the message that I had seen your special and you were right?"

"You tell me."

"I didn't see the special, but I knew the TV company was an Olympian front. And I knew that TV special would slander Kennedy while pretending to be a memorial. Very subtle. Very effective."

Lowell was shaking his head, as if lost in his own thoughts. "Brockway," Williams heard him say, and then, "Richardson." "The networks," he said, uncomprehendingly. "I thought after Watergate the networks were still free. I thought there at least. . . ."

"Last year the networks *wouldn't* use the slanted special once they saw what it really was," Williams said. "But *this year's* special—which will slander Kennedy just as subtly and just as effectively—is going on. Why? Because this year the networks have been reached."

And now Allen was staring at him with fright. "But they can't be that powerful!"

"They are, Allen," said Williams. "Your video tapes will never see the light of day. They'll disappear, I guarantee you. The Olympians will get them."

Allen, suddenly vulnerable and young-looking, buried his head in his arms. "Oh God, God. . . ." His body shook with sobs. "Then there's no hope! No way! . . ."

Allen looked up, his face slick with tears. "If I testify in court, they'll just say I'm an insane killer. I *need* those tapes, Williams!"

Williams was silent.

"All those killings . . . they were all . . . for nothing. Nothing. Jesus," he said in a low shaken voice, "what happened to us, Williams? What went wrong after 1963?"

"We had a chance and we lost it," said Williams softly. "But did we fall or were we pushed?"

"God, were we pushed," said Allen, almost in a whisper. "Nobody knows how we were pushed."

— 21 —

In 1963 Allen Lowell fell in love. The girl was a blue-eyed blonde from Lansing, Michigan, named Mary Knowlton who worked as a secretary at the Bureau of Standards. She was attending George Washington University at night, and Allen met her when he went there to apply for some courses. Both of them were ambitious. Mary wanted to join the Peace Corps, Allen wanted to make politics a career.

Mary lived in the second story of a house on upper Connecticut Avenue with two other girls, both government secretaries, and Allen spent many pleasant evenings with them learning new things about life: candlelight, Bartok and Bach, the right wines— and he took her to, and even enjoyed, the ballet. Mary told her roommates she liked Allen because he was "funny." He made her laugh all the time.

Coming out of south Chicago and the home of a repressive spinster aunt, Allen was in heaven in Washington; his horizons were opened wide; he loved his work at USIA—the little frames of film which passed before his eyes, lovingly cut and spliced, were windows through which his eyes saw a new world. He was part of it. He would be on those films himself someday; it was possible. Anything was possible.

Allen was cheerful, light-hearted and he loved Mary; even her roommates adored him. He was always doing something amusing. Like the time they asked him to pick up a second-hand rug they bought from a friend. The three girls piled into his beat-up old convertible, and they putt-putted over to a house in Georgetown, and a few minutes later the four of them staggered out of the house with the rolled-up rug.

The trouble was: how to carry it in the car? They finally jammed one end in the back seat, and the rest of the rug protruded like a telephone pole from the side, and Allen, with two girls in front and one behind with her hand on the rug, swept around a corner of Georgetown and there was a policeman on a horse, and the rolled-up rug struck the cop in the back and smacked him off his seat and in desperation he grabbed the horse's belly and the horse took fright and started galloping wildly up the street with the cop underneath, and Allen calmly turned the next corner and raced off home and they never did know what happened to that unhinged cop.

Allen and Mary talked of their plans which did not include marriage. Mary was fired up by Kennedy's demand, "Ask what you can do for your country," and she wanted to do something before she married. Early one rainy August morning she went to the Peace Corps and offered her services but was turned down because she was too young.

Later President Kennedy went to Dallas and after his death Allen decided to join the Berets. Mary was thrilled; for the first time she saw a note of seriousness in this fun-loving boy. That night to celebrate they rented a room in a hotel near the Capitol and made love, love that was intensified by the sudden new turning in their lives, the feeling that from now on, with Kennedy gone, things were up to *them*.

Allen went to war, and Mary never did join the Peace Corps. Two months after he left, she got word that her father in Lansing was seriously ill, and she went home to be with him and there she met a young